"You're mistaken[...]
"I'm not suggestin[...]
both mine. But I'm[...]

Valerie arched a[...]
breathless."

Interesting choice of words. Steven's gaze dipped to her lips. Their natural color made him wonder if she wore lipstick. Perhaps he could tell with a taste. "I thought you wanted a promotion?"

"I do. But on my merit, based on what I've worked for. Not because I'm serving as a shield between you and your fiancée."

That stung. "My *ex*-fiancée. And I'm not asking for a shield. I think it would be less awkward—for the firm—if you took the account."

"Your discomfort isn't going to keep me up at night. But if your conscience wakes up and decides to give me back *my* account, call me."

She slipped past him again, this time back to her conversation table. Right back to where they'd started. Just then, in his peripheral vision, Steven noticed Traci through the glass wall of Valerie's office, frowning at Valerie with a mixture of hostility and curiosity.

A plan to free himself from his dilemma sprang to mind. Steven didn't stop to think. He didn't measure the pros and cons. He had to act now or lose the momentum of this fast break.

He reached out, curving an arm around Valerie's slender waist and stepping closer to her. Her dark eyes flared wide. Her moist lips parted as though she was about to speak. Without hesitation or warning, Steven lowered his head and sealed her mouth with his own.

Also by Patricia Sargeant

You Belong to Me

On Fire

Sweet Deception

Published by Dafina Books

Heated Rivalry

Patricia Sargeant

Dafina
BOOKS

Kensington Publishing Corp.

http://www.kensingtonbooks.com

DAFINA BOOKS are published by

Kensington Publishing Corp.
119 West 40th Street
New York, NY 10018

All Kensington Titles, Imprints, and Distributed Lines are available at special quantity discounts for bulk purchases for sales promotions, premiums, fund-raising, and educational or institutional use. Special book excerpts or customized printings can also be created to fit specific needs. For details, write or phone the office of the Kensington special sales manager: Kensington Publishing Corp., 119 West 40th Street, New York, NY 10018, attn: Special Sales Department, Phone: 1-800-221-2647.

Dafina and the Dafina logo Reg. U.S. Pat. & TM Off.

ISBN-13: 978-0-7582-3144-4
ISBN-10: 0-7582-3144-X

First mass market printing: April 2010

10 9 8 7 6 5 4 3 2 1

Printed in the United States of America

To my dream team:
My sister, Bernadette, for giving me the dream
My husband, Michael, for supporting the dream
My brother, Richard, for believing in the dream
My brother, Gideon, for encouraging the dream
My friend and critique partner, Marcia James,
for sharing the dream
And to Mom and Dad always with love.

Chapter 1

"How did you find me?" Valerie Parker stood in the threshold of her Coral Gables, Florida, condominium staring at Steven Crennell. She blinked, but her rival didn't disappear.

"As junior partner of your family's ad agency, I have access to personnel files." Steven's baritone made Valerie think of warm, rich liqueur and John Legend songs.

Beneath her dismay, Valerie's pulse skipped once. Maybe twice. A flock of hummingbirds nesting in her stomach took flight. "I'll have to talk with my father about restricting access."

Why did she always react this way to him? Sure, the chiseled lines of his sienna features—high forehead, aquiline nose, square chin—were impossibly attractive. His tailored gunmetal gray suit and ice blue shirt looked casual and elegant on his long, lean muscles. But she wasn't so shallow as to be attracted to a man she disliked.

Was she?

Steven shifted on her front steps, lifting his right leg

to the step above. "You can do that in the morning. For now, may I come in?"

Her right hand already was on her doorknob. She raised her left to the doorjamb. Valerie didn't want him in her home. She didn't want him at her family's agency, either. "We said everything we needed to say at the office when you and my father decided to take my prospective client away from me."

Steven's sharp features tightened. "That's not what happened."

Valerie angled her head. "Am I going to be project lead, then?"

Steven sighed, rubbing the back of his neck. "No."

"Well, then." Valerie backed into her condo.

Steven stepped forward and braced his hand against the door to keep her from closing it. "Please, Val. I'll only take a few minutes of your time."

Resentment crawled through her like a parasite hoping to feed. But courtesy and professionalism kept her from shoving him off her doorstep. Valerie pulled the door open. "That's about all I have. I'm on my way out." She couldn't be late to her Thursday evening commitment.

Steven entered her home, carrying an energy and charisma that crowded her. His six-foot-four-inch frame made her feel delicate and small even though she was five-foot-seven-inches in her stocking feet.

She secured her door, then led Steven through her living room, past her dining room and into her kitchen. She gestured for him to take a seat at her blond wood, rectangular kitchen table with its matching chairs. "Would you like some apple juice?"

"Thank you." His voice followed her across the room. "Do you have a child?"

Valerie frowned at the nature of his question and the tightness of his tone. She grabbed the container of apple juice from the refrigerator before pushing its door closed. "No. Why?"

Steven gestured toward the drawings tacked to her refrigerator. "Who's the artist?"

Valerie glanced at the artwork covering her fridge. The makeshift gallery displayed a broad spectrum of artistic styles, from the painfully precise to the wildly abandoned and everything in between.

A faint smile eased her frown. She poured a tall glass of juice and handed it to Steven. "Artists. Plural. I volunteer at Miami Children's Hospital, drawing with the kids. Sometimes they give me their pictures."

Steven's lips, well-formed and firm, curved with pleasure. His black velvet eyes softened. "And you display them. That's nice."

The hummingbirds beat frantically in her stomach again. Valerie turned from him to pour herself a glass of juice. She crossed the room to return the container to the fridge and claimed the pint of fat-free milk. "What more is there to say about the Good 'N Healthy Foods account?"

Valerie steeled herself to discuss the natural foods and supplement company she'd hoped to bring aboard Parker Advertising, her family's agency. Unfortunately, her father, the agency's co-founder and senior partner, didn't think she was capable—or worthy?—of being the project's lead. Despite her protests, he'd assigned the campaign proposal to his junior partner. It had made a crummy ending to a promising day.

Steven swallowed some of his juice. "I've read your report on Good 'N Healthy Foods. It's very good, but it's not quite as thorough as the reports you've written in the past."

Seriously? He was complaining about the preliminary work she'd done for the client he stole? What nerve.

Valerie counted to ten as she deposited the pint of milk on the kitchen counter and pulled a box of Kellogg's Apple Jacks from a cupboard across the room. She finished counting and waved the box at Steven. "Would you like some?"

"No, thanks. Is that your dinner?"

"I need to go grocery shopping." She shook the cereal into a bowl she'd taken from another cupboard. "I'm sorry you're not satisfied with the background research I did on the company and its current ad agency. If I'd had more time, I would have gift wrapped the report for you."

Valerie looked up for his reaction. Was that a gleam of amusement in his black velvet eyes? Was he enjoying himself while her temper bubbled like Mount Vesuvius?

"Your work is excellent, as usual. But I think you withheld information." His eyes challenged her.

Valerie kept her gaze steady on his. "What information are you looking for?"

Steven angled away from the table and lifted his right ankle to his left knee. "You typically include your ideas on how to approach the campaign, what tone to use and insights the client might have shared with you."

Valerie lowered her eyelids. She poured milk over her cereal. "You mean my rough presentation outline. I believe, as the project lead, that's your job."

"But you spoke with the client."

"Yes, I did." She carried her dinner to the kitchen table and claimed the seat across from him.

Silence ensued as they locked gazes and battled wills. He didn't seem so amused now. In fact, there seemed to be a transference of frustration. Valerie swallowed a spoonful of cereal—and her satisfaction.

Steven spoke first. "For the good of the agency, I think we should try harder to work together."

"You mean *I* should try harder to work for *you*." She gave him a condescending smile. "I have a better idea. For the good of the agency, *I* should be the project lead for this presentation."

"How would that benefit the agency?"

Valerie had been right about that transference. His frustration was beginning to show.

"When I told Garry that we should diversify our client base, I suggested creating two account teams. Your team would focus on the sports industry clients like the ones we have now. My team would build clients in other industries, like Good 'N Healthy Foods."

"I can handle other industries. I know about things outside of sports."

"I'm sure you can. But sports *is* your area of expertise, as Garry tells me repeatedly."

In fact, the former NCAA basketball savior and NBA star shooting guard could walk into any sporting event and walk out with three new clients for the agency. She didn't know how he did it and didn't want to ask. But perhaps she should, because Mr. Congeniality had walked into their four o'clock meeting today with her father and walked out with her potential client.

Steven lowered his right foot to her kitchen's pale

gold tile. "I bring more to the agency than my basket-ball background. I do have an advertising degree, re-member? And I've worked on several presentations over the past year—"

"Eight months."

"Some of those presentations I worked on with you."

Did he have to bring up the projects they'd worked on together? Valerie shifted in her seat as her body temperature rose. She'd enjoyed those collaborations more than she cared to admit.

Valerie lowered her spoon. "One person can't keep up with the volume of work we'll get if we broaden our client base beyond the sports industry. We need a second team."

She sensed Steven considering her idea. What did he think? Did he agree with her? Would he add his support to her proposal?

"That's not the way Garry wants to handle it. And he's the senior partner." Steven finished off his apple juice.

His response disappointed but didn't surprise her. Valerie dragged her attention from the sight of Steven's throat muscles contracting as he drank. "So you were just following orders when you took my client this afternoon?"

Steven shifted in his seat. Was that a sign of guilt? "I didn't take your client. We can work on the project to-gether."

"With you as the lead." Was he hard of hearing or incapable of reason? "I want my own accounts. I've earned them."

Steven scanned her kitchen. What did he hope to find in the spacious pale gold room? She was neat, or at least she tried to be. She kept everything in its place, and drew the line at frills and knickknacks. Valerie had chosen the white wood trim, white stone counters, and pale gold walls and flooring to make the tiny area appear more spacious. The steel appliances were durable.

His eyes returned to hers. "We work well together. Our campaigns have earned industry awards."

Valerie nodded, finishing her meal. "I also received several awards before you joined the agency."

Steven treated her to another look of intense scrutiny. She had the sense he was adjusting his strategy to salvage a win. Those tactics had worked for him on the basketball court. Too bad for him, her career wasn't a game.

"You'll have other opportunities for promotion, Val. Your father's not ready to expand the firm now, but give him time. He'll see the wisdom of your proposal."

Valerie's shoulders rose and fell on a cleansing breath. "I hope so."

Tension lifted from Steven's features. "In the meantime, will you work with me on the campaign presentation for Good 'N Healthy Foods?"

"No." She stood to carry her cereal bowl and glass to the sink.

Steven followed her with his empty glass. A reluctant smile curved his full lips. "You're one stubborn woman."

Valerie felt her lips tip upward in response. "It's part of my charm."

"Only part of it?" Steven turned to face Valerie at the sink. "How will not helping with the presentation convince your father to give you your own accounts?"

He stood so close. Valerie could breathe his scent,

musk and sandalwood. She could feel his heat reacting with hers.

She stepped back and returned to the table. She wasn't running away. She just needed the distance to think. "My work with the agency isn't appreciated. Maybe by working on the presentation alone, you'll see the value I bring to our projects. Then, maybe Garry will stop treating me like your groupie."

Steven frowned. "Your father doesn't treat you like my groupie."

Valerie crossed her arms. "I'm curious. Why didn't you start your own agency? You have the money, and you can obviously get the clients."

Steven considered her as though he'd heard her unspoken wish that he leave her family's agency, her home and her life. "I don't have the experience of running an advertising agency. I thought your father would be a good mentor."

She'd thought as much. How long would she have to wait until the mentoring was complete and the great Steven Crennell left the agency?

Valerie turned to lead him back to her front door. "You're on your own with this project, Steve."

Steven followed her. "You're not being reasonable."

Valerie laughed. "Of course you'd say that. If you're not getting what you want, it's because *I'm* being unreasonable. And you probably believe that."

"You and I don't make the decisions, Val. Your father does."

"Are you going to tell on me because I won't help you?" She smiled as she made the childish taunt.

Steven stared at her mouth a moment before lifting his eyes. "I'm not your enemy."

She knew that. Deep inside, she knew that. But if it

wasn't Steven's fault that her father didn't see her worth, whose fault was it?

Valerie opened the door. "I don't know what you are, Steve. But I do know you're in my way."

Steven loved the familiar gym sounds. Squeaking sneakers, dribbling balls, shouts, grunts, curses and cheers. He walked from the locker room, showered and dressed after his workout. Steven wished he could as easily wash away the argument he'd had with Valerie earlier.

He pushed past that thought and instead watched the young men from the neighborhood battle on the basketball court. The small forward on the team that seemed to be losing was having a hard time getting his teammates to follow his direction. *That's life, kid. Get used to it.*

The ballplayers spied him watching and ran faster, jumped higher and tried harder. They'd reacted the same way earlier while he'd run the track above the court. Their basketball skills weren't what the center was about, though. The goal of the Nia Neighborhood Recreational Center was to prepare kids for what could happen if their sports dreams ended. Like his had.

"I hope you're thinking about the center's New Year's Eve party."

Steven turned to watch his former teammate and Nia Center business partner, Marlon Burress, saunter toward him. "I thought you were going to plan it."

A reluctant grin lit the NBA player's face. "No, man. You're not going to run that game on me. You're the one with all the rules. Six books *and* book reports per kid by December first or no New Year's Eve party? That's harsh, player."

Steven shrugged. "It's working. Most of them have already turned in their six reports."

He took in the suspended track on which he'd just finished running laps, and the basketball court with bleachers. Bordering the court's three sides were study rooms and a small library, complete with computers and Wi-Fi. He'd built this, he and Marlon with the help of family and friends. The center's purpose—its *nia*—was to encourage physical and mental fitness. Strong bodies, strong minds.

Marlon turned and moved to the bleachers. "If we don't get all the reports, will we still have the party?"

Steven followed him, sitting beside his friend on the first bench. "No. I'm not going back on my word."

"Well, it's not even Thanksgiving yet. The stragglers still have more than two weeks." Marlon rested his elbows on his thighs. His folded hands hung between his knees.

Steven watched as the teenaged boys tore up the court. They'd ramped up their game once Marlon Burress, star shooting guard for his former team, the Miami Waves, entered the center. Would he and his friend have to break up a fight? He hoped not.

Marlon cut short their companionable silence. "You heard Walt's divorce is final." He made it a statement rather than a question.

"No, I hadn't." Steven waited to feel something on learning his former teammate had divorced his ex-fiancée. Nothing. "That didn't last long."

Marlon shook his head. "Less than four years. He should've realized something was wrong when Tracé said she wanted to open her health spa in Colorado. Everybody else did."

After his career-ending knee injury, Steven's then-fiancée, Traci Greer, broke their engagement and married Walter Millbank. The end of their four-year relationship had been a vicious kick when Steven had already been down. "How's Walt?"

"His divorce is affecting his game."

Steven nodded. He'd noticed the power forward's game wasn't as sharp as it used to be. But at least, after the breakup, Walt had had a game to return to. "He's going to have to pull himself together."

The kids on the court kept playing. They'd been at it for at least two hours. Would they continue the game until he and Marlon left?

Marlon shifted on the bench beside him. "Marrying Trace was a mistake Walt's going to pay for for years."

"Literally. Trace got what she wanted."

"Yeah. Walt's money. You got off easy, my friend."

The pain, physical rehabilitation and uncertainty hadn't seemed easy to Steven. "How?"

"Walt got your lady. But you made all this." His spread arms took in the recreation center.

Steven's smile was part pleasure, part pride as he corrected his friend. "*We* made this."

"Right." Marlon nodded. "Now, Walt's paying Trace serious jack in alimony, while the center continues to benefit more and more kids. Who's sleeping better at night?"

Marlon was trying to make him feel better. Should he tell his friend it wasn't necessary?

Steven rubbed the back of his neck. "I feel sorry for Walt. Nobody likes to be played."

"Sometimes I wish I had a decoder ring when I meet a honey. Yeah, a Honey Decoder Ring. That's what we need. It would turn green if the lady just wanted to have a good time. Red would mean she was planning to set me up for a paternity suit."

"And gold would mean she's the one for you. To her, it wouldn't be about the money or fame. She'd care about *you*."

Marlon's expression suggested his friend wanted to drug test him. "That would be a neat trick. If you find a woman like that, ask her if she has a sister."

"It's not impossible." Steven had managed to run into two women on opposite sides of the spectrum. On one end, Traci had wanted him for his fame and paydays. On the other, it seemed Valerie disliked him for those same reasons.

Trouble brewed in the recreation room at Miami Children's Hospital. Valerie watched ten-year-old Courtney Washington give her six-year-old playmate a hard-eyed stare from the other side of the round blond wood table. The younger girl was oblivious.

Courtney was tired. Fatigue made the little girl, who was recovering from surgery, cranky. Her rich caramel skin was pale. Dark rings lay beneath her onyx eyes. Still her voice rang with authority as she corrected the other child. "Esmeralda, you have to color inside the lines. Watch me."

Esmeralda Cortes watched Courtney demonstrate the proper technique for coloring the sketch of a large, old maple tree.

Wrapped in a plum robe dotted with peach flowers and a matching kerchief covering her hairless head,

Esmeralda bounced her coffee-brown gaze between Courtney and the drawing. It didn't take long for her to lose interest, though. She disregarded her elder's counsel and returned to her broad strokes of kelly green across the top of the maple tree drawing.

"Esmeralda!" Courtney's scold was the warning bell for Valerie to intervene.

She crossed the emerald Berber carpet to the small, round table and joined the group of boys and girls of varying ages diligently coloring in various plant sketch books.

Valerie hunkered down beside the tired little girl. "Courtney, Esmeralda doesn't have to color within the lines. Her drawing is different from yours, but that doesn't mean it's wrong."

Courtney studied Esmeralda's sketch on which the colors ran free. "Can I color like that, too?"

Valerie cupped Courtney's cheek. "Of course you can, hon. You can draw anyway you want." For a few moments, she watched Courtney cover the sketch of the maple tree with vibrant hues, inside and outside the lines.

Crisis averted, Valerie moved on to spend time with and give encouragement to the other children.

"You handled that well."

At Gloria Shaffner's words, Valerie looked up from her conversation with a boy scheduled for minor surgery the next morning.

Her friend didn't look like a high-powered executive. The older woman—vice president of marketing at Good 'N Healthy Foods Company—wore an azure blue oversized T-shirt bearing a lemony yellow smiley face over baggy pumpkin-colored pants.

Valerie arched a brow. "No meetings today?"

"Speaking of which, how's the GNH proposal going?" Gloria settled into the chair across from Valerie, tucking her auburn hair behind her ears.

Valerie counterfeited a confident smile. "We've pulled together a creative team to work on it."

That wasn't a lie. She and Steven were a creative team. They just had a difference of opinion over who would lead the project. But Valerie would never admit that to a client. Airing the agency's dirty laundry would be bad for business.

Gloria's golden brown eyes brightened with enthusiasm. "Great. Great. Listen, Val. I'd like to schedule the presentation for right after the New Year. Things are crazy at work now. We're wrapping up projects from this year before taking on new ones. Then, of course, we're taking time off for the holidays. Will that be a problem?"

That soon? Valerie dug into her purse for her personal calendar, taking a moment to regain her breath. "No, that's not a problem." Even if that means the agency will be working while the client takes the holidays off. Those were the breaks, but it was worth it.

"Great. Great." Gloria pulled her day planner from her handbag and flipped through several pages. "Let's meet January second, right after the holidays. Everyone will be refreshed from the break. And it should still give you plenty of time to pull together a presentation."

Valerie swallowed the lump in her throat. Seven weeks? That was assuming they didn't have other projects. "That sounds fine." For now, she noted the date in her calendar. Later, she'd figure out how to make it work.

Gloria pushed her day planner back into her handbag. "Great. Great. So, what angle are you pursuing?"

"What do you mean?" Valerie mentally developed a schedule for the advertising presentation—the words, the images, the audience—and printing the materials. It would be tight.

"How do you see the campaign unfolding?"

Valerie stopped fretting about the schedule. Once she was alone, she could bang her head against the closest wall. Right now, she needed to concentrate on the client. "We're still tossing around ideas. We haven't settled on an approach yet."

"What are some of your ideas?"

Valerie bit her lip. "Gloria, I'm not comfortable reviewing ideas with clients before a presentation. They could—inadvertently—stifle my creativity."

Gloria's laughter was full and uninhibited. "Of course, you're right. I apologize."

Valerie covered her relief with a chuckle. "I understand. We're excited about your campaign, too."

"Will Steve Crennell come to the presentation?"

Valerie sobered. "I don't know. Why?"

Her friend's laughter was more self-conscious. "I'd love to meet him. Could you arrange that?"

Valerie looked away. "I can try."

That's what she was up against. Her father and her friend were more interested in Steven's celebrity than in her credentials. Steven's fame would always overshadow her experience. What could she do to change that?

Chapter 2

"But it was my idea." Valerie couldn't control the anger in her voice as she questioned her father. "Why did you give my prospective client to Steve?"

Garrison Parker leaned into his deep gold executive chair. Her father had always seemed larger than life to Valerie. The royal-blue and gold decor of his corner office underscored her sense of petitioning a monarch instead of addressing her parent—or even her boss. Photos of Garrison with high-profile clients were stationed around his office, and the numerous industry awards the eighteen-year-old firm had earned adorned the walls.

Valerie returned her attention to the russet brown angles of her father's aloof expression. Her mocha features more closely resembled her deceased mother, who'd passed away more than twelve years before, when Valerie had been fourteen.

Garrison picked up his Cross pen and bounced it against his desk pad. "The three of us had this conversation yesterday afternoon."

"And even after thinking about it all last night, I still don't understand your decision."

His ebony eyes bore into Valerie from across his cedar desk. "You don't have to."

Valerie took a deep breath to release the pain of her father's words. She kept her voice steady and tried again. "I'm just asking for a moment of your time."

Garrison hesitated. He leaned back into his throne. "I assigned the presentation to Steve because his success in the NBA gives us an edge."

Valerie clenched her fists in her lap. "But it's my prospect. I contacted the company. I researched its products and marketing campaigns."

Her father's expression remained inflexible. "We're only going to get one chance to take Good 'N Healthy from our competitor. We need every advantage we have. You can still work on the presentation."

"With Steve as lead."

"Why are you making a big deal about this?"

Her father's frown was disapproving—and daunting. But Valerie straightened her spine and argued her case. "I deserve to be the project lead. It isn't fair that I do the research and plan the campaign while he has the final say on the creative and the proposal, and makes the presentation to the client."

Garrison shifted impatiently in his chair. "You act as though you'd do all the work. Steve's planned campaigns before."

Valerie sighed. Her father didn't get it. "In that case, why doesn't *Steve* plan this campaign and *I'll* make the final decisions and the presentation?"

"Because *I* decide who makes the decisions and client presentations, and I've chosen Steve." Garrison's tone was final.

Even after swallowing her disappointment, Valerie could manage only one word. "Why?"

"Steve Crennell is a household name across the country, but especially here in Miami. He has been since he carried his alma mater, St. Paul University, to the NCAA Championship his senior year."

If she had to hear her father's sermon on the glory of Steven Crennell one more time, she'd pull her hair out by its roots. Valerie reined in her temper. "This isn't a presentation for sporting equipment or athletic gear. It's for natural foods and supplements. Steve's NCAA background and NBA connections aren't a factor. If you want to compare résumés, I have more experience."

"We aren't comparing résumés." Garrison doused her hope. "We're discussing intangibles, and Steve gives us an edge you can't deliver."

Valerie flinched. He'd taken away her breath, just as he'd taken away from her so many other things, including her confidence. "You've made your position perfectly clear. I'll do the same. Steve can have my prospective client, including my files on Good 'N Healthy, if that's what you think is best for the agency. But he's on his own. I'm not helping with the presentation."

Valerie stood and forced her shaking muscles to carry her from the room.

Two fast knocks on her office door ended Valerie's stiff-legged pacing. She glanced in the direction of the interruption. Who was that? It didn't matter. She couldn't let any of her coworkers see her so upset. It was bad enough her rival, Steven, knew she and her father were at odds. If anyone else knew how poorly she compared to the great Steven Crennell in her father's eyes, she'd be mortified.

Why did Garrison prefer Steven's company to hers? Why couldn't she have Garrison's approval?

Two more taps against her door. Valerie strode to her desk. She sat and opened a project folder, a prop to hide behind while she collected her composure. "Come in."

Manuel Lopez strolled into her office. The graphic artist wore a lavender shirt and white Dockers. His scarlet belt and matching canvas shoes lent strong accents. The artist in Valerie admired her friend's confident fashion statement and risky sense of color.

Manuel quirked his thick, arched brows. "I thought we'd be celebrating your promotion this morning." A hint of his Cuban ancestry seasoned his speech.

Valerie forced the words of defeat from her throat. "Steve's the one celebrating. Garrison gave the presentation to him yesterday."

Her friend sagged into one of her navy blue guest chairs. "Why?"

"Steve's NBA background should get the natural foods company to give us more attention." Good. Her tone didn't carry any of the resentment burning like acid in her gut.

"I was afraid of that."

Valerie frowned. Manuel's response didn't bode well. "You were?"

"Whenever we get a big account, Garrison gives it to Steve." Manuel shrugged one shoulder. "He usually closes the deal."

"You knew Steve would get the presentation?"

Manuel winced. "Pretty much."

How many other coworkers knew she didn't measure up to her father's standards? No matter how many successful campaigns she designed or awards she earned, Steven's intangibles would always overshadow her.

Valerie's gaze dropped and her stomach sank. "Why didn't you say something?" She stood as she asked the question.

"Because I knew it was important to you, and I didn't think it would hurt to try. To be honest, it's important to me, too."

Valerie paced to her office window. She stared past the vertical slants of the ivory blinds to study downtown Miami. From the fourteenth floor of the rented office space, she saw other steel and glass skyscrapers, coco palms and the Atlantic Ocean.

She spoke over her shoulder, using her friend's nickname. "Manolín, we've been working for the firm for four years. I'm more than ready for bigger challenges."

"So am I, Val. I was hoping this presentation was the opportunity we'd been looking for."

"Good 'N Healthy Foods is a multi-million-dollar company." Valerie turned from the window. "It would have meant a promotion to senior account executive with my own creative team, including you as the senior designer."

"Thank you."

She marched back to her desk. "Don't thank me. You've earned it. We both have." Valerie dropped into her chair, folded her hands behind her head and stared at the ceiling. "I probably have bad karma. I shouldn't have used my connection volunteering with Gloria at the hospital to advance my career."

"You didn't set out to do that. *Gloria* approached *you*."

Valerie shrugged. "I know, but still."

"I don't think it's your bad karma. I think it's Garry's fanaticism. He's a huge Miami Waves fan and, by extension, a huge Steve Crennell fan. Steve's like the son he never had."

The son he wished he'd had? Was that it? But she had to give the devil his due. "It's not that easy to impress Garry." She should know. "Steve's fame helps, but he's also good at his job."

"He does have the raw animal magnetism." Manuel affected a shiver of excitement. "I think it's his sexual magnetism the clients really like, not his basketball."

It was suddenly warmer in her office. Valerie touched the bun at the nape of her neck. "I appreciate your insight, Manolín, but I don't think Nathan would."

Would referring to Manuel's long-time lover get him to behave? Apparently not.

Manuel's chuckle was wickedly amused. He leaned into his chair and crossed his legs. "I'm in a relationship, but I'm not blind."

"You're not helping."

Manuel sobered. "Whatever happened to nepotism? You're the owner's daughter. That should count for something."

"Being related to Garry Parker is more hindrance than help."

"What are you going to do?"

"Keep trying, I suppose." Valerie pushed aside a couple of project folders and linked her fingers together in the center of her desk. "What choice do I have?"

"We could have handled reassigning the Good 'N Healthy campaign better." Steven sat in one of the visitor's chairs on the other side of Garrison's desk.

Friday morning had sped by. He'd even worked through lunch. Still, he couldn't get last night's confrontation with Valerie out of his mind. What had made him think she'd be easier to reason with away from the office? He hadn't known his opponent.

Garrison twirled his Cross pen between his fingers. "Don't worry. I'll talk to her again. She'll help you with the presentation."

Steven quirked a brow. In the almost nine months since he'd been with Parker Advertising, he'd worked on several campaigns and presentations, some with Valerie and some on his own. But Garrison seemed to think of him like a prop. "I can handle the presentation. I meant we should have considered Val's perspective when we decided I'd be the project lead."

"This is business. I don't have time to coddle her feelings."

"Val isn't talking about feelings. She's talking about fairness. She did the work. She should have the win."

Garrison tapped his pen on his desk. "It's not a win until the client signs the contract. And you want to talk about fairness? In this economy, how can I justify risking the jobs of more than thirty people for one person?"

Once again Steven was caught in the middle of strife between Valerie and Garrison, and unable to find a way to please both. But the memory of the disappointment in Valerie's dark chocolate eyes made Steven push a little more. "That's a bit of an exaggeration, isn't it? You wouldn't be risking the agency for this one account. Besides, it's not a risk when the person is as good at her job as Val is."

"We have to deliver more than 'good' to get ahead. As my partner, you should know that. Your investment allowed us to develop our Internet marketing services. You're responsible for this firm, too."

"Val's your daughter." Steven held his mentor's gaze as he delivered the quiet reminder. "She's responsible for the firm, too. She wouldn't do anything to jeopardize it."

"I don't treat Valerie any differently from my other employees."

I've noticed. But Steven had pushed hard enough. He didn't want to antagonize his boss any further. "It's your agency. You know best."

Garrison grunted. "Maybe you can convince Valerie."

"I don't think I have much influence with your daughter." Steven stood to leave, grabbing the folder that contained Valerie's research on Good 'N Healthy Foods.

"Steve, don't worry. I'll get Valerie to help you with the presentation."

Steven turned from the doorway, keeping his smile steady and his tone light. However, he was growing impatient with Garrison's misinterpretation of his concern. "I'm not worried. I can handle the presentation myself."

"But you and Valerie make a good team. Several of your campaigns have won advertising industry awards."

Satisfaction eased the tension from Steven's shoulders. He enjoyed working with Valerie. The awards were icing on the cake. "We've done good work together."

"Yes, you have."

Garrison's speculative look made Steven cautious. He lifted the project folder. "But this time, I'm on my own. I think the lady made herself perfectly clear."

Chapter 3

Steven parked his silver BMW in front of his parents' house, pulling in behind his sister's bronze Lexus SUV. He'd been looking forward to dinner with his family. Actually, he looked forward to every moment spent with his family. With them, he was just Steve Crennell, not a former NCAA phenom or an ex-NBA star.

But not everyone viewed former professional athletes in a positive light. Valerie Parker seemed to consider them one, maybe two, steps above a viral strain.

Steven climbed from his almost five-year-old BMW and reached back for his contribution to tonight's dinner—his famous green bean casserole. He balanced the dish in one hand, shoved the vehicle door closed with the other, then turned toward his parents' home.

Sparring with Valerie gave him an adrenaline rush as powerful as his NBA games. The only problem was Steven liked Valerie. And, while the sparring was fun, he wished he knew how to make her stop hating him. As he'd told her, he wasn't her enemy.

Steven used his key to let himself in to his parents'

home. Laughter greeted him at the door. He followed the sound to the kitchen, where his mother and sister were putting the finishing touches on the food, and his father and brother-in-law were collecting utensils and glasses to prepare the table.

His sister turned as he entered. Barbara Crennell Green was older than him by three years and shorter by four inches. Her dark, almond-shaped eyes teased him. "Ah, the green bean casserole is here."

"Funny." Steven failed to suppress an answering smile. He set the casserole on the counter beside the other dishes. "If you wanted variety, you should have let me pick up something from a restaurant or a grocery store."

Barbara kissed his cheek. "How would that be a home-cooked meal?"

"You can't have it both ways."

His sister stepped aside so Steven's mother could greet him. Macy Crennell's head didn't quite reach his shoulder, but she wrapped him in a warm embrace. Her scent, baby powder and fabric softener, enfolded him in thirty years of memories.

Macy stepped away to look up at him. Her still-dark curls framed her round face. Her loving tone chided him. "We need to widen your repertoire. Green bean casserole isn't a meal."

Steven patted his flat stomach. "I'm not starving, Mom."

Macy waved her hand dismissively and turned to peel the foil from the casserole dish. "You eat out too often."

Barbara made a face at him, regressing back to their preschool years.

Steven wouldn't give her the satisfaction of a reaction.

He plucked a cucumber slice from the top of the artfully arranged bowl of salad and jabbed it toward Barbara. "Want to do something useful, like tutor science an extra day next week at the center? Some of the high school kids have midterms coming up."

An expression of mock surprise settled on Barbara's dark brown features. "So now you need me. Now you're glad your sister's a high school science teacher."

Steven gave her a long-suffering sigh. "Whatever."

A heavy hand gripped his shoulder. "I'm tagging you out." Steven's father, Phillip Crennell, used the wrestling term for being rescued. "Help Emmett and me set the table."

Steven took the salad bowl from the counter and followed his father and brother-in-law, Emmett Green, into the dining room. He set the bowl in the center of the table. "Emmett, could you tutor math an extra day next week?"

"Sure." Emmett looked around as his wife strode into the room. "We should be free Wednesday."

"Thanks, man. It really helps to have an investment advisor in the family, in more ways than one." Steven moved past his father, who was laying silverware at each place setting.

"How many kids do you expect to show up for the tutoring?" Barbara chose a cherry tomato from the salad bowl and popped it into her mouth.

Steven paused in the doorway between the kitchen and dining room. "I'm not sure. Maybe a dozen."

She frowned at her brother. "Is everything okay? You seem a little off."

"Trouble with a project at work." Steven reentered the kitchen, took the bowl of seasoned rice from the counter, then returned to the dining room. He placed the rice beside the salad.

Emmett filled the last glass with lemonade. "I don't understand why you put yourself through all this stress. It's not like you need the money."

"But he does need to work." His father followed his mother into the dining room. Phillip waited while Macy made room on the table for the controversial green bean casserole. "What would he do otherwise? Lie around his house all day? He has to be useful."

Emmett found room on the crowded table for the pitcher of lemonade. "Steve could find some other less stressful way to be useful. He could work at the center."

Phillip snorted. "Hanging out with a bunch of kids playing basketball all day isn't work."

Some of the air leaked from Steven's lungs. His father had helped launch Nia. His entire family had contributed to the project. But Phillip had never understood Steven's motivation in opening Nia or the goals he'd set for the center.

Macy stared at her husband in wide-eyed incredulity. "Phil, Nia is more than a place for kids to play basketball. You know that. Barb and Emmett aren't the only volunteer tutors. And Steve employs career counselors and social workers."

Phillip faced Steven sheepishly. "I didn't mean to downplay what you've done, son."

Steven nodded. "I know, Dad." And he did. He knew his father was proud of him and the center. But he wasn't drawing a paycheck from Nia. And, according to Phillip Crennell, if you weren't making money, it wasn't a job. It was a hobby.

Steven exchanged silent communication with his

sister. Maybe his father's attitude had rubbed off on him without his realizing it. Maybe Phillip's inflexible work ethic had something to do with his investing in Parker Advertising and accepting the junior partnership. But in the end, he stayed with the agency because he liked the work. He enjoyed the challenge. And he loved sparring with Valerie.

Phillip took his seat at the head of the table. "Nia is a valuable contribution to the community."

"Yes, it is." Macy's voice was firm and carried a hint of censor. She wouldn't soon forget the slight against her child, even if the criticism had come from his father.

From her end of the table, Steven's mother handed the bowl of seasoned rice to Barbara, who sat on her right. His sister served herself, then gave the dish to Emmett. A contented silence—broken by teasing and the occasional "thank you"—settled over the family as they passed dishes around the table and filled their plates.

Macy dripped dressing over her salad. "I heard Trace's divorce is final."

Steven stopped eating his salad. His mother's casual tone didn't conceal the concern underneath. "Where did you hear that?"

Phillip answered for his wife. "Your mother's addicted to those gossip shows. She was watching one last night. They showed some pictures of Trace with her husband."

Macy stabbed her salad. "Ex-husband. Smart man."

Bittersweet memories of his family's caring and concern after his knee injury and failed engagement made Steven melancholy. They'd helped him battle back depression and pull his life together. With his family beside him, he'd found the strength to leave the past hurt and disillusionment behind. "Trace's divorce doesn't have anything to do with me."

His father's stare bore into him as though searching for the truth. "Are you sure?"

"Positive. I don't feel anything for her anymore." Steven ate more of his salad.

Macy pointed her fork in Steven's direction for emphasis. "You may be over Trace, but she's not done with you. Mark my words."

Steven frowned at his parents. "What are you saying?"

Barbara looked across the table at Steven. "Now that she has *what* she wants—money—she's going to go after *who* she wants—you."

Steven wrestled with his sister's logic. "What makes you think that?"

Barbara gave him an impatient frown. "Trace has her own money now."

"Sort of," Emmett interjected.

"Right. Sort of." Barbara nodded to Emmett. "But she's looking for that perfect male accessory, an advertising executive is better respected than a guy who chases a rubber ball up and down a court."

"Chasing that rubber ball is a lot harder than you think." Steven slid his salad plate aside. "And breaking off our engagement was a strange way for Trace to show how much she wanted me."

"You'll see." Barbara shrugged. "Now tell us about this project that's causing you trouble."

Steven heard the laughter in his sister's voice. "I'm glad I can entertain you."

Barbara's smile widened. "Little brothers have so many uses."

He laughed outright at that. With his height, he

hadn't been her "little" brother since he was ten. "My boss's daughter is angry because she thinks he gave me her client. She won't work on the project."

Barbara paused with her fork above her plate. "Val?"

Steven nodded. How many of the comments he'd made about Valerie did Barbara remember?

Macy passed the dinner rolls to her daughter. "*Did* your boss give you Val's client?"

Why did his mother assume Valerie's complaint was legitimate? "Garry didn't give me the client. He wants us both to work on the project."

Phillip chewed, then swallowed a mouthful of salad. "What makes her think it's her client?"

Steven sliced into the grilled chicken breast. "Val identified the company. She did the research and spoke with the client."

Emmett stabbed a slice of chicken. "She can do that? Meet with clients on her own without checking with you and Garry first?"

"She's the boss's daughter." Barbara's comment came on an empathetic tone.

Steven ignored her. "Val knows the company's vice president of marketing, Gloria Shaffner. They volunteer together at Miami Children's Hospital. Gloria invited Val to do an advertising presentation."

Barbara sipped her lemonade. "Then her father gave the invitation to you."

Steven heard Barbara's disapproval. He couldn't mask his defensiveness. "What am I supposed to do?"

"Tell him no." Barbara was serious.

"Do you want me to say, 'Sorry, Garry, but your daughter's angry with me so I can't do the project'?"

Barbara shrugged once more. "Something like that."

"Steve, it's not your client." Macy's chastising tone was as baffling as Barbara's disapproval. "You can't take credit for work you didn't do."

His father came to his rescue. "Macy, he's not taking credit. The project was given to him. Obviously, his boss thinks he would do a better job."

Steven started to correct his father's misperception when Barbara spoke.

"If her father thinks you'd do a better job, why do you need Val to help you?"

Steven had never noticed before how similar in attitude Valerie was to his mother and sister. It must have been his curse—blessing?—to be surrounded by strong-minded women. "Val's account summary is missing some important information."

Barbara chuckled. "Well, good for Val."

Steven gave her a surly look. "Thanks for your support, sis."

Emmett shook his head. "She's got you, man. Do you think she knew her father would give you the client?"

"The thought had crossed my mind." Steven chewed and swallowed some of his green bean casserole. Delicious.

Phillip snorted. "So how are you going to convince her to work with you?"

Steven shook his head. "I don't know. I tried talking with her again this evening, but she's being stubborn."

Barbara waggled her fork. "That's not stubbornness. That's survival. She knows what she wants but you're in her way."

Steven stiffened as Barbara's words brought back Valerie's comment the day before. "How do I convenice her to work with me?"

Barbara chuckled. "Turn on your infamous charm."

Steven shook his head. "Val's immune."

His sister feigned shock. "Are you sure she has a pulse?"

Steven set down his lemonade. "Positive." It wasn't her heart he was worried about. It was his.

"Steve, could you step into my office? I want you to meet our new client." Garrison's voice sounded hesitant over the phone line.

The request also confused Steven. He adjusted his grip on the phone as he called up his online calendar. He found today's date, Monday, November nineteenth. "I don't have a client meeting on my schedule."

"I'm sorry. This is an impromptu meeting. Could you join us?"

Steven frowned at the tension in Garrison's voice. "Is something wrong?"

"You'll see."

He smothered a sigh at the senior partner's continued secrecy and frowned at the proofs multiplying on his desk. He didn't have time for games. "I'll be right there." Steven recradled the telephone receiver and shoved away from his desk. Valerie was right. The firm had been growing, and there was too much work for one account team.

Steven pulled on his suit jacket and straightened his tie as he strode from his office down the hall. It was time Garrison created another account team and gave his daughter a well-deserved promotion. He stopped in front of Garrison's closed door and knocked twice. Through the glass wall to the right of the door, Steven glimpsed a woman ensconced in one of the guest chairs.

"Come in." Garrison's voice carried into the hallway.

Steven pushed open the door and stepped into the senior partner's office. His attention bounced from his boss seated behind the heavy desk to Garrison's new client.

Steven tensed. There was something familiar about the glossy raven curls that tumbled past the client's shoulders. When she shifted in her chair to face him, Steven's heart sank.

Traci Greer Millbank gave Steven a wide smile. "Hello, Stevie."

Chapter 4

Steven had never considered Traci would show up at the agency. If he admitted, at least to himself, that he'd ever imagined seeing his ex-fiancée again, he pictured her standing on his doorstep. Maybe she'd come by the center. Never had he considered she'd show up at Parker Advertising. Why would she?

Garrison leaned back in his thick-cushioned executive chair. An apology dimmed his eyes. "Thanks for joining us, Steve. Introductions aren't necessary. Traci didn't realize she needed an appointment, but I was happy to make time to meet with her."

Steven wanted to accept Garrison's apology, but his boss had just shown his loyalty could be bought. The betrayal hit him hard. Steven shook off his surprise and returned his attention to Traci. "What are you doing here?"

Traci lowered her chin and lifted her gaze to his. The angle made her eyes look bigger. The hazel green tinted contact lenses were new. "You aren't going to ask how I've been?"

Steven had played enough games for one day. He held on to his patience as he sat in the spare guest chair.

It seemed more like four days than four years since he'd been in the same room with Traci. The last time he'd seen her alone, she'd returned his ring. A few months later, he'd seen her at a team function, wearing a much bigger diamond. That's when he'd realized his family had been right. Traci was always scouting a bigger payoff.

The woman before him today had more polish than the one he'd thought he'd loved. She'd gone from the college student who tried to look her best to a confident woman who wore wealth with ease. The knee-length, purple dress hugged her full curves and showed off her toned, crossed legs. The matching, open-toed stilettos cupped her small feet.

Looking at her, Steven didn't feel anything, neither love nor hatred. He lifted his gaze and saw the knowing gleam in Traci's eyes. Did she think he wanted more than a look? She was wrong. "What can we do for you?"

Her grin was greedy. "You can start by taking me to lunch."

Steven checked his watch. It was almost noon on Monday. Where had the morning gone? A paper explosion—design proofs, copy drafts, invoices—waited on his desk. The already knotted muscles in his neck and shoulders tightened. "Sorry, I can't. I'm busy."

Traci's expression turned pouty. She trailed a purple-painted fingernail across the back of his hand. "Oh, come on, Stevie. Don't hold a grudge."

Garrison swiveled his chair toward Traci. "I'd be happy to escort you to lunch."

Traci glanced at the older man before turning back

to Steven. "Thank you, Garry, but Stevie and I have a lot of catching up to do."

"No, we don't." Steven removed Traci's hand from his forearm, placing it instead on her chair.

She went back to pouting. "Oh, come on, Stevie. Don't make me beg."

Garrison's stillness communicated his discomfort. "Steve, could you change your plans and take Traci to lunch?"

Steven didn't have the patience to cater to Traci's whims. But he read Garrison's request in the older man's brown eyes. His mentor was asking for a favor. Steven didn't want to have lunch with his scheming ex-fiancée, but how could he say no? An hour of his time wasn't that much to ask.

Fine. Steven would take Traci to lunch, but Garrison would have to do something for him. Steven stood, holding Garrison's gaze. "I'll get those invoices for you to approve."

Garrison arched an eyebrow, seeming to acknowledge Steven's message. "I'll take care of them."

Steven nodded. "Thanks. They're payable within thirty days, and the clock's ticking." He turned to his ex-fiancée. "Are you ready?"

Traci extended her arm for his assistance in rising. Steven clenched his teeth and took her hand.

"Thank you." With her four-inch stilettos, Traci came almost to his chest.

Steven stepped back to allow Traci to precede him from the office. Her full hips swung like a flag in the breeze.

His boss's voice stopped him at the doorway. "Enjoy your lunch."

Steven spoke over his shoulder. "I'll bring you the receipt."

Valerie checked her watch before knocking on her father's half-open office door. It was a little past twelve in the afternoon. "Do you want to get some lunch?"

Garrison pulled his attention from the advertising industry magazine lying open on his desk. She couldn't wait to read the issue. Judging by her father's reluctance to be interrupted, the articles must be fascinating.

Her father looked at his watch. "Maybe another time. I have plans today."

Why did his refusals continue to disappoint her? He managed to have lunch with Steven at least once a week. Valerie couldn't remember the last time she'd had lunch with her father, just the two of them.

She lowered her hand from his door and tried to keep her voice steady. "Are we still on for dinner?"

Garrison looked puzzled. "When?"

"Tomorrow night. Our remembrance dinner for Mom. Tomorrow would have been her fifty-fourth birthday. We talked about this last week. Remember?"

"Yes, I do."

Still skeptical, Valerie nodded and started to leave. Before she crossed the threshold, she reconsidered. "Actually, do you have time now? I'd really like to talk to you."

"What about?"

Valerie crossed his office, her sensible black pumps sinking into the royal blue carpeting. She settled into one of his crimson guest chairs. "We need another account team."

Garrison picked up his silver Cross pen and rolled it between his thumb and forefinger. "With you as the senior account executive?"

Was he patronizing her? The look on his face, the sound of his voice gave her the sense he wasn't taking her seriously. Valerie shifted in her seat, crossing her legs. She wouldn't leave until she'd said all she had to say. "We've grown our client base, and that's great. But we don't have the staff to keep up with the extra work. Steve can't manage all of those projects on his own."

"I haven't heard him complaining."

"He won't complain. You know that. Steve's the kind of person to do everything himself because that's what's expected of him."

Garrison inclined his head. "And he's never disappointed me."

Was there a message for her in that comment? Why didn't he just tell her how she'd disappointed him instead of forcing her to guess? "There are only so many hours in the day. That level of expectation isn't fair to Steve or to our clients."

Garrison settled deeper into his chair. His throne. He looked comfortable and in charge. She felt tense enough to shatter.

Her father dropped his pen onto the table and linked his fingers across his torso. "We're in a recession. The economy isn't stable. It wouldn't be smart to expand now."

She'd had college professors who were less pedantic. "We had more revenue this year than last year, and more last year than the year before. We can add another team."

"What happens if the economy gets worse, and we lose clients?"

"We won't. With a second team, we'll be able to provide even better service to the clients we have, and use those same resources to bring in new ones."

The silence was long. Valerie struggled not to squirm under her father's scrutiny. Instead she distracted herself with a perusal of his office. Was that a new project folder on his desk? Strange. Her father didn't manage projects anymore.

Was he wearing a new tie? The light blue and green harlequin pattern reminded her of a Vincent van Gogh painting. Where did he get it?

Garrison pulled his chair farther under his desk. "You really want this promotion, don't you?"

That was everything he'd taken from all she'd said? Seriously? She'd put it on the table. "I've earned it."

"Have you?"

Anger ignited in her belly. "Yes, I have."

He gazed at her with that long, silent scrutiny again. "You've only been here four years."

She had to give her father her résumé? "I interned here even before I started working for you full time. This isn't about my being your daughter, and it shouldn't be about how long I've worked here. This is about the quality of my work, and what I've brought to the firm. I deserve this promotion. I *have* earned it."

"I recognize what you've brought to the company, but this isn't the right time to promote you."

Valerie's frustration started to boil. "When will it be the right time?"

Garrison spread his arms. "I don't know, Valerie. I don't have a crystal ball."

Her lips parted in disbelief. "You need a crystal ball to know your own feelings?" She couldn't take any more. Valerie stood and spoke over her shoulder as she strode to the door. "When you're done with your crystal ball, can I borrow it? I'd like to know what you're feeling, too."

Steven should have known better than to let Traci decide where to eat. The Cuban restaurant she'd selected was one of his favorites. The food was delicious. The service was great. But the clientele was here to see and be seen. And they'd all been staring at him ever since he'd entered the restaurant with his ex-fiancée. Not what he'd call a relaxing lunch hour. But, judging by Traci's constant primping, she was having the best day of her life.

Steven kept his eyes on the menu and pretended at least twenty other people weren't staring at him. "Do you know what you want?"

"From the menu?"

Steven saw the heat in Traci's gaze. Her hazel green tinted contacts were disconcerting. During their four-year relationship, he'd gotten used to her dark brown eyes. "Yes. From the menu. Nothing else is being offered."

She pouted again. He was starting to hate that.

Traci tossed her long, layered ebony locks and glanced over her shoulder. "How long are you going to hold a grudge, Stevie? It's been four years."

And most of the time, she'd been married to another man. Had she forgotten that part?

"I'm not holding a grudge." Steven leaned back as

the server brought their drink orders. He'd asked for unsweetened ice tea. Traci had ordered a mojito.

The young woman provided ice water as well. "Are you ready to order or do you need more time?"

Steven waited for Traci to request Chicharrones. He added his Chicken Havana with meat sauce to the order. Their server had barely stepped away before Traci returned to her pouting.

"Well, if you're not holding a grudge, you should stop being so mean to me." She shook her glossy locks again, glancing around to see who was watching. The answer would be half the restaurant. At least. "Now that my divorce is final, and since you're still single, there's no reason we couldn't pick up where we left off." She sipped her mojito and licked the moisture from her red lips.

If the seductive gesture was meant to imply where they'd left off, her memory was faulty. They'd "left off" with her returning his engagement ring.

Steven spoke as gently as he could. "Trace, I don't have those feelings for you anymore."

She frowned her confusion. "What do you mean? I still look the same. Actually, I think I look even better. Of course you're still attracted to me."

"Is that what this is all about? Did you come to Parker Advertising to pick up where we left off?" Steven was more irritated than surprised. More of Traci's games.

Her lips tightened as her pout disappeared. "I don't need to chase after you. Men chase after me. I came to Parker Advertising because I'd heard it was a good advertising company. I want someone to plan a campaign for my health spa."

Steven drank some of his ice tea. "I heard you'd

opened a health spa. In Colorado, right?" With Millbank's money.

Pleasure brightened Traci's brown features. "That's
right. It's called Fit in Time, and it's in Vail, near a
lot of rich people." She spent the next several minutes
describing the spa—its square footage, facilities, interior decorating, and staff—in great detail. Traci was
so enthusiastic about her project she seemed to forget
her audience. Just as she was winding down, the server
brought their meals.

Steven thanked the young woman, then cut into his
Chicken Havana. "I'm happy for you, Trace."

She glowed. "I want the ad campaign to be off the
hook. Something no one has ever done before. And I
want *you* to plan it for me."

Steven saw the lust in her eyes. "I'll work on your
campaign, but we're not getting back together."

Traci sipped her mojito, then licked the droplets
from her lips again. "You're still attracted to me,
Stevie. I can tell. You won't be able to deny yourself
for long."

On the one hand, Steven didn't want to mix working on an advertising campaign with fending off Traci's
advances. That wasn't his idea of a good time. On the
other hand, he didn't want to lose Traci's account.
Garrison wanted this client. He wouldn't have asked
Steven to take Traci to lunch otherwise.

If he was going to work on this account, he'd need
help handling his ex-fiancée.

"Val, can I have a minute?"

Valerie looked up from the stack of proofs on her
conversation table. Her mouth went dry. Steven

rested one broad shoulder in her doorway. He looked like a *Gentlemen's Quarterly* model after a tiring shoot. The top two buttons of his pearl-white shirt were undone. He'd loosened his mango orange tie. His black pin-striped pants traced his hips and covered his long legs with the kind of care and attention she'd use.

She'd seen him in that suit before, of course, but it was a sight worth repeating.

Valerie sipped her lemon-flavored green tea, trying to dislodge the hummingbirds perched on her vocal cords. "Sure. Come in."

His long strides reflected Steven's strength and confidence, and that animal magnetism Manuel had alluded to before. He was the bad boy of the boardroom, the Prince Charming whose happily-ever-after came with a price. But there wasn't a woman alive who didn't want to give him her IOU.

He leaned his hips against the front of her desk. "I wanted to talk with you about—"

"Oh, there you are, Steve." Manuel appeared outside her door. He shoved a mug toward the other man. "Would you like some coffee?"

Valerie's jaw went slack. Had her friend joined the bandwagon of coworkers who felt a need to pamper the former NBA superstar? "Et tu, Brutus?"

Manuel wrinkled his nose at her accusation of his betrayal. He smiled at Steven. "I noticed you take it black and without sweetener."

Steven nodded toward the mug Manuel held. "Is that for me?"

The graphic artist shrugged. "I poured an extra cup."

Valerie couldn't let that comment pass unchallenged. "You *happened* to pour an extra cup of black, unsweetened coffee? Why didn't you just add your usual half cup of cream and six sweeteners, and drink it yourself?"

Steven took the coffee from Manuel. "Thank you. I appreciate it."

Manuel blushed. "You're welcome. I thought a cup of java would give your afternoon a boost."

Valerie dropped her head into her hands. "You were saying, Steve?"

Manuel backed out of her office. "I'll let you two get back to work. Sorry to interrupt."

"Don't worry about it." Steven gestured toward Manuel with the coffee mug. "Where's your silver chain? I don't think I've ever seen you without it."

Manuel touched the base of his neck where his chain usually lay. "Nate borrowed it. He has a casting call today for the role of a villain in a movie project. We thought the chain made him look edgy."

Steven's brows jumped. "A movie role? Cool. I hope he gets it."

Manuel smiled. "Thanks." Flustered, the graphic artist's gaze darted around the room, finally meeting Valerie's frown.

She lifted her tea mug. "Don't you have something to design?"

Manuel lifted both hands. "As a matter of fact, I do."

Valerie watched Manuel disappear through her doorway before turning on Steven. "Did you know Manuel's gay?"

Steven folded his long body into the extra chair at her conversation table. "So?"

His response cooled her temper by several degrees. "He has a crush on you."

"So?"

Valerie's mind went blank. Steven had completely disarmed her. And charmed her. She didn't want to like him. Valerie touched the bun at the nape of her neck. "What did you want to talk about?"

Now that he had her attention, Steven didn't know where to begin. He surveyed her office. The walls and shelves were crowded with plaques, certificates and trophies of accomplishments. The display probably compensated for Garrison's lack of encouragement.

The only personal effect displayed was a painting of a butterfly hovering over wildflowers. The artist's signature read Marilyn May-Parker—Valerie's mother.

His gaze came back to her. She looked good in the short-sleeved dark blue coatdress. Her golden brown skin glowed and her inky black hair looked darker. He wished she'd worn her hair down, as it had been Thursday night when he'd gone to her condo. The pulled-back style highlighted the delicate bone structure of her heart-shaped face, but it also made her look cool and unapproachable. Then again, she *was* cool and unapproachable, at least to him.

Valerie sipped her tea and prompted him again. A concerned frown wrinkled her brow. "What's on your mind?"

Steven wandered past her to her window, from where he could contemplate downtown Miami. After lunch, he'd escorted Traci to Garrison's office so they could discuss the client contract. This was the perfect time to talk with Valerie, except for one thing.

"I don't know where to begin." What could he say to guarantee her support instead of her usual opposition?

"Don't they always say you should start at the beginning?" Valerie's amused tone relaxed him.

Steven turned from the window to face her. "I know you're disappointed you're not the lead on the Good 'N Healthy campaign. But I may have another opportunity for you."

Her suspicion was palpable. "What is it?"

"We're signing a new client right now. Her name's Traci Greer Millbank. She wants us to create a campaign for her health spa, Fit in Time. It's in Vail and opens this spring. She wants something modern and unique. It's a great opportunity. You can do something different and really creative." Was he overselling the account?

Valerie stood. She settled her hands on her slim hips, drumming her fingers on her hip bones. "That sounds like the type of challenging project I've been waiting for." Her voice was slow and thoughtful. "It's almost as challenging as the Good 'N Healthy campaign. So, what's the catch?"

Steven walked toward her, closing the distance between them. "There's no catch. It's a new client. She's with your father now, reviewing the contract."

She maneuvered around him toward her desk, carrying her mug. Her shoes were silent on the thick blue carpet. "She sounds like a very important client. Garry usually gives you the high-profile ones. Why didn't he give you this one?"

He should have known Valerie wouldn't blindly jump at being lead on the account. Her keen mind was one of the things he admired about her.

Steven stood on the other side of her desk. "The client asked for me. But there could be a conflict if I took the account."

"What kind of conflict?"

Steven hesitated, perhaps too long. "She's my ex-fiancée."

Valerie crossed her arms over her chest. "I can see how that could be a problem for you."

"A conflict." Referring to working with his ex-fiancée as a problem made him sound weak. "Since you're interested in being lead on an account, I thought I'd tell you about the Fit in Time campaign. Then we'd both have an account."

Valerie was silent for one contemplative moment. "I have a better idea."

A cold breeze blew into Valerie's office and moved over Steven. "What?"

"You keep your account with your ex-fiancée, and I'll keep Good 'N Healthy Foods." Valerie slipped from behind her desk and marched to her window.

Steven tracked her movements with his gaze. Why didn't she stay still? He was getting tired of chasing her around her office. "What difference does it make which account you get?"

"I can turn that question back to you. Why does it matter whether you work with Gloria Shaffner or Traci Greer Millbank?"

He met the challenge in Valerie's eyes. "I'm not opposed to working with my ex-fiancée. But, since she's admitted to having an ulterior motive for hiring us, it wouldn't be a good idea for me to spend a lot of time with her."

Valerie cocked her head. "We'd each be starting from scratch if we switched accounts now. I've already done the research on Good 'N Healthy, and I have a relationship with Gloria. You already have a relationship—of sorts—with Traci."

Steven paced toward Valerie and her window. "You're mistaken. I'm not suggesting we exchange accounts. They're both mine. But I'm willing to give one to you."

Valerie arched a brow. "Your generosity leaves me breathless."

Interesting choice of words. Steven's gaze dipped to her lips. Their natural color made him wonder if she wore lipstick. Perhaps he could tell with a taste. "I thought you wanted a promotion?"

"I do. But on my merit, based on what I've worked for. Not because I'm serving as a shield between you and your fiancée."

That stung. "My *ex*-fiancée. And I'm not asking for a shield. I think it would be less awkward—for the firm—if you took the account."

"Your discomfort isn't going to keep me up at night. But if your conscience wakes up and decides to give me back *my* account, call me." She slipped past him again, this time back to her conversation table. Right back to where they'd started.

"You're not being reasonable."

Fury from her dark chocolate gaze burnt him. "That's the second time you've accused me of being unreasonable, and again, it's when you're not getting what you want."

In his peripheral vision, Steven noticed Traci through the glass wall of Valerie's office. How long had she been standing there? His ex-fiancée was frowning at Valerie with a mixture of hostility and curiosity.

A plan to free himself from his dilemma sprang to mind. Steven didn't stop to think. He didn't measure the pros and cons. He had to act now or lose the momentum of this fast break.

He reached out, curving an arm around Valerie's slender waist and stepping closer to her. Her dark eyes flared wide. Her moist lips parted as though she was about to speak. Without hesitation or warning, Steven lowered his head and sealed her mouth with his own.

A shiver went through him like a jolt of electricity. He hadn't reacted like that to a kiss since junior high school. But he couldn't help it. A similar tremor moved over Valerie, prompting him to hold her closer still.

Steven nibbled her lips. She tasted so good—a little sweet, a little spicy—and felt even better. Her lips were so hot and full. Moist.

His groin tightened, urging him to deepen the kiss. Valerie's lips were parted under his. Steven wanted to slip his tongue inside. He wanted that more than anything, but even he recognized taking that liberty would be crossing too many lines.

Valerie moaned, whether in protest or pleasure, he wasn't sure. But he could hazard a guess based on their most recent argument. Steven pulled back, at great pain and discomfort to himself, and searched her eyes. They looked hazy and confused. Her lips were moist and swollen from his. Still, he didn't regret what he'd done. In fact, he wanted to do it again.

A sound in the doorway pulled him back from temptation and recalled his purpose. Traci stood in the threshold with her mouth hanging open. Behind her, in the open area where the graphic designers worked, several coworkers also gaped at them. One thing at a time.

Steven loosened his embrace around Valerie, but kept a hand on the small of her back. He didn't want to lose her warmth. Not yet. "Trace, have you and Garry gone over the contract?"

His ex-fiancée made an obvious effort to pull herself together. "I signed the contract. Garry offered to

walk me out, but I told him I could find my own way."
She tossed her long, glossy locks, and jerked her
head toward Valerie. "Who's that?"

Beneath his palm, he felt Valerie's back stiffen.
"Valerie Parker, Traci Greer Millbank. Valerie's my
fiancée."

Chapter 5

His fiancée?

Whose fiancée?

Valerie's brain and body shut down, as though someone had hurled her into a pool of freezing water. But she needed to process that kiss.

The hummingbirds had been right. Steven Crennell was quite a kisser. A secret part of her had wondered about his taste ever since they'd met. He was sexy, sweet, thoughtful. He took his time making a connection with her, even for such a chaste kiss. The birds still flapped wildly in her stomach, causing a racket and keeping her from thinking straight.

But she'd heard Steven tell Traci she was his fiancée. Steven must have lost his mind. Unfortunately, there was no graceful way out of his lie.

Valerie fixed a smile on her face. Did it look as false as it felt? "It's a pleasure to meet you."

Traci stared at Valerie's proffered hand before accepting it. "Stevie, why didn't you tell me you were engaged?" Her voice blended sulk and suspicion.

Steven glanced at Valerie before answering Traci. "The subject never came up."

Valerie wanted to kick him. That was the best he could come up with? Seriously? If he was going to lie, the least he could do was sell it. "What Steve means is that we try to keep our personal and professional lives separate."

She stiffened and her eyes stretched. Had she just defended him? Her rival was involving her in a farce for his own selfish reasons, and she was helping him? What was she thinking?

Valerie met his gaze. His eyes were warm with gratitude. How incredible that her rival made her feel more treasured than she'd felt in twelve years. Heat flooded her body.

She turned from Steven to face his past. This was the woman he'd asked to marry him. Valerie had a hard time picturing the two of them together. Was anything about Traci real? The other woman's glossy Eva Longoria locks were extensions. Her dark coffee complexion meant her hazel green eyes were compliments of tinted contacts. And even with the other woman's full curves, Valerie bet her annual membership to the University of Miami's Lowe Art Museum that Traci's bustline was enhanced.

Was this the type of woman Steven—her father's favorite—preferred? She questioned both men's judgment.

Traci's attention dropped to Valerie's hands. "Why isn't she wearing a ring?"

Steven lifted Valerie's left hand. "She doesn't wear her ring to work. As Val said, we're very private people."

Valerie fought against a shiver of pleasure at the

feel of his large, rough palm cupping hers. Why did she react to him this way? She had every reason to dislike him. He'd stolen her account, and her father liked him better. Still she felt drawn to him. Professionally, they were creatively in sync. And personally . . . she wanted to taste him again.

Traci gave Valerie a scathing once over. "She doesn't look like your type, Stevie. She's so boney. And gigantic."

The barb bounced off Valerie. She'd long ago realized her height wasn't the problem. Besides, compared to Traci, she was a giant. Even wearing four-inch stilettos that could double as weapons, Traci was at least five inches shorter than her.

"Val is exactly what I want." Steven's firm tone could make even Valerie a believer. It frightened her how much she wanted to believe.

Traci's sulk returned. "Not so long ago, *I* was exactly what you wanted."

"We can't go back, Trace." Steven gentled his voice. "We have to move forward."

The pain that flashed across the other woman's features tugged a chord in Valerie. Rejection hurt. The words and actions left bruises deep beneath the skin. How well she knew this.

But Traci's vulnerability didn't last. Her expression hardened. "If you think *she's* moving forward, you'd better check your GPS. It's giving you the wrong directions." With a toss of her extensions, Traci turned and stomped from the room.

Striking out was one way to deal with rejection.

Valerie caught her breath. She hadn't realized she'd been holding it. "I think you owe Walter Millbank a fruit basket or something."

"Yeah. He did me a favor four years ago."

That was one of the things she enjoyed about working with Steven. He could follow her train of thought. Their connection on that level was disconcerting. Sometimes he even finished her sentences. Strange.

Valerie started to return to her desk, but paused when she realized the graphic designers were staring at her through her office's glass wall as though watching a movie. "How am I going to recover from this?" She grabbed the proofs from her conversation table.

"You're the boss's daughter."

Valerie faced Steven with a frown. "What's that supposed to mean?"

"You don't have to explain anything. No one's going to comment on your office relationships."

Seriously?

Valerie put her desk between them, dropping the proofs to its surface. "First, I don't have office relationships. Second, being the boss's daughter doesn't give me any advantages. Garry treats me like everyone else." Maybe worse. "The only reason people suspect he and I are related is that we have the same family name."

Steven moved to the other side of her desk. "You resemble him."

"I look like my mother."

"Then she was a stunner."

"Stop trying to get on my good side."

"You have one of those?" Steven's smile—wicked and seductive—curled her toes.

"It's reserved for people with a modicum of common sense."

Steven folded his arms across his broad chest. "You don't think I have even a modicum of common sense?"

Valerie tipped her chin toward the door. "What do you call that show you put on?"

He dropped his gaze. Was he embarrassed? "A desperate attempt to avoid an awkward situation."

Valerie widened her eyes in feigned amazement. "You were trying to *avoid* one?"

"Actually, yes." He *was* embarrassed.

She propped her hands on her hips. "You failed miserably. I'm sure the situation was awkward for Traci. It was definitely awkward for me." She gestured toward her doorway. "And, judging by the expressions on our coworkers' faces, I'm going to continue to feel awkward for quite some time."

"Don't worry. No one's going to say anything to you about it."

He couldn't be that obtuse. Could he? "That's not the point. You should not have kissed me, especially not here at work."

"I'm sorry I offended you."

Valerie gave him a suspicious stare. He didn't sound sorry. He didn't look sorry either. A knock on her door broke her concentration. She looked up as Yamile Famosa, their executive secretary-cum-receptionist, walked into her office.

Yamile stopped less than an arm's length from Steven. "I brought you your mail." Her sultry Cuban accent steamed up Valerie's office.

Steven studied the mail as he took it from her. "Thanks, Yamile."

Valerie glanced between the two of them. "Do *I* have any mail?"

Yamile kept her eyes on Steven. "I put it in your mail slot."

Valerie blinked. "You came to *my* office to deliver *Steve's* mail but left *my* mail in the reception area?"

"Yes."

Valerie looked at Steven. Why was it taking him so long to scan the two envelopes Yamile had given him? She returned her attention to the back of the younger woman's head. "You don't see anything strange about that?"

Yamile shrugged. "No." The secretary swung her curtain of shiny, ebony locks to one side, baring the left side of her long neck, apparently for Steven's benefit. "See you later." She gave Steven an I'd-like-to-see-you-naked smile, then turned to saunter from Valerie's office. Her hips swung slow and steady like a pendulum in a clock.

Valerie pinched the bridge of her nose. Was she more irritated or amused? "Women are always throwing themselves at you."

Steven finally looked up from his mail. "You don't."

She huffed out a rush of air. "And I won't."

"Pity." Steven eased into one of her guest chairs.

Valerie scowled at him as she sat. "Speaking of women throwing themselves at you, I'm surprised you don't want to get back together with your ex-fiancée."

"That's insulting. You think I'm only interested in an easy score?"

Valerie's cheeks heated. She had thought that. "I'm sorry I offended you."

He arched a brow. "Funny. That's the same apology I gave you. Is this payback or are you sincere?"

"I'd wondered the same thing about your words."

"Not all athletes sleep with every woman who knocks on our door. Some of us can say no."

"Then why don't you just say no to Traci?" Valerie

forced herself to remain still under Steven's intense scrutiny.

"Trace won't take no for an answer, and I don't want to lose her account."

"So you're willing to take one for the team?" Through the tense silence, Steven maintained eye contact. Valerie recognized his controlled anger.

"I have more self-respect than that." Steven exhaled a deep sigh. "I can't read you, Val. You seem disgusted by the stereotypes of NBA players, and you've apparently put me in that category. But you don't know me well enough to have made that opinion."

Valerie felt the sting of shame. "I'm sorry. But it's obvious Traci's eager to rekindle your relationship, and you'd wanted to marry her."

"Past tense. I realized Trace wasn't the right person for me when she broke our engagement right after my injury. Nothing's changed since then."

"I'm sorry."

"How sorry?"

Valerie's lips curved in a surprised smile. "Not sorry enough to take her account."

"You said yourself it was a good opportunity. What difference does it make which account you work on as long as we both get what we want?"

Valerie stared at him. He was as dense as a basketball. "I want a promotion, but your grand scheme doesn't include that. According to your plan, you're the only one getting what you want—someone to protect you from your ex-fiancée."

"I don't need protection." Steven stood. "The offer's open, Val. Think about it. If it plays out, we may both get what we want."

Valerie watched Steven's long, lean form disappear

through her office door. What was that supposed to mean? He had a great job, her father's respect, women falling all over him and her potential account. What else could he want?

Valerie went back to her proofs, but it wasn't long before she was interrupted again. Manuel knocked once, then entered without permission. "Why didn't you tell me things were *like that* between you and Steve?"

Valerie turned away from her proofs. "Because things aren't 'like that' between me and Steve. And you can go back and tell that to your little friends."

Manuel settled in to her guest chair, crossing his legs. "That's not fair, Val. You know I don't gossip about you."

Regret soured her stomach. "I'm sorry, Manolín. You're right. I'm just embarrassed."

"Ah, and who could blame you." Laughter deepened his Cuban accent. "I'm sure any woman—or man, for that matter—would be embarrassed to have Steve Crennell press his long, hard length against them and fuse his lips to theirs. Oh, how embarrassing!"

Valerie's face warmed. "Knock it off, Manolín."

"How will you ever recover from this embarrassment?" He sighed, shaking his head. "Your reputation has been shredded."

Valerie's cheeks burned even hotter. She turned away from the graphic artist to fiddle at her computer. "Steve didn't press anything against me. Where do you get that stuff?"

A part of her had enjoyed Steven's taste and the feel of his long, hard body pressed to hers. But she'd take that confession to her grave.

Wicked humor gleamed in her friend's bright brown eyes. "So what's between you and Steve?"

"Nothing's between us."

"Ah, that's even better."

Valerie closed her eyes and rubbed her temples. With friends like Manuel . . . "I'm this close to smacking you."

"Again, you're being unfair, Val. You didn't smack Steve."

She dropped her hands and lifted her startled gaze to his. He was laughing at her. Again. Even after four years, there were times she didn't understand her friend's sense of humor. It was probably better to change the subject. "The woman who was in my office is Traci Greer Millbank, Steve's ex-fiancée."

Manuel sobered a little. "I thought I recognized her."

"How do you know her?"

"I watch the entertainment news. Her divorce from Walter Millbank of the Miami Waves is final."

"Steve kissed me so Traci would think he and I were engaged."

Manuel's eyes widened. "Engaged?"

"Engaged." Valerie clenched her fist as renewed outrage stirred in her system. "I should have exposed him. Right there on the spot, I should have told her he was a liar."

"Why didn't you?"

She dropped her head into her cupped palm. "He caught me off guard. At the time, it just seemed easier to go along with his story."

"It was a kinder, gentler way to let Traci know Steve isn't for her anymore." He waggled his thick, black brows. "And think of the benefits."

She gave the designer a disgusted look. "Steve's love life isn't my problem."

Manuel held up a hand. "No one said it was. But it's very nice of you to do Steve this favor."

Valerie shrugged a shoulder. "It's not as though he gave me a choice. Besides, it was just this one time."

Manuel chuckled. "What are you going to do when Traci comes in to meet with Steve?"

"She lives in Colorado."

"Not yet. She's not moving to Vail until her spa opens in the spring."

"How do you know that?"

"I watch the entertainment news."

Valerie went numb. What had she done? She couldn't go through any more kisses like the one this afternoon. It was nice. It was great. But it was Steve.

She took a calming breath. "Then I guess we'll have to break up. I'm not continuing this lie until the spring."

Manuel pursed his lips and lifted his hand again. "I have a better idea. If you do Steve this favor, he's going to owe you a favor."

"What are you thinking?"

Manuel lowered his hand to his knee. "I'm thinking that, if you do him the favor of pretending to be his fiancée, Steve should talk to your father about promoting you."

"And he should wash my car and mow my lawn."

"I'm being serious, Val. He should also let you co-present to Good 'N Healthy."

Valerie's outrage returned. "He should *let* me co-present to Good 'N Healthy? It's my account!"

"No, it's Steve's." Manuel's voice was gentle.

"But it should be mine—all mine. And I don't want

Steve's help getting my promotion." That was pride talking, but Valerie couldn't muzzle it.

"He may have a better chance of convincing your father. Garry listens to him." Although hard to hear, Manuel's words were true.

"I deserve a promotion, Manolín. We both do." Valerie propped her chin on her fist. She was drained. "I'd much rather expose him and this fake engagement to Traci."

"That won't get you the account or the promotion."

"No, but it would make me feel better if, for once, Steve Crennell didn't get his way."

Chapter 6

"When are you going to leave your father's firm and work for me?"

John T. McGee's question interrupted Valerie's thoughts. She looked up to find the chief executive officer and owner of JTM Agency casually and confidently assuming Steven's seat beside her. Her father and Steven were still making their way through the AdFed's buffet line. The advertising industry organization met the third Tuesday of every month. Valerie tried not to miss the networking opportunity.

Valerie forced a smile. She felt disloyal doing even that. Her father couldn't stand the younger man. But Valerie didn't see the harm in being professional. "Hello, John. How are you?"

The executive ran his fingers through his dark blond hair. "I'd be even better if you told me you were leaving your father's firm to work for me."

His audacity made her want to laugh out loud. "You say that every time we see each other. You can't expect me to take you seriously."

"You should." John's expression sobered, surprising

Valerie into paying closer attention. "Your father's stifling you. All Parker's interested in is Crennell's star power. That's fine, but where's the substance? At the end of the day, it's creativity and ideas that get and keep the clients. And that's what you bring to the table."

As a compliment, it was wonderful. The words were a balm to her ego, which recent work events had dented and bruised. But the sentiment's shine dimmed with the realization that even an industry rival knew her father didn't value her.

Valerie put down her fork and set aside her salad. "Steve has substance. He's creative and offers a lot of good ideas. His star power may blind people at first but, once they listen to him, they see all the rest." She'd never admit as much to either Steven or her father, though.

John leaned back in Steven's seat. "But you're the glue holding that operation together. Everyone knows that."

Everyone but her father. However, even Valerie wouldn't take things that far. She wasn't Parker Advertising's glue. The whole team worked together to raise Parker Advertising's profile in the industry.

Valerie started to ask John to leave before her appetite deserted her. But her father arrived before she could make the request.

Garrison's voice conveyed outrage and anger. "And you hope that by removing the glue, as you call her, my agency would fall apart?"

Valerie's mouth went dry. He'd heard John's comments? Her gaze swung past her father to Steven, standing just behind him. How much had they heard?

"I hadn't realized you were back." Valerie's cheeks trembled with the effort to keep her smile in place.

"Would it have made a difference?" Judging by the frost in her father's tone, he hadn't quite gotten into the networking mood. The present company wasn't helping.

Valerie's spine stiffened. She didn't deserve to have her loyalty questioned. "No, it wouldn't have. I haven't said or done anything to regret."

Garrison confronted John. "Are you hoping that by luring away my daughter to work for you, my company would fall apart?"

John stood to relinquish Steven's chair. "We both know that's a distinct possibility, Parker."

There was no emotion in Garrison's gaze. No reaction at all. "I don't know any such thing."

John shrugged. "We may never find out." He glanced at Valerie before turning back to her father. "But it's my fondest wish that Valerie would agree to work for me."

Garrison sneered. "Wishing won't build your company, McGee. It takes diligence, intelligence and talent. Everything you lack."

Steven placed his free hand on Garrison's shoulder. "We're beginning to draw attention that I don't think any of us wants."

Valerie pulled her fascinated gaze from the argument in front of her and caught the stares of some of the other members. What little remained of her appetite shriveled and died.

Garrison muttered something under his breath and took his seat. Steven settled into the empty chair between Garrison and Valerie.

Valerie felt a gentle weight on her shoulder. She looked up to meet John's gray eyes.

"I'm sorry for the interruption." The advertising executive straightened away from her. "I hope you can enjoy the rest of the meeting."

Somehow she thought that would be impossible. "Thank you."

John squeezed her shoulder. She stiffened under his touch. "I know how much creativity you bring to a campaign. My offer will always be open."

"Go peddle your wares elsewhere, McGee." Garrison waved his fork at the younger man. "No one here's interested."

Valerie wasn't so sure about that. She watched John disappear into the crowd before picking up her glass of ice tea.

"It would be hard to replace you, Val." Steven spread his napkin across his lap.

Garrison cut into the broiled chicken entrée. "Hard, but not impossible."

A dry chuckle escaped Valerie. Her father hadn't given her even a moment to enjoy Steven's words. "What a relief. Knowing that it wouldn't be impossible to replace me makes it easier for me to sleep at night."

Garrison didn't appear to have heard her. "Why do you talk to him? You know you can't trust him. He's a used car salesman pretending to be an ad executive. He gives the industry a bad name."

Valerie considered her salad, but didn't think she could eat it even if it were her last meal for weeks. On the other hand, her father's appetite appeared impervious to stress or embarrassment. He stabbed a broccoli floret and shoved it into his mouth.

Valerie didn't want to have this debate in public.

She didn't think Steven was comfortable in the middle of this argument—literally—either. "It's over now, Garry. John's gone back to his table."

Garrison swallowed before responding. "It's not a good idea for you to get friendly with him."

Now he wanted to issue her paternal orders. Where had he been for the past twelve years? "He approached me. But he's gone now. Let's just drop this subject."

Garry swallowed another forkful of chicken. "It doesn't matter who approached whom. And there's every need to continue this conversation. You have to understand that, not only is McGee our competitor, but his being seen talking to you is bad for our firm."

She should have known her father's concern was for the company, not her. She unclenched her teeth and forced an even tone. "Whatever you say, Garry."

Finally, silence settled over the table, but it wasn't a comfortable one. Tension was thick enough to cut with a steak knife. Valerie checked her watch. There was plenty of time before the meeting's scheduled presentation.

From the corner of her eye, she saw an old colleague approach her father. After a warm greeting, the other man remained to chat with Garrison. Judging by the joviality, it couldn't all be business. Good. Maybe an old friend could help Garrison shake his bad mood.

Steven broke the rest of the tense silence. "Would you really leave the agency?"

Valerie turned to him. The agency's junior partner looked genuinely interested in her response.

"No. My roots are here. My mother helped my father start this agency. They built it together." She shrugged, trying to ease the weight of her heritage. "Besides, I've brought a lot to the company."

"I feel the same way. I belong at the firm, too." Steven pushed away his plate. Judging by the amount of food left on it, he didn't have much of an appetite, either. Was it the meal or the tension around them?

Valerie drank more ice tea, but she couldn't wash away the bad taste left from the argument with her father. "Why do you feel that way?"

"I've made a mark on the company. I've helped the agency grow."

Valerie nodded. "I was hoping to help the company grow, too, through the Good 'N Healthy account."

"I'm sorry, Val. If it were up to me, I'd give you the account."

She didn't want to soften toward him. "Are you saying that because it's true or because you want me to handle Traci's account?"

Steven smiled. The warmth of his expression, the teasing light in his eyes made Valerie forget what they were talking about.

Steven leaned toward her. "It's true. *And* I want you to handle Trace's account."

She laughed. "At least you're honest."

Valerie trekked to the back of the agency's suite where the partners worked secluded from the staff. She saw Steven through the glass wall that framed the front of his office. He was still here well past six o'clock in the evening. That wasn't a surprise. Long days seemed the norm for him, yet he never complained. Maybe there really was more to him than the pampered ex-NBA star. He stood behind his desk, packing page proofs and marketing material mock-ups into his briefcase.

Valerie continued to his doorway and watched him for a few moments. "Are you really going to review those tonight?"

Steven raised his head. His tie was loose and the first few buttons of his shirt were undone, revealing the hollow at the base of his throat. He gave her a smile, though his dark eyes were tired and lines of fatigue bracketed his well-shaped lips. "Of course. Otherwise, I wouldn't pack them."

From sharp and sexy this morning to rough and rumpled—but still sexy—this evening. Valerie almost felt sorry for the guy. Almost. "It's Tuesday. Isn't there a game on tonight?" There was. The Waves were playing the Cleveland Cavaliers. She'd been looking forward to the game all week.

Steven shrugged. "I'll watch some of it."

Valerie's gaze dropped to his briefcase again. "That's a lot of work for one person to keep up with."

He winked at her. "I'm more than just a pretty face—or a well-known name."

Valerie scanned his office. One of these days, she'd tell him it reminded her of an ESPN newsroom: framed newspaper and magazine articles with action photos of the great man himself decorated one wall. His jerseys—high school, college and pro—appeared on another wall, and sports trophies posed on his dark wood bookcase.

Her attention shifted to the thick project folders, stuffed campaign binders and proofs littering his desk before lifting to his eyes. "It's all right to ask for help. We won't take back your superhero membership card."

The left side of Steven's mouth lifted, revealing his dimple. Humor brightened his tired eyes. "I can manage."

No, he couldn't. Guilt prodded her again as it had since that afternoon's AdFed luncheon meeting. He'd been so kind. "You're going to get a lot busier, Steve."

Wariness replaced humor. "What does that mean?"

Valerie crossed his threshold. "I spoke with Gloria Thursday. She wants to see the presentation January second."

Steven's stare bore into her for several silent beats. "Tell me you're joking." His tone was flat.

"I'm not." Valerie battled guilt and regret. Where was her bravado now? Good 'N Healthy was her account, and she wanted it back.

Steven lowered himself to his thickly padded black executive chair. "Both campaigns are due right after the first of the year."

He made it a statement, but Valerie nodded as though he'd asked a question. "It looks that way."

"Did you call her, or did Gloria call you?"

"I saw her at the hospital Thursday night."

"Did it occur to you to ask for an extension?"

Valerie ignored Steven's sarcasm and slipped into the closest visitor's seat. "No, but it did occur to me that *I'd* be able to make her deadline. All you'd have to do is give me back my account."

Was that checkmate?

Steven's gaze was hard. "I never realized how selfish you are."

Valerie's blood ran cold. "What?"

"You're jeopardizing the firm's reputation for delivering

quality work on time and on budget so you can get your way."

Valerie sprang from her seat and jabbed a finger toward Steven's desk. "You and my father are the ones jeopardizing our reputation."

"That's ridiculous. Your father wouldn't risk his own company's reputation."

"That's exactly what he's doing." She waved a hand toward his briefcase. "Look at yourself. You've already worked an eleven-hour day. Now you're stuffing your briefcase with more work to bring home. You can't keep up."

Steven set his jaw. "I'm doing just fine."

"*I'm* the one who got us the opportunity with the account. *I'm* the one who researched the prospective client. But does my father give me the presentation? No. Instead he's sending someone without any knowledge of the account to present."

Steven stood now, too, his arms spread. "Then help me. Give me the information I need to make a successful presentation."

Valerie gaped. "Don't you hear how unfair you're being?"

Steven stepped back as though she'd slapped him. "I offered you Trace's account."

"This isn't a game, Steve. It's not *Let's Make a Deal*. It's my career, and I want what I've earned."

Steven crossed his arms, the very picture of stubbornness. "What about what the client wants?"

Valerie heard again Gloria asking whether she'd get to meet Steven. She wanted to bury her face in her hands and scream her frustration. Her friend would just have to settle for an autographed eight-by-ten glossy. "The client wants to sell their product. In the end, we'd all get what we want."

Steven shook his head as he secured his briefcase. "You're a trip, Val." He marched to his coatrack and snatched his jacket from its hanger. "Thanks for screwing me over." He gripped the material in his fist and strode past her out of his office.

Valerie stared after him. A deep breath released her tension. Great. Just swell. He steals her account and she's the one who ends up feeling guilty.

Now what?

"I don't think he's coming." Valerie's aunt, Loretta Parker Post, stared at the clock across the wide, shiny kitchen as though reading a crystal ball.

Valerie considered her father's younger sister. What an odd thing to say. "Dad has to show up sooner or later. This is his house."

Loretta turned her round cocoa gaze toward Valerie. "Are you sure he remembered he was having dinner with us tonight? You know how forgetful your father can be."

"I reminded him this afternoon." Valerie checked her wristwatch again. It was after seven-thirty. Garrison was more than half an hour late. "The two of you live together. Have you talked about the dinner?"

Her aunt shrugged. "No, not really."

Valerie frowned. Why wouldn't they talk about it? "I don't understand. He left work before me. I thought he'd already be here."

Loretta busied herself around the kitchen, wiping down already clean counters and polishing spotless appliances. "Are you hungry? Do you want me to fix you something?"

Childhood memories warmed and relaxed Valerie. How often had she watched Loretta glide across the kitchen, cooking, baking, and cleaning while Vallerie had provided her brand of help? Valerie remembered her father's widowed sister moving in after her mother passed on. Loretta had become her surrogate mother.

Time had stood still for the older woman, though. Her hair was still a deep, dark brown, her skin a flawless caramel. Her figure was full and firm in the casual butter cream slacks and sepia brown jersey.

Valerie wandered to the kitchen table and settled into one of its chairs. "No, thank you, Aunt Lo. I'll wait a little longer. But I don't want to keep you from dinner."

Her aunt's frown made Valerie feel guilty. "It's already so late. Are you sure you don't want to eat something?" Loretta asked again.

Valerie hesitated. She didn't want Loretta to worry, but neither did she want to eat two dinners. "If it's not too much trouble, I'll have a cup of tea."

Loretta gave her a skeptical look. "Tea isn't a meal." But she put the water to boil anyway. "I'm going to make myself a sandwich."

Valerie drew her cell phone from her purse. "I'll eat when Dad gets here. I'm going to try calling him again." She selected the preprogrammed number for her father's cell phone and waited for the call to go through.

"You've already left a message." Loretta pulled two mugs from a cupboard and placed an herbal tea bag inside each. Then she gathered the ingredients for a ham and cheese sandwich.

"I'm getting his voice mail again." Valerie pushed out an impatient sigh and waited for the beep. "Hi, Dad. It's Val." She rarely called her father Dad, and he never called her Val. But tonight, she used the monikers deliberately. Now, what message should she leave this time? "Just checking to see when you're coming home. It's almost seven-forty. I'm still waiting to have dinner with you—our remembrance dinner for Mom. Could you call me when you get this message? Bye."

Valerie and Loretta exchanged looks as Valerie rested her cell phone on the kitchen table. The atmosphere in the kitchen went from comfortable to strained as Valerie tried not to let her disappointment show. It was a losing battle.

"He's probably having dinner with Steve." She glared at her cell.

Loretta turned toward the stove when the kettle whistled. "You think so?"

Valerie approached the stove as the other woman filled the two mugs with steaming water. "They get along well. Dad enjoys Steve's company."

"Maybe it's male bonding." Loretta's humor sounded forced.

"Maybe." Valerie claimed her mug. "But I don't like feeling as though I'm in competition with Steve."

"Why do you feel that way?" Loretta took her tea and sandwich, then followed Valerie to the kitchen table.

"I've been working my way up at the firm since high school. Steve comes in and, right away, Dad makes him a partner."

Loretta sipped her tea. "Steve did invest a lot of money in your father's agency. Enough to start an Internet marketing division for the company."

Valerie wrapped both hands around the mug. Its warmth seeped into her and battled back her cold resentment. "The Internet division has been profitable. But I don't want to spend the rest of my career playing second fiddle to Steve Crennell."

"Why would you?"

"He gets the accounts. Even the ones I'm cultivating." Resentment stirred again inside her. Valerie took another soothing sip of hot herbal tea.

"You're not second fiddle to anyone, Valerie Grace." Loretta used her Mama Bear voice. "Don't ever think of yourself that way."

"It's not the way I see myself, but it's the way other people see me."

"I've told you before, people see you the way you see yourself, and treat you the way you expect to be treated. That includes your father." Loretta's tone didn't entertain challenges.

"I don't see myself as second to Steve, so why does Dad keep putting him ahead of me?"

"What makes you think Garry's doing that?"

"It's like I said—Steve has strategy meetings with my father. Dad confides in him."

"Val, don't ask for what you want, especially from your father. Take it. If you want Garry to have strategy meetings with you, schedule them. If you want him to confide in you, make him."

"How am I supposed to do that? I can't even get him to have dinner with me in his house." She frowned at her watch. Another ten minutes had gone by.

"If you want affirmation from your father, you'll be

waiting a long time." Loretta sounded as tired and hopeless as Valerie felt.

Valerie rose to pace the kitchen, walking off restlessness and nerves. She paused with her back to Loretta. "Am I looking for affirmation?"

"What do you think?"

Valerie faced her aunt. "I think it's time I was promoted to senior account executive and given my own accounts."

"But Garry's already said no." Loretta bit into her sandwich.

"Then I have to decide what's more important, a promotion or my father's approval."

The older woman swallowed a mouthful of ham and cheese. "I think, to you, they're the same thing."

Valerie began pacing again. "You could be right. So what do I do?"

Chapter 7

Valerie shifted in her seat again. She divided her attention between her Friday morning planning meeting with her father and Steven, and the nerves bowling for organs in her stomach. She recognized these bowlers. They were the remnants of her resentment toward her father for blowing off their dinner last night.

Where had he been? And why hadn't he called?

Garrison pushed himself away from his desk and crossed to the coffee station against his office's far wall. "I need more caffeine. Anyone else want some?"

"No, thanks." Steven wrote something on his notepad.

What were his notes for? Valerie tried to peek at Steven's writing tablet. He'd rested his right ankle on his left knee, then laid the notepad on his inner thigh. Valerie shifted her gaze and noticed the proximity of the notepad to Steven's crotch. Her breath shortened and her cheeks heated.

"Valerie?" Garrison demanded her attention.

Valerie started. She looked toward her father. In

her peripheral vision, she saw Steven turn toward her. "Yes?"

Garrison lifted the coffee pot. "Would you like some?"

Was her father offering an olive branch? Did he think coffee would make up for missing their remembrance dinner? If so, the gesture would mean more if he remembered she didn't drink coffee. "No, thank you."

Steven lowered his right leg to the floor. "Would you like me to get you a cup of tea?"

Valerie's surprised gaze met his expectant one. How was it that her rival realized she didn't drink coffee, but her father couldn't remember? She glanced at Garrison, who was making his way back to his desk.

Valerie shook her head. "No, I'm fine. But thank you."

Steven held her gaze. Valerie looked away, unable to face the concern in his eyes. How could he tell something was wrong? And had he really forgiven her for "screwing him over"?

Garrison sank into his chair, still stirring his coffee. "Okay. Where were we?"

Valerie tapped her notepad. "I'll e-mail you and Steven the cost estimates for the athletic shoes commercial shoot and the print advertisements in the national magazines."

"And I'll send you both the rates for the network and cable times." Steven captured her gaze, and Valerie felt her pulse hop again.

"That's a good idea." She dragged her eyes from his and scribbled a meaningless note on the top sheet of her writing tablet.

Garrison gulped his coffee. "Okay. I'll expect an update on this project in two weeks."

Valerie closed her steno pad. She met Garrison's gaze. "Can I talk to you?"

Steven stood, glancing between the two of them. That discomforting concern was back in his eyes. "I'll see you both later."

Valerie waited until Steven closed the door behind him. She shifted again in her seat, trying to interrupt her stomach's bowling league before confronting her father. "I waited for you until nine o'clock last night. We were supposed to have dinner together."

"I'm sorry. Something came up." Garrison didn't look sorry. He didn't seem to care.

"Something to do with the agency?"

"No."

She waited, but he didn't appear inclined to elaborate. "I wish you'd returned my calls. That dinner is very important to me."

The remembrance dinner had been her idea. They'd started it twelve years ago. As an adolescent, it had comforted her to spend time with her father on her mother's birthday, although they hadn't talked much during the meals and certainly not about anything personal or important.

At first, the silence hadn't mattered. All she'd wanted was to be with her father on that important day. But as she'd grown up, Valerie had wanted more. She'd wanted Garrison to confide in her. What were his memories of her mother? What had her mother meant to him? What had the family meant to him? How had he gone from being a caring, loving parent to this impenetrable block of ice?

"We could reschedule."

Her father's comment pulled Valerie from her

thoughts. "We have the remembrance dinner on her birthday. It's not a day you can reschedule."

Garrison rubbed his forehead. "Valerie, either reschedule the dinner or drop it. The agency isn't the place for this conversation."

Did he think his exasperated tone would intimidate her? She was beyond intimidation. Valerie sat up. "If we don't talk at the agency, where are we supposed to talk? You didn't show up for dinner with me—at your own home."

Garrison's frown darkened. "I told you something came up."

"I matter so little to you that you didn't consider calling to let me know you weren't coming? And when I called you, you didn't return any of my messages."

Garrison sighed again. Another attempt at intimidating her into silence.

"I've offered to reschedule with you," he said, his patience obviously wearing thin.

"I need to make an appointment to speak with you?"

He shook his head. "Don't twist my words, Valerie. You're getting emotional."

Maybe she was. And maybe he needed to.

"You're right, Garry. We need to keep things professional between us." Valerie collected her pen and notepad, then stepped away from his desk. "Will you join Aunt Lo and me at the cemetery on Thanksgiving? I know that's a week away, but I thought you might pencil me in now."

Garrison gave her a sharp look. He must not have liked her tone. "I have other commitments."

Am I anywhere on your list of priorities and commitments? Number four, maybe? "Of course. Will we spend any time together on Thanksgiving?"

"Of course. You and Loretta should be back before dinner." Garrison checked his watch. "Anything else?"

The bowling league broke free. Valerie's gaze shifted from her father's cool, dark eyes to his white gold Movado wristwatch, and back to his eyes. "Thanks for your time."

Valerie strode from Garrison's office, her back straight and her shoulders tense. How much longer was she going to settle for the crumbs her father doled her? Was this struggle for his approval worth the pain?

Manuel sauntered into Valerie's office and flopped into one of her two guest chairs. "You're going to have to make a deal with the devil, Val."

Valerie settled back into her chair. "I've been waiting for you, Manolín. You're like the Terminator. Relentless. Once you have a plan, you just won't stop until it's implemented."

Manuel crossed his legs and spread his arms. "That's just one of the many things you love about me."

"Yes, that and your courageous fashion style."

Today, the graphic artist was much more conservative in mustard-colored jeans, a maple brown silk jersey and plum canvas shoes.

Manuel waggled a finger at her. "Your compliments—no matter how true or well-deserved—will not distract me from my purpose."

Valerie sobered. "What's it like, Manolín?"

Concern dimmed the battle lights in his eyes. "What's what like, sweetie?"

"What's it like to be so comfortable in your own skin? You are who you are, and if others don't like it, they don't have to be a part of your world." She couldn't imagine her friend wasting twelve years of his life trying to earn his father's approval. What was it like to be that self-assured?

His expression softened with understanding. "It's easier to be comfortable in your own skin when your family supports you."

The corner of Valerie's mouth tipped up in a smile. "Which brings me right back where I started." She dropped her red pen and gave the graphic designer her full attention, infusing her tone with an energy and assurance she didn't feel. "So, you're here to convince me to pretend to be Steve's fiancée."

Manuel hesitated. "Val—"

She lifted a hand. "I appreciate your caring, Manolín. But this is what I want to talk about. I don't want to deal with the other right now."

Her friend nodded. "Then, yes. I do think you should do Steve this favor. And, in return, tell him he should talk to Garry about giving you a promotion."

"Suppose he can't convince Garry to promote me?"

"You know he has a better chance with Garry." Manuel leaned forward in his enthusiasm. "He would also have to let you copresent to Good 'N Healthy."

"I don't know, Manolín. Now I'll be presenting as well as doing the research, developing the creative and getting it produced. All that extra work on the promise that Steve will *try* to get me a promotion?"

"You're not doing the entire project alone. Steve helps with that, too. He comes up with the words and you do the illustrations."

Valerie wouldn't give in that easily. "So? If he can't guarantee my promotion, what do I get out of this engagement farce?"

"You get the experience to add to your résumé."

Valerie read the cold, hard truth in her friend's dark eyes. "I could wait forever, and my father may never give me that promotion. Or I can take my experience and leave."

"I know that's not what you want to hear, but it is time to look at the broader picture. I don't want you to leave, but I do want you to be happy."

"You're right." A deep breath eased the band tightening her chest. "We'd have to set some ground rules for this fake relationship, though. First, no more public displays of affection."

Manuel tossed both arms up. "Oh, sometimes you suck all the joy out of life."

Valerie smiled as she knew Manuel intended her to. "I'm serious, Manolín. This is a temporary solution to his problem. Once Traci moves to Colorado, Steve and I will have to return to our professional relationship."

"Are you afraid that, after a few more embraces and kisses like the one the other day, you will not be able to be professional around him?"

The thought had crossed her mind. "Of course not."

"Then just enjoy yourself. What do you have to lose?"

Valerie didn't want to find out.

Steven saved a rebound, battling three sets of arms grasping for the basketball. He spun, planning to hand off the ball to a teammate in this pickup game taking place on the Nia Neighborhood Recreational Center's indoor court.

"Hey, Shorty. You got game?"

His twelve-year-old teammate's comment broke

Steven's concentration. "Colin, keep your head in the game." He searched the court, seeking the source of the boy's distraction.

Valerie stood alone, watching the game from the sidelines. She looked confident and sexy in casual black denim cropped jeans that showed off her shapely calves and an orange top that teased him with cleavage. She'd worn her hair loose again. The straight dark locks hung just below her shoulders. His fingers itched to play with the strands.

She looked amused by Colin's question. Was it the flirtatious tone or the invitation to join the game? Her presence had brought the competition to a standstill. Colin wasn't the only one waiting for her answer. Steven was curious, too.

With a smile, Valerie pointed toward her strappy sandals before responding to Colin's invitation. "Sorry, player. I left my sneakers at home."

Steven tossed the basketball to Colin, then used the back of his wrist to wipe sweat from his upper lip. "I'll handle this, guys."

A series of catcalls and teasing followed Steven across the court. As he jogged toward Valerie, her gaze moved over his sweat-soaked T-shirt to his Nikes. He almost tripped over his feet at the look of admiration in her eyes.

Steven stopped an arm's length from her, conscious of his less-than-well-groomed appearance. "So, how 'bout it, Shorty? *Do* you have game?"

The teasing lights in Valerie's dark chocolate eyes invited him to join in. "That depends," she replied. "Can I take my shots from the pity line?"

Steven's smile grew into a grin. He gestured toward

the dark blue line behind which players took their free throws. "It's called a free-throw or charity line."

Valerie laughed, shaking her head as he tried to correct her. "Not the way I shoot. It's a real pity."

Steven chuckled, enjoying her self-deprecating humor. She was so much more relaxed away from work. Away from Garrison. Steven wanted to spend more time with this version of the woman who'd fascinated him since the moment they were first introduced.

"What are you doing here, Val? I didn't know you knew where the center was."

Valerie arched a brow. "I read the papers. The center was the top story for weeks when it opened."

"How did you know I'd be here?"

"Manuel told me you usually stopped here after work." Valerie surveyed the area, looking toward the offices beyond the basketball court. "Those are the tutoring rooms, right?"

Steven furrowed his brow. "How did you know?"

She shrugged, seeming uncomfortable with the simple question. "I came here for a tour after you started working for Garry."

But she hadn't asked him to show her around. Delayed disappointment dampened his mood. "I'd have been happy to give you a tour."

Valerie shifted her weight from one foot to the other. Why was she uncomfortable? "The center's great. It's wonderful what you've done for the community. But that's not what I'm here to talk about."

"What do you want to talk about?" Steven tried to reclaim eye contact.

Valerie gestured toward his sweat-soaked clothes. "Do you want to clean up first?"

Steven stepped back, embarrassed. "Sorry. I probably reek."

Color climbed into her high cheekbones. "No, you're fine. I mean, you smell fine. I just didn't want you to catch a chill."

Steven gestured for Valerie to join him on the bleachers. "I'll be all right." He grabbed the sweat jacket he'd tossed there before the pickup game. Turning toward her, Steven pulled on the jacket. "Have a seat."

"If you're sure." Valerie stepped onto the bleachers, taking a seat on the second row.

Steven sat beside her, leaving some distance between them. He didn't believe he didn't reek. But he didn't want to take the chance that Valerie would disappear if he left for the showers. She seemed to be in a strange mood. "Now, what can I do for you?"

"It's about what you want *me* to do for *you.*"

Steven frowned. "What's that?"

"You want me to pretend to be your fiancée to protect you from Traci."

He felt a spurt of irritation. "I don't need protection."

Valerie waved a hand. "Okay. Sorry. You just need a fiancée."

"Having another woman in the picture will help Trace believe we're never getting back together."

"Whatever. I'm willing to be your fake fiancée. But I want something in exchange."

His heart beat harder and faster than it had while he was keeping up with a bunch of prepubescent kids on the basketball court. She was willing to pretend with him? What did this mean? "What do you want in exchange?"

"I want to copresent our campaign to Good 'N Healthy."

"You're going to work with me on the presentation?"

"Provided you agree to give me a role in the client presentation."

He'd take it. Steven offered his hand to seal the agreement, keeping his voice steady. "That sounds fair."

Valerie's gaze dipped to his hand before rising again to his eyes. "There's more."

Steven let his arm drop to his thigh. He eyed her suspiciously. "What is it?"

"I also want you to convince Garry to promote me to senior account executive. He won't listen to me, but your support could sway him."

Steven noted her defensive tone, her increased tension. It had cost her to make the request of him. But she was asking for a miracle. "Val, your father doesn't listen to me any more than he listens to you. When his mind is made up, there's no changing it." He felt her disappointment as his own.

"He *does* listen to you, Steve. He admires you. Part of the reason he doesn't think we need a second account team is that he thinks you can handle everything. He sees you as some sort of superman."

Embarrassed, Steven looked away. "I'm not any kind of superman. But I'm doing okay keeping up with the projects."

"No one can keep up with that pace. Not for long." She sounded emphatic. "Sooner or later you're going to burn out. Then what will happen to Parker Advertising's reputation for getting projects done on time and on budget?"

That's what he was afraid of, too. He didn't want to disappoint Garrison. "I'll talk to him, Val. But I can't guarantee I'll be able to change his mind."

"Fair enough." Valerie extended her hand to seal the deal.

Steven glanced at her long, elegant artist's fingers. Her manicured nails were short and coated with a clear polish. He remembered from too few and too brief encounters the softness of her skin.

He didn't take the hand she offered. "Now I have a condition."

Valerie let her hand drop to the bleacher. "What condition? I'm already pretending to be your fiancée. What more do you want?"

A lot. But he'd start small. "I want you to manage Trace's account."

Valerie shook her head emphatically. Her hair swung behind her shoulders. "Oh, no. No. No. I'll pretend to be in a relationship with you. I'll keep her from crawling all over you. But I will not manage her account. You're on your own with that one."

"How are you going to keep her from crawling all over me—your words—if I'm meeting with her alone?"

Valerie sighed her exasperation. "Why don't you tell her you're not interested?"

"I did. She doesn't believe me."

"It would be too unfair for you to manage the account I went after while I got stuck dealing with the diva."

"Those are my terms." He knew he was driving a hard bargain, but he needed a starting point for his negotiations.

Valerie glared at him as she took to her feet. "Your terms are unacceptable."

Steven stood, taking her arm to prevent her from leaving. Her slender muscles vibrated with anger under his hand. "Wait. Maybe we could find a compromise like we did with the Good 'N Healthy presentation."

She turned on him. "To this point, I've done all the compromising. I'm giving up my prospective client. I'm pretending to be in love with you. What are you giving, Steve?"

Maybe he had pushed too far. "Okay. Would you at least work on Trace's account with me?"

Her chest rose and fell with a temper he hadn't anticipated but should have expected.

Valerie turned away, staring into the distance. After a few moments, she faced him again. "Fine." Steven offered her his right hand, but she pinned him with a direct challenge. "One more thing. No more public displays of affection."

Steven reached for her right hand and placed it between both of his. "Fair enough. No more public displays of affection."

He could agree to keep that part of their pretense private.

Chapter 8

Monday morning, Valerie sat in Steven's office and thrust her chin in his direction. "We should work on the Good 'N Healthy presentation first. It's due January second. That's five weeks from now."

From across his desk, Steven considered Valerie's mulish expression. Her brows were knitted and her brown eyes glowed. "I have a love-hate relationship with your stubborn streak."

Valerie blinked. Her shocked expression gave way to humor. "Should I feel sorry for you?"

Steven ignored her comment. "I love the way you're not shy about stating what you want."

"How big of you."

"But your stubbornness is difficult to work with. Then again, my father always said nothing worth having ever came easily."

Color bloomed in Valerie's high cheekbones, conflicting with the cool image she presented in her figure-hugging cream skirt suit.

She crossed her long legs. "Really? And has it occurred to you that you've been spoiled by all those people who'd say anything and do anything to spend a moment in your glory?" She checked her watch with exaggerated concern. "Hmm. Manuel's late with your coffee. Maybe he and Yamile are fighting over which you'd want first, your coffee or your mail."

Steven cocked his head. "For the record, I don't have a preference."

Valerie's laughter poured over him like cool spring water. "What arrogance."

Steven's smile faded as he faced his next challenge. "We should start on Trace's account first. She's meeting with us in a week. We need to show her something."

Valerie sobered. "Trace's spa doesn't open until March. We have plenty of time for her campaign."

"We can't wait until the spa opens before we start promoting it. You know that."

"And *you* know that we have a small window of opportunity to lure Good 'N Healthy from its current agency."

"Our contract with Trace includes delivery dates." Steven held up a hand, palm out, as Valerie started to speak. "Let's stop trumping each other. It doesn't get us anywhere."

Valerie uncrossed her legs and responded in a reasonable tone. "I'm not trying to trump you. I'm trying to talk some sense into you."

"That's the second time you've implied I'm senseless. You're hard on a brother's ego."

"Your ego can handle it."

Could it? "We could work on both accounts simultaneously. You can walk and chew gum at the same time, can't you?"

Valerie arched a brow at him, but remained silent.

She watched him watching her. Steven sensed her weighing the pros and cons of his suggestion. Would she see it as one too many compromises and reject it? Would she refuse to help him?

"Yes, I can walk and chew gum at the same time." She waved the folder in her hand. "You want to start with Fit in Time, don't you?"

"We do have that meeting Monday."

"It must be nice to get your way all the time." Her smile took the sting from the words.

"It certainly is." Steven opened his folder on Traci's health spa. "Trace didn't give us much information. Floor plans, decorating schemes and an equipment list, but no personal impressions or ideas." He looked up and found Valerie studying him. "Did you look over the information?"

"I read it last night."

"What do you think?"

Valerie took a deep breath. "Traci's going to need a lot of guidance, not only with the marketing campaign, but with planning the spa. The decorating scheme is at least five pages long with details down to the number of threads in the sheets. But the equipment list isn't even a page."

"I noticed." Steven brought the inadequate list to the top of his folder. "But we're responsible only for the campaign."

"And her brand identity. So, what are your ideas?"

Steven stood to pace. "I want to focus on the physical fitness. The exercise."

"That's not surprising. Fitness is your specialty."

He turned to her. "Why else would someone go to a health spa if not to work on his physical fitness?"

"The real question is, why would someone go to *this* health spa? To Traci's health spa?"

"To get in shape."

Valerie raised the equipment list, drawing his attention. "If Traci's so concerned with her customers' fitness, why does she only offer basic exercise equipment like treadmills, yoga balls and Jacuzzis?" She frowned, studying the list. "Are yoga balls and Jacuzzis even considered exercise equipment?"

Steven walked back to his desk to scan his copy of the list. "There's also an indoor swimming pool and a hiking path."

"No one in their right mind is going to pay twenty-five hundred dollars a night to walk on a dirt path."

Steven settled his hands on his hips. "What's your idea?"

It took Valerie a beat to raise her gaze from Steven's hips to his eyes. She may not like him, but that didn't stop her from finding him attractive.

Valerie closed her project folder. "We should focus on the spa's amenities. They're obviously what Traci's most interested in."

Steven sat again. "If no one would spend twenty-five hundred dollars a night to use a weight bench, no one's going to spend twenty-five hundred dollars a night for a bed." He cocked his head. "Unless it comes with company. And, even then, she'd better be damn good."

"Sleepovers aren't mentioned in Traci's decorating schemes."

"An oversight." Steven continued, "People go on vacation to a health spa to work out with professionals and get into shape. Otherwise, they'd go to a regular hotel."

"Maybe Traci thinks her guests want to feel at home while professionals help them get in shape."

Steven acknowledged that possibility. "It would be cheaper to stay home and have the professionals come to you."

"Tell that to Traci."

"Do you belong to a gym?"

Valerie blinked. "No. Why?"

"You have the discipline to exercise on your own. But some people go to spas hoping to find that same discipline and motivation. That's why we should work the exercise angle."

Valerie shrugged. "I'm just interpreting the information Traci gave us."

"Her information includes trainers, aerobic classes and equipment."

Valerie leaned forward to tap his copy of the list. "It also lists monogrammed robes, sunken bathtubs and eight-hundred-thread sheets." She raised a brow. "If I slept on eight-hundred-thread sheets, it would be very hard to get out of bed at five in the morning to use a treadmill."

"Is that when you work out? At five in the morning?"

"Focus, Steve."

He sighed. "It looks like we have two angles to offer Trace during Monday's meeting, physical fitness and interior design."

Valerie shook her head. "Your ex-fiancée wants to emphasize the interior design, not me."

They spent the next several minutes reviewing Traci's paperwork and the questions they wanted to ask to help develop a campaign style for the resort.

After some time, Steven glanced at his watch.

"Would you mind if we talked about Good 'N Healthy this afternoon? I'm meeting someone for lunch."

A humorless smile parted her lips. "Why am I not surprised? You got your way. We talked about Traci's account and now you're done."

Valerie stood. Her suit traced the slender curves of her figure, and Steven's gaze followed her suit.

Steven stood also. "It's not that way, Val. We'll talk about Good 'N Healthy this afternoon. Fit in Time took longer than I'd thought."

"That's because you wasted time defending an idea that was indefensible."

His eyebrows jumped. "My idea's not indefensible. It's a health spa, not a bed-and-breakfast. Who cares about the decor?"

She tucked her folder and notepad into the crook of her arm and capped her pen. "Fine. We'll write up our separate proposals and see which one Traci chooses."

Steven crossed his arms. "Unless you come to your senses beforehand and admit my idea has greater appeal."

A spark of challenge brightened her brown eyes. Steven had recognized the competitor in her. It walked hand-in-hand with her stubborn streak.

Valerie settled her free hand on her slim hip. "You're pretty sure of yourself. Do you have insider information?"

"No. Confidence."

"I'm confident, too."

"Care to put a wager on it?"

She furrowed her brow. "What kind of wager?"

Could it be this easy? "Winner takes the loser to dinner."

A sassy smile curved her lips. Valerie turned toward the door. "I'm not a cheap date."

He'd already come to that realization.

Valerie pulled the hot water lever attached to the office coffee maker. The tea bag steeped as the mug filled, carrying the lemon scent of the green tea to her. She shifted her stance. Her hip bumped against the ancient white refrigerator.

With her peripheral vision, Valerie checked out the supplies crowding her—stacks of coffee filters, bags of caffeinated and decaffeinated grounds, packets of napkins, and boxes of sugar and sweeteners.

If the agency's kitchenette were any smaller, it would be a closet. And it reeked of coffee, probably because someone was always brewing a fresh pot.

Garrison probably didn't devote much space to the kitchenette to discourage people from treating the tight quarters as a break room. The strategy worked with some employees. Valerie, for one, never lingered.

"How did the meeting with Steve go?" Manuel's voice startled her.

She lowered her mug to the counter and grabbed a napkin to dry the hot water she'd splashed onto the back of her hand. "It was okay. I don't object to working with Steve. I object to him taking the lead on my prospective account."

"At least this way, you are not completely out of the project." Manuel's smile grew into a grin. "Any more kissing?"

"*No.* We were working." She gave Manuel the full force of her exasperation.

"Boring."

Valerie stirred sweetener into her green tea, then led Manuel from the suffocating kitchenette and down the hall toward her office. "Manolín, you're a good friend. You're also a horrible instigator."

Manuel's grin never wavered. "What are friends for?" He paced beside her down the hallway. "What are your plans for the campaigns?"

"We haven't decided yet. We have different ideas on how to approach Traci's account." She sipped the hot tea. "We also didn't have time to discuss Good 'N Healthy. He has a lunch date."

Manuel followed Valerie into her office. "He's having lunch with another woman while he's engaged to you?"

She was embarrassed to admit the same question had occurred to her. "*Pretending* to be engaged to me. The engagement is fake, Manolín. Remember?"

"Sure. Right. But still. Who's this other woman?"

Valerie rounded her desk, blowing air on her tea to cool it. "Probably some basketball groupie."

"I hope Traci doesn't see him stepping out on you. It could ruin our whole plan." The graphic artist was practically vibrating with outrage.

Valerie chuckled. "We wouldn't want that."

Manuel turned to leave. "Go ahead and laugh. But if Traci smells blood in the water, she'll go back on the hunt."

"Steve didn't specifically say he was having lunch with a woman."

That seemed to mollify Manuel. Slightly. "He'd better not be."

"Manolín, what are you doing for lunch?"

Manuel paused. "I'm meeting Nate. Do you want to join us?"

Valerie shook her head, masking her disappointment. "No, but thanks. Tell Nate I said hi."

Manuel hesitated. "Are you sure? Nate won't mind. He loves you."

"No, really. I've got a salad in the refrigerator."

"Sounds delicious. Not."

Valerie noticed the spring in his step as Manuel left her office. Now she was doubly glad she hadn't accepted his invitation to be a third wheel in his lunch with Nathan.

She thought of the salad she'd shoved into the tiny, overstuffed kitchenette fridge. It was the remains of the dinner she'd picked up from a take-out restaurant the other night. Packing it for lunch had seemed like a good idea this morning. But now she wanted more of a meal.

Her wristwatch read a few minutes past noon. Perhaps if she hurried, she'd see whether Garrison would surprise her by agreeing to be her lunch date. Just the two of them.

Valerie strode the hall to the partners' offices in the back of the agency. Steven rounded the corner. A tall attractive woman walked beside him, smiling as though she enjoyed his company. Valerie hesitated between satisfaction and disillusionment. She'd been right. Steven was having lunch with a basketball groupie. Why did she care? And why had he asked *her* to protect him from Traci when he had a legion of women more than happy to fawn all over him?

Steven noticed her a few feet away and his smile brightened. "Val, we were on our way to your office."

"You were?" Her gaze cut across to the beauty beside him. She noted that the other woman must be six feet tall, five inches taller than Valerie. But the three-inch heels of her fashionable boots brought her much closer to Steven's six-foot-four. Her lightweight ruby sweater and jet black jeans complemented her figure in a way that would make other women emerald green with envy. Her raven hair fell in waves past her narrow shoulders.

Her makeup emphasized her ebony eyes and high cheekbones. But the woman's true beauty was in her expression. Welcoming, intelligent, confident. She'd give Steven credit. This woman was a vast improvement over Traci.

Why did that depress her?

Steven put his hand on the woman's shoulder. "I wanted you to meet my sister, Barbara Crennell Green. Barb, this is Valerie Parker. Val's our account executive and art director."

Barbara extended her hand with a smile. "It's a pleasure to meet you, Valerie."

Stunned, Valerie shifted into automatic pilot. She returned Barbara's handshake, staring hard at the other woman. Now she could see a family resemblance between the tall beautiful woman and her taller, handsome brother. "Please call me Val. It's very nice to meet you, too."

Steven dropped his hand from Barbara's shoulder. "We're on our way to lunch. Would you like to join us?"

Valerie blinked. She was tempted to join them. They seemed happy in each other's company. Her gaze moved between them, noting the smiles, the laughter, the warmth. Steven's sister had come to the agency to meet her brother for lunch. Her father worked down the hall from her. She could count on two fingers the times they'd had lunch together. Neither time had they been alone.

Valerie stepped back from her thoughts and the two people in front of her. "I don't want to intrude."

Barbara offered an encouraging smile. "You wouldn't be intruding. We'd love for you to join us."

A stranger would rather have lunch with her. Why did that make her feel worse? "I appreciate the offer. Perhaps another time?"

Steven's gaze shifted toward Garrison's office. Concern clouded his eyes. Had he heard the desperation in her voice?

His smile looked forced. He put his hand on the small of his sister's back. "We'll hold you to that."

Valerie stepped aside to let them pass. "I look forward to it."

Valerie watched a moment as brother and sister continued down the hall before returning to her own journey. Outside of her father's office, Valerie almost bumped into Yamile—literally—as the other woman emerged.

Yamile rocked back on her heels. "Garry's already left for lunch."

That surprised her. Her father usually didn't break for lunch until closer to half past noon. "Did he have an appointment?"

"I don't know. I gave him the market reports he asked for, then he flew out of here like his pants were on fire." Yamile laughed at her own humor.

"Thanks, Yamile." Valerie turned toward the kitchenette.

Manuel was having lunch with Nathan. Steven was joining his sister. Valerie's lunch would be leftover salad alone at her desk. She was used to eating while she worked. But today, she'd wanted something more.

Chapter 9

"Steve's not a complete jock. I've worked with him long enough to realize that." Valerie accepted the pre-scrubbed dinner plate her aunt handed her and loaded it into the dishwasher.

She could still smell the spaghetti and meat sauce Loretta had made them for dinner. The wall clock in the kitchen marked the time at just minutes before eight. It would be nice if her father made it back home before Valerie left.

Loretta scrubbed the second plate. "Then what's worrying you?"

Valerie straightened and nodded toward the dish. "You know, you don't need to wash the dishes before you put them in the dishwasher. It's a waste of time and energy."

"So you've told me many times." Loretta handed her the second prewashed plate. "And as I've told you an equal number of times, the dishes get cleaner this way."

Valerie accepted the dish, dutifully bending to settle it into the machine. "Yes, Aunt Lo."

She worked in silence with her aunt until the dishes and pots were cleaned and the kitchen returned to order.

Then Loretta led her back to the table and settled into her chair. "Stop stalling and tell me what's bothering you."

Valerie took the chair across from her aunt. "I'm afraid Steve's more interested in his ex-fiancée and her health spa than in the Good 'N Healthy presentation."

"What makes you think that?" A frown of concentration knotted Loretta's brow.

"He insisted on working on Fit in Time this morning. Then, this afternoon, he said he didn't have time to talk about Good 'N Healthy." Her skin still prickled with irritation at the memory. Perhaps Steven didn't have time to talk with her, but he had plenty of time to meet with her father. What did they have to discuss without her?

Loretta crossed her legs. "But if he's so interested in this other woman, why would he try to get you to take her project from him?"

Valerie exhaled a short, sharp breath. "Who knows? He claimed he doesn't want to work with her, but he's working with her now, isn't he?"

"He is, but he has you as a buffer."

"That's right. I'm a buffer, not protection." Valerie snorted. "He even scheduled a status meeting with her for Monday. That gives us four days to come up with a campaign plan. And we have to have Garry approve it before we can present it to her. A little anxious, isn't he?"

Loretta looked more amused than concerned. "He is, but would it be such a bad thing if it were successful? You'd both share the credit."

"But it would be another client *he* brought to the company. Good 'N Healthy would be a client *I* brought to the company. How do I make sure he understands how important it is to me that the Good 'N Healthy presentation succeeds?"

"Since when have you had trouble expressing yourself?"

Valerie's breaths were coming faster. Nerves. "I *have* been expressing myself. He's not listening." Another trait Steven shared with her father.

"Maybe he is. Give him time. This is only the first day you've worked together on these projects."

"I have to make it successful."

Awareness cleared Loretta's expression. "This is about your father again."

Valerie's back stiffened in response to Loretta's obvious concern. "No. This is about my promotion."

"But you think your father promoting you would be his way of saying he loves you."

Heat burned in Valerie's cheeks. Embarrassment churned in her stomach. "I deserve this promotion, Aunt Lo." She was beginning to feel like a broken record.

"Yes, you do deserve your father's love. Every child does." Loretta set her chin at a stubborn angle. Her dark eyes glowed with a protective light. "But, Val, your father's not going to change. After twelve years, you should realize that."

Fear spread like ice through her system. "What do you mean? You don't think he'll promote me?"

"This isn't about a promotion and you know that." Loretta reached out and squeezed Valerie's forearm. "After your mother died, your father shut himself off from everyone, including you. I'm sorry for that, Val.

But it doesn't mean he doesn't love you. He does. He just can't express it."

Valerie needed to pace the kitchen, though she regretted the loss of Loretta's touch as she stood to move away. Her touch carried a warmth and comfort she'd leaned on for a very long time.

The clock read well after eight PM now. Still no sign of her father. Where was he?

Valerie folded her arms against the cold inside her and walked across the kitchen. "He doesn't talk about Mom. Every year, I invite him to go to the cemetery with us. He always says no."

"He loved your mother very much."

Valerie nodded. Her back was to the older woman. "I remember. And I've seen photos of them together taken before I was born. That's why I don't understand why he's put so much distance between himself and me and Mom's memory."

"He's the only one who can explain, and he doesn't want to talk about it."

Valerie turned to face her aunt. "And I can't make him."

"No, you can't. You can't control what your father says or what he does. But you can control your attitude."

Valerie cocked her head. "What's wrong with my attitude?"

Loretta stood and walked toward her. Valerie remained still as Loretta cupped her hands around Valerie's shoulders. "I've told you many times before. You have to love yourself, respect yourself and accept yourself. Then, it doesn't matter what other people think. Not even your father."

Valerie placed her palm over one of Loretta's. "It shouldn't, but it does."

Steven's e-mail leaped into Valerie's in-box Tuesday afternoon. The subject heading read, *Please. Come to my office.*

Why? What did he want?

Valerie opened the message, expecting an answer to those questions. But the e-mail itself was empty, keeping the mystery intact. Seriously?

What was the point of his secrecy? Valerie set down her mug of strawberry kiwi green tea and started to type a request for an explanation. Steven might think he was her boss, but he wasn't. He shouldn't expect her to ask how high when he told her to jump.

But he'd said please, a part of her whispered. Valerie sighed. True. He may be bossing her around, but at least he was being polite about it. She cancelled her reply and pushed away from her desk.

It was a brisk walk to Steven's office, but she stopped before she got to his door. Through the clear glass wall fronting his office, she saw the answer to her questions.

Why had Steven summoned her? Because Traci had come to visit. His ex-fiancée posed opposite Steven in one of his two guest chairs.

Valerie shifted her scrutiny to Steven. How was the big, strong, former NBA star taking this surprise visit from his past? Steven seemed cool, confident and in control. But Valerie wasn't fooled. She'd sensed the desperation in the e-mail he'd sent her. He needed her protection.

Valerie took a moment to prepare for her role as

Steven Crennell's fiancée. Then she knocked on his door. "Am I interrupting?"

Steven stood up. The warmth in his eyes must be gratitude. "Of course not, sweetheart. Come in."

Sweetheart? Valerie's hesitation almost gave them away. She noted Traci's scowl as she crossed to the empty guest chair. The other woman's glossy ebony locks cascaded in artful disarray around her shoulders. Was the red material—what little there was— molded over her full curves real silk? Traci's perfume was a powerful presence between them.

Valerie settled into the chair beside Steven's ex-fiancée. "I thought our meeting wasn't until Monday. Was I mistaken?" She indulged in one last visual feast of Steven's well-toned physique in his pale lemon shirt and pleated chocolate brown pants before he re-claimed his seat.

Steven pulled his chair back under his desk. "You're not."

Traci gave Valerie a secretive smile. But her eyes glittered with hate. "Oh, this isn't a business visit. I thought I'd drop by to take Stevie to lunch."

Surprised, Valerie checked her watch. "It's almost two o'clock."

Traci shrugged a shoulder as she kept eye contact. "You don't mind, do you?"

Steven interrupted. "I told Trace we'd just had lunch."

Together. The word hung between them, unspoken but understood.

Valerie angled her body to face Traci. "That's right. Steve and I just had lunch."

In reality, Steven had eaten at his desk. Valerie knew this because she'd waited her turn while he'd heated his leftovers in the diminutive kitchen's miniscule microwave. Afterward, he'd walked her back to her office before continuing on to his own. Ah, the glamorous life of advertising—eating microwave lunches at your desk to meet a deadline.

She saw the approval in Steven's eyes. A promise was a promise, and she'd pledged to pretend they were a couple. The scary thing was, she was enjoying herself.

Valerie turned her attention to the woman who considered her a rival for Steven's affection. How long would Traci pursue Steven? And what was her purpose? True love? Not possible. It was more likely Traci saw Steven as a symbol, proof she could have any man she wanted. Even one she'd turned her back on years before in favor of someone who could fulfill her every material wish.

Traci's voice was breathy, but her smile tightened. "Stevie and I will plan to get together for lunch another day. You don't mind, do you? I mean, after all, Stevie and I have a past. A very long and intimate past."

Valerie struggled against a laugh. Traci was trying hard to find her buttons, but Valerie didn't have any to push. However, she was willing to play along. "You may be his past, but I'm his future." Not bad. Very daytime drama-ish.

Steven cleared his throat. "Val and I have lunch together every day."

Was that a smile Valerie glimpsed in his eyes?

Traci laughed, a harsh grating noise mixed with anger. "You can't have lunch together every day."

Steven looked baffled. "Why not?"

Traci wrinkled her nose in disgust. "That's so boring."

His confusion didn't clear. "Why?"

"It's so routine and predictable. Unless—" Traci gave Valerie a scathing look that made her feel as though she were wearing a tattered bathrobe and fuzzy slippers instead of a fitted forest green jacket, black pants and three-inch pumps. The other woman returned her attention to Steven. "You don't expect me to believe you have a nooner every day, do you?"

Steven's expression hardened. "I'm not discussing my private life with you, Trace. And I'm not having lunch with you, either."

"Or a nooner." Valerie muttered the words under her breath.

Traci gave her a fast glare before affecting a coy look for Steven. "You won't have lunch with an old friend?"

Traci's dogged determination impressed Valerie. If she used her powers for good, the other woman could probably end world hunger.

Steven folded his hands on his desk. "Trace, let's stop circling the truth. We aren't old friends. We aren't anything. Any relationship we could have claimed was destroyed when you broke our engagement to marry someone else."

Traci leaned forward. A sense of urgency surrounded her. "I made a mistake, Stevie. Can't we start over?"

Valerie's muscles went tight. How disconcerting to feel so threatened. "Uh, no. We're working for you, Traci. Of course we're going to dedicate ourselves to creating a successful campaign for your company. But we need to keep our relationships strictly professional. It's in everyone's best interest."

Traci gave her a hard stare. Valerie returned it

without wavering. Finally, the other woman addressed Steven. "Is that how you feel, too?"

Steven nodded once. "Of course. Val and I are more than business partners." He gave Valerie a smile that curled her toes in her pumps. "Still, I couldn't have put it better myself. We're already working on some strong, creative ideas to show you Monday."

Traci stood. She adjusted her little red dress over her video vixen curves. The hem ended well above her knees. "If that's the way you want it, Stevie, then that's the way it will be. But you're making a mistake." She gestured disdainfully toward Valerie. "She can't give you what you need. Look at her body. It would be like having sex with a mannequin."

Traci stomped from Steven's office, her full hips spinning angrily in the tight dress.

Steven clenched his teeth to trap the words he wanted to call after Traci. The language and tone were less than chivalrous and would make Valerie even more uncomfortable than she probably was already. "Are you okay?"

"Do you think she'll keep our appointment Monday?" Valerie sounded curious, not angry.

Steven eyed her with caution. Was she going to lull him into a false sense of security before exploding over Traci's words? "She'll show if she's serious about advertising her health spa. And, knowing Trace, she is."

Steven studied the elegant lines of Valerie's profile while she stared at his doorway. Her high cheekbones, delicate nose, full lips and pointed chin. Not for the first time since meeting her, he wished he could draw.

Traci's strong perfume lingered in his office, overpowering Valerie's soft scent. She usually smelled of lavender and vanilla. Steven wanted to circle his desk and bury his face in her neck. Would she excuse his action if he explained he needed her fragrance to remove Traci's scent?

"Do you think she'll pay any attention to what I said?"

"No." He settled back into his chair, still wary of Valerie's reactions. "What Trace wants, Trace gets. Her marriage is a perfect example. She didn't let her engagement to me stand in her way."

Valerie finally looked at him. "Now she wants you back. It will be an interesting battle of wills."

"One Traci's going to lose."

Valerie tilted her head. "I think she missed her true calling."

"What do you think it is?"

"With all of her drama, she should have been an actress."

Steven grunted. "True." He kneaded the back of his neck. Tension stiffened his neck and shoulders like quick-drying cement. He still worried Valerie would displace her anger onto him. Not that he'd blame her. "I'm sorry about this."

Her eyes danced with humor. "About what? Fabricating our engagement? Talking me into working on this project with you and Traci? E-mailing me to protect you?" The words may have stung, but Valerie didn't speak them in anger.

"I didn't ask you for protection."

She laughed outright. "Oh, come on, Steve. You sent me a cryptic e-mail begging me to come to your office. What did you want if it wasn't protection?"

She was verbally backing him into a corner, trying to trap him into a false confession. But he'd spent enough years playing basketball to know how to elude his opponents. "I wanted your company."

Valerie tossed her head back as wave after wave of hilarity rolled from her. Once again, he enjoyed the sound, letting it flow over him like cool spring water. Valerie's full, pink lips were parted, displaying perfect white teeth. Her eyes were closed and thick lashes lay above her high cheekbones. Her long graceful neck arched. Steven wanted to move behind her, pluck the clips from her tight bun and watch her hair swing free.

"That's a good one, Steve. You wanted my company." Valerie wiped tears of laughter from her cheeks. "You know, I should get more out of this partnership if I'm also supposed to act as your bodyguard."

"I didn't call you for protection." The left side of his mouth tipped up as this time he chose to be amused rather than annoyed by her accusation.

"Oh, that's right. You called for my company." A few final chuckles escaped Valerie. "One day, you'll admit it's more than my company you want."

He did want more than her company. But he doubted that what he wanted and what she thought he wanted were one and the same. "Why do you find it amusing that I'd want to spend some nonworking time with you?"

"Why would you want to? We're not friends—"

Steven interrupted her roll. "Why can't we be?"

She blinked at him as though he'd changed lanes without warning. "We don't have anything in common."

"I don't think you know me well enough to decide that."

She swung a hand toward him. "You're Steve Crennell, former NBA superstar, community benefactor and junior partner in my father's ad agency. I'm Val Parker. Period."

"A successful account executive, a talented artist, a caring volunteer at Miami Children's Hospital and someone I'd like to know better."

Valerie narrowed her eyes at him. "Why?" She gestured toward his door. "I've already seen what type of woman attracts you, and I'm nothing like that."

"Trace was different when we were together. Her lifestyle with Walt changed her."

"Or brought out something you'd never noticed before."

He shrugged. "Maybe. I realized years ago I probably never really knew Trace."

Valerie smiled. "But now you're older and wiser?"

"Yes."

"And you know what you want?"

He caught his breath. "Yes, I do."

Valerie stood. "Well, I hope you get it."

Steven watched her leave. He hoped so, too.

Chapter 10

"You've started without me."

Valerie looked up at Steven's voice, a potato chip caught between her lips, to find him in the center of her doorway. His arms were braced on either door-jamb, emphasizing the width of his chest and shoulders in his iceberg blue shirt. The hummingbirds in her stomach launched into action. Her mouth went dry.

Valerie lowered the potato chip. "What are you talking about?"

"You're having lunch without me."

Her brows knit. Steven's conversation was like mental yoga. "Yes. I have before, and I probably will again."

"Yesterday we told Trace we had lunch together every day. I thought we should start doing that today."

She didn't see how that would help her digestion. The hummingbirds wouldn't sit still that long. "Why?"

"Because we're supposed to be a couple." His tone implied the answer should have been obvious.

One of them wasn't thinking clearly. Her money was on Steven. "We're just pretending, Steve. Remember?"

"If we're going to convince Trace we're a couple, we have to spend more time together. What if someone tells her we're not actually engaged?"

Valerie returned her attention to her page proofs. "Everyone knows about the fake engagement. You know how office gossip works. They'll keep our secret. Now, if you don't mind, I've got a lot of layouts to approve."

"Maybe that's why you're always so tense. You never take a lunch break. You should try getting away from your desk once in a while. That might help your disposition."

Valerie smothered a sigh and gestured toward the piles of paper asserting their dominance over her desk. And it was only Wednesday. "Today isn't that day."

Steven held her gaze a moment more. Then, without a word, he left. Shaking off a vague sense of disappointment, Valerie returned to her soup and chips. And proofs. The never-ending proofs.

Minutes later, footsteps tracked closer to her office. Valerie looked up as Steven folded his long, lean form into a seat on the other side of her desk. "What are you doing?"

"Having lunch with you." He made space on her desk for his bottled water, napkin and plastic ware before pulling the lid off his microwaveable bowl of chicken and green bean casserole. The scent of pepper, cumin and garlic made her mouth water.

Valerie swallowed and nodded toward his bottled water. "That's going to leave a wet ring."

He dragged her pad of medium-sized Post-Its toward him, then settled his bottled water on top of it. Valerie shrugged her brows. That wasn't quite what she'd had in mind.

Valerie pondered her microwaveable bowl of tomato basil soup and her grab bag of baked potato chips. What had made her think that would be a satisfying lunch?

She returned to her proofs, though she didn't recognize the words. She couldn't comprehend the sentences. Valerie felt Steven's presence like a phantom touch. She sensed his every movement like a psychic link. And if she tried, not even very hard, she could taste him, just as she'd tasted him when he'd stolen that kiss. Her fingers clenched around the stem of her red pen.

Steven's voice broke the lengthening silence. "Ignoring me won't make me go away."

She refused to look up, refused to meet his eyes. "I still don't understand what you're doing here."

"I thought we'd progressed past the I-hate-Steve-for-no-apparent-reason tantrums."

Valerie's expression was shocked surprise. "I don't throw tantrums."

Steven arched a brow. "What are you holding against me?"

Her heart stuttered. She had an image of what she wanted to hold against him. "I don't—"

"Don't lie. I know it takes a while for people to get comfortable with each other. But it's been almost nine months, Val."

Valerie leaned away from her desk. "Why don't we talk about the Good 'N Healthy presentation instead? Since you haven't had time to meet with me, I've been brainstorming on my own."

"I'm not your enemy." Steven's tone was firm, but not unkind.

"Why are you baiting me?"

He gave a brief, dry laugh. "That doesn't take much, does it? At least not where I'm concerned. Why do you dislike me?"

Her gaze bounced from Steven, to her desk, to the wall behind him. "Why do you care?"

"If you dislike someone, you should have a reason. It only seems fair."

She sat straighter, frustration coursing through her. "You want to talk about fairness? We do the same work. But, as the senior account executive, you have final say on the project and creative, and you're the one who presents our ideas to the client."

"That's not my decision."

Valerie dropped her pen and crossed her arms. "I don't believe you aren't allowed an opinion on the project leads. You're a partner."

Steven set his bowl of half-eaten chicken and green bean casserole on her desk. "Your father wants to use my name to sway clients."

"The name you established on the basketball court."

"It's worked."

Valerie uncrossed her arms and laid her hands flat on the desk. She wasn't getting through to him. "We're an advertising agency, not an NBA team."

He nodded toward the wall behind her. "I have several of those trophies, too."

"But you're not bringing them with you to the meetings, are you? You're bringing your NBA record."

"Do you think that NBA reputation fell into my lap? It's decades worth of hard work and sacrifices, mine and my family's. I didn't roll out of bed one day and end up in the NBA."

The anger in his tone brought Valerie up short. "I'm not saying that you did."

"Not everyone makes it into the NBA."

"I know that."

"It's a *competitive* sport."

"Yes, it is."

"And every accolade a player gets is earned. Nothing is handed to him."

Valerie's cheeks burned. A pulse beat in her temple. She leaned into her desk to drive home her point. "I wasn't belittling your accomplishments. But we're an advertising agency. Holding your NBA accolades in higher regard than my campaign successes undermines *my* accomplishments."

Steven sighed. "That's not intentional."

"Then why were you assigned my prospect? The client *I've* been working with."

"Your father made that decision and the decision for me to do the campaign presentations." He paused, holding her gaze and refusing to allow her to look away. "I understand you're frustrated, but that debate is between you and your father. Instead, you're projecting your anger onto me."

The truth of his statement dealt Valerie a stinging blow. "You're right."

Steven blinked. "I expected more of an argument."

Valerie offered a smile. "You didn't think I could admit when I've been wrong?"

"I thought it might take a bit more persuasion."

Her heart beat faster as she struggled to keep an even tone. "No, I can admit when I'm wrong. And I apologize for treating you unfairly. But, in fairness to me, I think my projecting my frustration with my father's decisions onto you is an honest mistake."

Steven frowned. "What do you mean?"

Her voice was breathless. "If you didn't agree with using your name, or doing the presentations I prepared, or reassigning the Good 'N Healthy proposal, you could have said no."

Steven stared. "I'm the junior partner. It's your father's company."

Valerie shook her head over his protestations. "That's not the reason you don't challenge his decisions."

"I'm not averse to confrontation." His voice deepened.

Valerie sensed his growing temper in the tension seeping from his body. "No, but you're a people pleaser."

"What?" Steven's brow furrowed as anger redirected to confusion.

"You want everyone to like you. That's important to you. And it doesn't matter whether you agree with them."

Steven cocked his head. His black velvet eyes gleamed. Was it anger or amusement? "That's crap."

His inelegant phrasing was out of character, but Steven's pronouncement didn't surprise her. What professional athlete would admit to an insecurity?

Valerie rested her chin on her fist and gave Steven a knowing look. "So you wanted to participate in that bachelor auction for the cancer research fund-raiser?"

"It was a worthy cause."

"You could have written them a check." When he remained silent, Valerie continued. "And the fashion show for the public television station? Another worthy cause?"

"What's your point?"

Valerie pursed her lips. "It's interesting that you're anxious to please my father and these social benefactors, but you're not as concerned with pleasing me. Why is that?"

Steven collected his barely touched lunch and half-empty bottle of water, then stood. "I don't think there is any pleasing you."

The buzzer sounded, ending the first half of the Miami Waves game. His former team was playing in New York and facing the worst shellacking of its season. Disgusted, Steven sat in his parents' family room listening to the broadcast announcer voice inanities about what the Waves needed to do to get into the game.

"They need to score." His mother gave her opinion in a muted growl.

Steven gestured toward the television with his glass of lemonade. "They need to play defense."

Phillip grunted his agreement from the sofa. "Some offense wouldn't hurt, either. Millbank's one of the tallest guys on the court, and he can't buy a basket."

"He'd better get his mind out of the divorce court and focus on the basketball court." Macy turned toward Steven. Concern tightened her features. "How are things between you and Trace?"

Steven drew his attention from the Gatorade commercial. His mother had been asking that same question every day since he'd told his family Traci had indeed reentered his life. "Stop worrying, Mom. Trace and I aren't getting back together."

Macy pursed her lips. She rested her hand on her

husband's thigh as he sat beside her on the sofa. "I told you that woman was going to come looking for you."

Steven nodded. She'd said that every day, too. "You were right."

"And she won't stop until she's got you."

"She knows it's over between us." Steven settled deeper into the cream armchair and sipped his lemonade. The cool liquid eased his parched throat as he came under the scrutiny of both parents.

"What makes you so sure?" His father sounded suspicious.

Steven gripped the chair's overstuffed arm with his free hand. The cotton fabric was warm and soft under his palm. "Because I told her I was engaged to someone else."

What was he opening himself to by confiding his subterfuge to his parents?

Phillip snorted his amusement. "You think that's going to work?"

Macy shook her head and breathed a heavy sigh. "She's not going to take your word for it. She'll keep after you until she meets your supposed fiancée."

"She has." Steven sipped more lemonade as his parents' eyes grew wide.

His mother regained her voice first. "She has what?"

"Met my fiancée."

"You're engaged?" Macy's volume approached a screech.

"Mace, Steve's not going to get engaged without telling us first." Phillip turned toward Steven. "Right?"

"Right," Steven agreed quickly. "We're not engaged. We're just pretending so Trace would know there isn't any chance of our reconciling."

Steven frowned. Maybe Valerie had a point about

their pretense. His explanation sounded a little childish now that he thought about it.

"Who's *we*?" His mother's voice was sharp with impatience.

"Val and I."

Macy's brows slid almost to her hairline. "Val agreed to this pretense?"

Steven didn't appreciate his mother's incredulity. "In exchange for copresenting the Good 'N Healthy proposal."

Macy crossed her arms. "She's the one who brought in Good 'N Healthy. If you ask me, she should do the presentation herself. It's only fair."

Phillip patted his wife's hand as it rested on his thigh. "That wasn't Steve's decision."

His father's words drew Steven's brows together. "Maybe I should have objected more strongly."

Phillip shrugged. "I'm sure Garry knows what's best for his company."

Steven tilted his head. "But I've invested in it. It's my company, too."

Macy studied her son's features with a mother's concern. "What's wrong, Steve?"

Steven stared at the television. The broadcast announcers were back to build anticipation for the game's second half. Steven didn't hear a word they said. Memories of the last conversation he'd had with Valerie blocked their voices. "Am I a people pleaser?"

"What do you mean?" His mother sounded bewildered.

Steven faced his parents. "Am I more concerned with other people's approval than I am with doing what's right for me?"

Phillip glanced at his wife before meeting Steven's eyes. "Only you can answer that, son."

Steven stood to pace the room. "I've played competitive sports all my life. It's laughable to think someone who'd played in the NBA would be confrontation averse. Isn't it?"

"Then what makes you think you are?" His father sounded as baffled as Steven felt.

"Not what. Who." Steven turned to study the floor-to-ceiling bookcase built into one corner of the family room's left wall. The polished mahogany wood shelves were full of classical literature, popular literature, fiction and nonfiction titles. And he'd read them all. "Val thinks I don't question her father's decisions because I'm a people pleaser."

Macy inhaled a sharp breath. "Maybe you agree with his decisions."

This from the woman who, a moment ago, chastised Steven for taking Valerie's client.

"Not always." Steven wandered to the matching bookcase built into the opposite corner of the left wall. He'd read these books, too.

"If you disagree with Garry's decisions, say so. You owe it to yourself to speak your mind." His father's advice was reasonable and right.

Then why hadn't he disagreed with Garrison in the past? Was Valerie right?

"Why does Val's opinion matter to you?" His mother echoed the question occupying his mind.

He faced his parents. "Val doesn't care about my celebrity. I can be myself with her." She challenged him. She was real with him.

Phillip twined his fingers with Macy's. "It doesn't

matter what we think or what Val thinks. What matters is what you think, and what you want to do about it."

Macy nodded. "That's right. Do you want to be a people pleaser or not?"

Steven wandered back to his armchair. Glancing at the television, he saw Miami and New York were just starting the second half of their game.

He met his parents' gazes from across the room. "The only person I want to please is myself." And Valerie.

Chapter 11

Valerie stood beside Loretta in front of her mother's grave site as she had every year for the past twelve years during the month of her mother's birth.

It felt right, sharing this day with Loretta. The other woman had been friends with her mother long before Valerie's birth, long before Marilyn May had married Garrison Parker. Then, after her mother's death, Loretta had stepped in to guide Valerie through her awkward adolescence to womanhood.

"I don't know what I would have done without you." Valerie had said those words before. She meant them every time.

Loretta wrapped an arm around Valerie's waist and squeezed. "I don't know what I would have done without *you*."

Valerie was grateful for her aunt's company. On this day especially, she needed to be with someone who knew her and who'd loved her mother. Still, Marilyn May-Parker's headstone read, BELOVED WIFE AND MOTHER. Her father should be here with them, remembering her mother. Remembering his wife.

"What could Dad possibly have to do that he couldn't be here with us?"

Perhaps Thanksgiving wasn't a convenient time for her father, although she couldn't understand why not. It was a holiday. What other commitment kept him from his wife's grave site?

Loretta released Valerie's waist to slip her hand into the side pocket of her butter yellow coat. "I found this photo in a scrapbook. You should have it. I have another copy in an album."

Valerie accepted the wallet-sized picture, running her fingertips over the image. "I've never seen this before." She breathed the words, mesmerized by the happy scene frozen in time.

In the photo, she was a toddler, wiggling in her father's arms and laughing up at her mother. Her mother stood behind her father's shoulder, aiming a loving smile at her baby daughter. Marilyn had curved one hand around Garrison's shoulder. The other rested lightly on Valerie's chubby arm. Garrison sat with Valerie held safely in his care. In the picture, he was beaming at her. His expression conveyed love, joy and pride. For her.

Valerie stared at the image a moment longer, then opened her purse and carefully placed the small photo in her wallet. "Thank you." The words came out watery as Valerie pushed them past the lump in her throat.

"I knew you'd want it."

Valerie raised her head and let her gaze travel over the rich green lawn. The late-November breeze was warm and sharp with the scent of cut grass. A scattering of fat old trees sat around the cemetery's perimeter. A mental image of her father's expression from the photo was superimposed over the landscape.

"When I was fourteen, I thought Dad didn't talk with me about Mom because he thought I was too young." Valerie tucked her hands into the pockets of her lightweight black jacket. "I'm twenty-six. What's his excuse now?"

Loretta joined her arm with Valerie's, bringing the two of them closer together. "We talk about your mother all the time. What more can your father tell you?"

Valerie contemplated the modest arrangement of long-stemmed pink roses she'd rested beside her mother's headstone. "Did he love her?"

"Of course he did. He loved your mother very much. You know that."

Valerie sensed Loretta's surprise and heard it in her voice. "Why?"

Loretta hesitated. "For a lot of different reasons."

Valerie turned to her father's sister. "That's one of the things that only he can tell me, if he'd ever talk to me about Mom."

Loretta rubbed Valerie's back. "Give your father time, Val."

"I've given him twelve years, Aunt Lo. How much more time does he need?" She faced the other woman as she gestured toward her mother's headstone. Loretta's arm fell away. "Why won't he come here with me? Has he even been back since her funeral?"

Loretta looked away. "Your father has his own way of dealing with his grief."

"And that's to forget the past and push me away?" She felt her emotions climbing to take over. She struggled to hold them back.

Loretta met Valerie's gaze with worry in her own. "What do you want him to do? What do you want him to say?"

Valerie stared across the cemetery, this time seeing the sorrow and emptiness. "I know the little things. Pink roses were her favorite. She liked butter-almond ice cream and pop music, especially The Deele."

"Don't mention that. The Deele was one of her guilty pleasures. But that group did have some good songs. Remember 'Two Occasions'?"

Affection for the other woman filled Valerie. Even after Marilyn's passing, Loretta still felt loyal to her friend.

Valerie blinked to ease the sting of tears. She returned her attention to her mother's headstone. "And, of course, she loved the Miami Waves."

A giggle burst from Loretta. Her hold on Valerie's arm slipped away. "She would scream at the TV when they were losing. And her language." The older woman shook her head, still giggling.

"Dad hated that. He'd say, 'Lyn, they can't hear you, you know.'" She deepened her voice to mimic her father.

Loretta giggled again. "Your mother was pretty loud. Even if the players couldn't hear her, your neighbors across the street and down the block sure could."

Valerie's smile grew into a grin. "Probably." With more memories, she sobered. "And she was a beautiful artist."

Loretta slipped an arm around Valerie's waist and squeezed. "Just like you. You're very much your mother's daughter."

"I look like her. I draw like her." Valerie clenched

her teeth. Where should she begin? She'd had twelve years, but she still didn't know how to ask the questions she needed answers for. She was better with pictures. Steven was the wordsmith. She'd give her right arm if he would appear and give her a tagline that explained her feelings.

She squeezed her eyes shut, straining for the words. "I want him to tell me why I'm not enough. Why couldn't he care enough about me to hold what was left of our family together?" She opened her eyes and met Loretta's stricken look. "What could I have done to make him care?"

Loretta pulled Valerie into her embrace. "Of course you're enough for him. Why would you think such silly things?"

Valerie stepped back to look down into the other woman's eyes. "Aunt Lo, you know why. He doesn't talk to me. My God, he won't even show up to share dinner with me in his own house."

"Val, just because he doesn't act the way you want him to doesn't mean your father doesn't love and care about you. You're his daughter."

"By birth. For the little we know about each other, we might as well be strangers." Valerie paced away, too agitated to stand still.

"That's not fair. Your father's not good at expressing himself. That's something you have in common with him. Lyn was the life of the party. But you and your father are introverts."

Keeping her back to her aunt, Valerie rubbed a knuckle under each eye. "I wouldn't think you'd have to be an extrovert to be interested in knowing your own child. You'd just have to care."

"He does care."

Valerie cradled her head in her hands. "Why can't I get past this? Why am I allowing him such a stranglehold on me?" She turned toward Loretta. "On my life?"

"Put yourself in his shoes. He lost his wife, the woman he loved."

"But he still has a daughter. Does that mean anything to him?"

"Of course it does."

Valerie frowned at her aunt. "Why are you so adamant about defending him?"

"I'm not defending him. I'm freeing you. Let him go, Val, and move on with your life."

Valerie threw her hands up. "I want to, but I don't know how."

"All you need to do is accept yourself the way you are. You're a strong, independent, intelligent, successful person. Accept yourself."

Valerie turned away, shoving her hands back into her pockets. "I don't see myself that way. I can't until I know . . ."

"What?"

Valerie shrugged, the gesture more restless than careless. "Why he won't accept me."

"He may not even know why he's keeping a distance from you." Loretta's voice came over Valerie's shoulder.

Valerie breathed a short, humorless laugh. "He's had twelve years to figure it out, Aunt Lo. He's running out of time."

"Whose idea was this movie?" Marlon stared at the credits flying up his sixty-five-inch, high-definition, plasma screen, surround-sound television. He was sprawled boneless in his armchair.

Steven scooted forward in the matching armchair. "That would be yours, player."

Marlon grunted without shifting his attention from the screen. "Well, you let me pick it. What kind of friend are you?"

Steven stood and stretched the stiffness from his muscles. "That's two hours and forty minutes of my life I'll never get back." He carried his empty juice bottle to his friend's recycling box, navigating the obstacle course of athletic shoes, gossip magazines and unidentifiable items littering his path.

"Maybe we should've gotten that Thanksgiving movie." Marlon rolled out of his chair carrying his empty bottles of fruit juice and a bowl of popcorn. "The previews looked good."

Steven glanced over his shoulder to find his friend following him into the kitchen. "That's what happens when you pick a movie based on action instead of script."

"Enlighten me."

"I don't have that much time." Steven rinsed the empty plastic bottle, then dropped it into Marlon's recycling bin.

"That's mean, man." Marlon took Steven's place at the sink, going through the same process of washing, then recycling the empty bottles. "I appreciate your cutting Thanksgiving with your family short so you could stay over to take me to the airport in the morning."

"No problem." Steven slipped into the easy familiarity of the exchange. "I appreciate your continuing our pretravel tradition even though I'm not on the team anymore."

Marlon slapped his shoulder. "It's a good tradition. I hate traveling. Movies distract me so I can relax and get some sleep."

"It works better if you watch a good movie. You've picked some losers over the years." Steven chuckled at those memories.

"You have no appreciation of fine films." Marlon glanced at his wristwatch. "I'd better get some sleep."

Steven checked the time. It was only after ten o'clock, but his friend had an early flight.

He followed Marlon from the entertainment room to the main part of the mansion. "Did you remember to put sheets in the guest room this time?"

"Yeah." Marlon tossed the response over his shoulder.

"Are they clean?"

"That's mean, man."

"Mar, I love you like the brother I never had." Steven spoke to Marlon's back as he mounted the winding walnut wood staircase. "But you're a slob. You need a cleaning service."

"I've got one."

Steven stopped and glanced around. "You need a new one, Mar."

"The sheets are clean, man. Stop fussing. You sound like a little girl." Marlon forced his baritone into a high soprano in an attempt to impersonate a little girl. "I need clean sheets." He crested the top of the staircase and turned left toward the bedrooms.

Steven shook his head as Marlon led him to the guest room. The room was large, bright and plain. His friend hadn't put much thought into the space beyond furnishing it to accommodate guests.

The same dark green carpet from the hallway extended into the room. Heavy white drapes covered windows that spanned the width of the far wall. The dressing table, chest of drawers and nightstands were made of plain, brown oak. The walls were bare except for a mirror hanging above the dressing table.

Steven spotted the sheets lying on top of the king-size bed standing in the middle of the room. "This is an improvement. At least the sheets are in the room. Maybe next time the bed will actually be made."

"Just like a fussy little girl. You've got complaints, take them up with management." Marlon gestured toward the sheets. "You need help?"

"No, I'm good." Steven stepped forward and shook out the fitted sheet before tucking it onto the bed. "Is Millbank ready for Chicago? My parents are still angry with him after the loss to the Knicks. If he drops another away game, they aren't going to forgive him this season. Or maybe even next."

Marlon grunted. "They aren't the only ones pissed at him. He'd better pull himself together before he steps on the court to play the Bulls." He leaned against the wall beside the bedroom door and crossed his ankles. His red T-shirt and black shorts were a strong splash of color against the white wall. "Speaking of Millbank, is Trace behaving herself?"

Steven shrugged. "As much as Trace can."

Marlon barked a laugh. "That means no. Is Val still helping you with that?"

Steven pulled the third corner of the fitted sheet over the mattress. The unpleasant memory of their surprise meeting with Traci Tuesday made his back tense. "Yeah. But I don't think Traci's buying the pretense."

"She's a woman on a mission." Marlon crossed his arms over his chest. "I still think pretending to be engaged to another woman is a dumb idea."

"Do you have a better one?"

"Change your name and leave the country."

"I'll reword that. Do you have a *realistic* plan?"

"What are you going to do when Val stops pretending?"

Steven reached for the top sheet he'd left on the dressing table. "Val won't go back on her word."

"That's not what I meant. What are you going to do when she falls in love with you?"

Steven stilled, waiting to get his wind back. The idea of Valerie loving him made his heart speed up and his stomach muscles clench with an almost painful longing. He took a breath and measured his words. "What makes you think that would happen?"

"What makes you think it wouldn't?"

"Val's not going to crumble at my feet just because I used to be a ballplayer." More's the pity. "In fact, with her, my former career is a strike against me."

Marlon spread his arms wide. "What? Every honey wants a baller. We've got the fame and fortune."

"Val pays her own bills."

"When she decides she's in love with you, what are you going to do? Fake another engagement? Something tells me that play won't work a second time."

"You don't know Val. She's the opposite of Trace. She's not on the hunt for a man to take care of her. She's about making her own way."

Marlon stood away from the wall. "You didn't realize what Trace was really like until after she broke your engagement. A damn close call."

"I've learned from my mistake."

Marlon shook his head. "You're asking for trouble, man."

Steven leaned against the dresser and shoved his damp palms into the pockets of his khaki pants.

"Maybe I think she's worth the risk." He held his friend's gaze, watching for his reaction.

Marlon's eyes widened, then narrowed. "Why?"

Steven shrugged. "I respect her. She's smart, talented and works hard. She's real, and I can be myself with her. And I think she's sexy as hell."

His friend sighed, shaking his head. "What color's your Honey Decoder Ring?"

Steven's lips tugged upward in a reluctant smile. "It's amber. Proceed with caution."

Marlon nodded once. "I'd listen to it."

Chapter 12

"John? Why are you calling me?" Valerie gripped the receiver of her office telephone in one hand. In her other hand, she squeezed a red pen between two fingers.

Muscles in her neck and shoulders bunched as memories of her last encounter with John T. McGee of JTM Advertising ten days ago assailed her. As she recalled, Garrison had been furious. If he found out John was calling her at work, he'd be enraged. Valerie didn't want to deal with that.

She checked the time on her computer monitor. It was just after nine o'clock Friday morning. Hopefully, Garrison was in his office on the other side of the suite and not roaming around the agency where he could possibly overhear her conversation.

"I wanted to remind you of my offer." John's voice was smooth as silk. "I know you're not taking me seriously, but I want to assure you I'm very sincere."

Despite John's charm, Valerie couldn't get past the discomfort of conversing with her father's competitor.

Garrison may have given up on their family twelve years ago, but her loyalty was proving a lot more tenacious.

Valerie kept an eye on her door. "I'm not leaving my family's agency to work for our competitor."

John's laughter rumbled low. "Don't think of me as a competitor. Think of me as an alternative. I'm another option for your career aspirations."

Oh, he was good. And Valerie was tempted. "My career goals are being met right where I am."

Yes, she was lying. But she wasn't about to give a competitor information that could damage her parents' company.

But John appeared to have his own suspicions. "Really? Because I think you have a lot more to offer an ad agency, opportunities that Crennell's star power is taking away from you. Am I right?"

John's assessment was too close to the truth. Was he guessing or did he know?

Valerie stared at her computer, her stomach tied in knots. "I appreciate your concern, but I'm really not interested. I'd also appreciate it if you would stop contacting me."

"I can't make that promise, Val. I really want you to work with me. With my company."

Was it her imagination or was John flirting with her? "Thank you, but no. Good-bye, John."

"Val, wait. Don't hang up. Why don't we meet for lunch and discuss this some more?"

Valerie cupped her forehead in her palm. She should just hang up. "There's nothing more to say. Now, please, don't ever call me again. Not here, and not at home." She wanted to be clear.

"You're not doing your career any favors, Val. You should at least consider my offer."

Valerie glanced across her office. The framed painting of a butterfly floating above wildflowers hung on that wall. Her mother had painted it as a gift for her on her twelfth birthday. "This isn't just about my career. Parker Advertising is about my family."

There was a brief pause before John answered. "It might be time to separate your work from your family."

Her grip on the receiver tightened to the point of pain, but Valerie couldn't let go. John had touched raw emotions. "I disagree."

"I'm sorry, Val. That was too personal. Please let me make it up to you. Meet me for lunch."

"John, you can make it up to me by never calling me again. Ever." Valerie recradled the receiver, then wrapped her arms around her torso to keep her body from shaking apart.

"That campaign isn't working for me." Two hours later, Valerie rose from the conversation table in Steven's office.

"Give me a chance to sell it to you." From his seat on the other side of the table, Steven tracked her progress as she passed him. She left behind the light, clean scent of her perfume. Lavender and vanilla.

Valerie stopped in front of the window. The early afternoon light cast a soft glow around her, framing the silhouette of her slender figure. The vision fed his fantasy of greeting her the morning after a night in each other's arms.

She spoke with her back to him. "We need a fresh approach. Your idea is good, but it's too similar to our sports campaigns. I can tell you rushed the concept."

The criticism brought Steven back to reality. "The healthy living angle is a fresh approach."

Valerie faced him. Her hands went to her waist. The pose emphasized her slender figure in the narrow dark purple skirt and cream blouse. "We've used similar angles with sports shoes and exercise equipment. Good 'N Healthy makes primarily nutritional supplements."

Steven propped an elbow on the table behind him. "There's a connection between these products. Exercise equipment and nutritional supplements work to keep people healthy." He shrugged. "I don't see a problem using the healthy lifestyle angle."

"Your idea takes the focus off the supplement by bringing in sports. As an agency, we need to show that we can do other types of promotion."

Steven arched a brow. "Do you think a pill alone will get you in shape? Physical fitness is a lifestyle, not a supplement."

Valerie paced before the window. "Our client base and campaigns work together. If we're going to grow the agency, we need to diversify both. If we keep contracting with the same types of clients and keep designing the same types of campaigns, companies will think we can only do one thing." She stopped to meet his gaze.

Steven smiled at her persistence. "We can't force a campaign that doesn't fit the product."

Valerie pivoted back to the window. "These walls are closing in on me."

Steven barely caught her words. Valerie had muttered them as though she hadn't wanted to admit her feelings. But she didn't have to voice them. He'd sensed them from across the room. Work wasn't the sole cause of the tension and frustration emanating from her. Valerie had been on edge since she'd walked into his office fifteen minutes ago.

What had upset her? Was it her father again? Was she upset about the project? Was it another man? He cut away from that train of thought.

Steven checked his silver Rolex. "It's a little after two." It had been a long day. It probably didn't help that he'd gotten up at 4 AM to drop Marlon off at the airport by five o'clock that morning. "I don't have any other meetings this afternoon. What about you?"

Valerie shrugged. "This is my last one, too."

"Let's get out of here for a while."

She frowned. "And go where?"

Steven stood and removed his suit jacket from the hanger behind his door. "A change of venue will help us think. I'll drive."

"You have someplace in mind?" The tone of her voice and the look in her eyes questioned Steven's sanity.

"Yes." He shrugged into his jacket and patted his pants pocket to check for his car keys.

"Where?"

"It's a surprise."

Valerie reclaimed her seat at the conversation table. "I don't like surprises. Let's stay here."

"You'll like this one." Steven walked back to her, putting his hand on the top of her chair in a silent invitation to join him.

Valerie met his gaze over her shoulder. "All of our files are here."

He sensed her softening toward the idea. "We can take them with us." Steven gathered her files from the table.

She lifted her eyes from the folder to his face. "This isn't a good idea." Her voice was a thin breath.

"Because you feel safer here, surrounded by coworkers and with your office on the other side of the suite."

Valerie frowned. "I'm not afraid to go off-site with you."

Steven offered his hand to her. "Prove it. All I'm asking for is a chance."

"How did you know this was one of my favorite places?" Less than an hour later, Valerie stood with Steven in the University of Miami's Lowe Art Museum. They were in the Art of Africa room studying a Komo helmet mask.

"My first hint was the postcards you have from the museum." Steven spoke in a dry voice.

Valerie's tension and turmoil from the visit to her mother's grave site yesterday and this morning's conversation with John McGee were blowing away like dust on a river breeze. She sighed her contentment.

"You're very observant." She pictured the two small postcards propped beside the box of facial tissues on her desk. No one would consider them prominently displayed, yet Steven had noticed them. What else had he noticed about her?

"I didn't realize you were a member, but I should have." Steven bent to read the card beside the mask.

He stood close enough for Valerie to breathe his scent, musk and sandalwood. Pulses all over her body tripped alert.

Valerie dragged her attention from Steven and focused on the display. She'd seen it before. The card explained that the horizontal mask was from the Bamana people. The leader of the Komo secret society wore it.

She wandered to the display of the Ukara cloth of the Igbo people. The intricately patterned black-and-white material was about six feet wide by seven feet tall. Valerie was familiar with most of the pieces in this room. She visited the museum several times a month. The cool, quiet rooms were therapeutic, stimulating the mind while easing the spirit. No one could carry their stress past the doorway. The minute she'd crossed the entrance, her tension had dissolved. Yes, Steven was quite observant. She was both flattered and frightened.

He caught up to her at the Ukara.

Valerie kept her eyes on the cloth. "What's your favorite place? Where do you like to spend your time?"

"Bookstores." Steven circled her to study the double-faced helmet mask of Nigeria's Ejagham people. Once again he had to bend to read the information card.

Valerie blinked. "Bookstores?" That wouldn't have been her first guess.

Steven straightened with a smile. "You thought I'd say gyms, right?"

"Could you blame me?" She gave his long, fine form a deliberate once-over. Her eyes traveled over his taupe blazer, mint green shirt and gray and mint green patterned tie, down to his slate-gray pleated pants and black Italian shoes. Her gaze returned to his face. She could forgive his cocky smile and the deep dimples that accompanied it. "You look like you work out. A lot."

"Thank you." He looked as though he were fighting a blush. Good.

"Which bookstore do you prefer?"

"I like them all." Steven shrugged. "I like the musty old stores that sell gently used books. The well-organized chains with the latest best sellers. The independent stores that know their regular customers by name."

His descriptions warmed Valerie. "I should have guessed. You're an athlete and a wordsmith."

"You didn't think I was much of a wordsmith earlier." Steven's crooked smile made the muscles in her thighs relax.

She turned away to gesture toward the artwork on display. "You see with words. I see with images. That's why you like to spend your free time in bookstores while I have a membership to the museum."

"What images do you see when you think of the Good 'N Healthy campaign?" Steven placed a hand on the small of Valerie's back and guided her from the Art of Africa room toward the outside courtyard. The heat from his palm woke the hummingbirds in her belly.

"When I think of being healthy, I don't automatically think of lacing up my running shoes and heading for the hills."

"What do you think of?" Steven paced beside her, leading them toward a bench.

"I think of being confident and beautiful."

Steven stopped and focused on her. "Go on."

"I know that a pill alone can't make you physically fit or confident or beautiful. Nutritional supplements are one part of a healthy lifestyle, like you said." At his nod, Valerie continued. "But in my mind, I see a woman taking a Good 'N Healthy vitamin supplement before she faces the day."

Steven picked up the story. "Then she's stuck in traffic on her way to work."

"And at work, she has a stressful meeting."

"And on her way home, her car breaks down."

Valerie held up a hand, palm out. "Let's not get carried away. We're talking about a nutritional supplement, not Valium."

Steven flashed her a smile. "You're right. That's enough for one day."

"We can offer them more than one version of the campaign. We could pitch this one with the working woman and another with a man running a bunch of errands on the weekend."

Steven's eyes took on a contemplative expression. "Healthy. Confident. Strong."

"Beauty from the inside out. That's it. That's the one." Valerie bounced on the tip of her toes. She threw her arms around Steven's shoulders and hugged him tight.

She felt Steven's arms wrap around her waist to return the embrace. Euphoria rushed through her body. They'd come up with a totally different pitch for a totally different company. They were on their way to diversifying their client base. She pulled back, a helpless grin still in place.

Until she saw the heat in Steven's black velvet eyes.

The hummingbirds went wild. She may have stopped breathing. She wasn't sure. Steven's eyes held so much heat and desire and wanting. Valerie was overwhelmed. Her body started to shake. She would have fallen if she didn't have a grip on his broad, thick shoulders. If his well-muscled arms weren't holding her close.

Steven's gaze dipped from her eyes to her mouth and stayed there. A prelude to his kiss. Did she want the real thing? Valerie wasn't sure. She wanted to feel his lips on hers. She wanted to taste him with her tongue. But what would happen afterward? After the holding and the heat? How would their relationship change after the intimacy of such an act? She didn't doubt that it would.

Did she care?

Should she?

Steven's embrace tightened around her waist, bringing her body closer to his. She breathed his scent, musk and sandalwood. Valerie melted into him. Steven parted his lips and lowered his head toward hers. His movements were slow, giving her time to decide. Did she want this? Did she want him?

Valerie closed her eyes, parted her lips and made her decision.

Steven's mouth landed softly over hers. Taking his time, drawing out the moment, the anticipation. Driving her wild. Valerie rose higher on her toes and leaned in closer to his body. Steven nibbled at her lips. The friction turned up her body temperature. He rubbed her top lip, then the bottom. He planted slow, soft kisses at the corners of her mouth.

He was mesmerizing her. Valerie was wrapped in a sensory haze. Her world was just his scent, his taste, his touch. And all she wanted was more.

Steven traced his tongue around her lips. Valerie's tongue reached out to meet his. He tasted the way she imagined sin would taste. A little sweet. A little spicy. Very hot. His tongue played with hers. Sliding over. Stroking under. Wrapping around. She moaned for more. Her blood was rushing in her ears. Her body was melting over his.

Steven's hands slid down her back, tracing her spine before settling low. His palms curved around her buttocks, then lifted her against his hips. Valerie sensed her feet leave the ground. Her heart drummed in her chest. Or was that his heart? His heat pressed against hers.

Valerie gasped and tore her mouth from his. "Wait."

Steven lowered her down his body. Her nerve endings trembled every inch of the way.

He pressed his forehead against hers, breathing deeply. "I'm sorry. Are you okay?"

How was she supposed to answer that? Every erogenous zone on her body was swollen and on red alert. "You promised. No public displays of affection."

He took a deep breath, then let it out. "We aren't in public."

Valerie lifted her head away from his to look at him. He had the sexiest smile. She stepped back before she gave in to the need to kiss him again. "We're in a museum courtyard."

"Look around. Do you see anyone?"

Valerie looked around the empty courtyard. She didn't even see anyone through the glass doors. They were completely alone.

She turned back to him, shaking her head and struggling against a smile. "You are indeed a master wordsmith."

Chapter 13

Steven considered the irritable expression on Traci's face. Perhaps ten o'clock Monday morning wasn't the best time to have a client status meeting with her. His ex-fiancée sat to his left at the table in the agency's conference room. Valerie, masquerading as his current fiancée, was on his right. Steven folded his hands on the conference table to keep from toying with Valerie's fingers.

Traci hadn't been a morning person when they were in college. Chances were that hadn't changed, considering the pampered lifestyle she'd been rumored to have had as Mrs. Walter Millbank.

In contrast, Steven had always been a morning person. He enjoyed the still hours before the rest of his community was up and about.

Was Valerie a morning person? He'd like to find out.

Traci was barely covered in a very little, very tight black dress. She'd angled her chair to face him, displaying her long, toned, bare brown legs. As she crossed them, the dress rose to even more immodest heights.

Steven diverted his attention to his meeting notes. "We've come up with a couple of angles to promote your resort. One option showcases the health spa's luxury accommodations. Another option emphasizes the exercise facility as the primary selling feature."

Traci looked thoughtful. "I like it." She combed her fingertips through her dark locks, repeatedly lifting the strands, then letting them tumble back to her shoulders. Her hair gleamed in the overhead lighting.

Steven waited a beat. "Which idea?"

Traci hesitated. "Which one did you come up with?"

Before Steven could respond, Valerie did. She leaned forward, catching Traci's attention. "Without knowing who came up with which idea, which one more closely reflects your brand identity?"

Steven enjoyed the way Valerie appeared in her modest orange and green checked blouse. It topped a narrow knee-length green skirt. Valerie was a soothing summer day to Traci's dangerous summer night.

"What's a brand identity?" Traci addressed the question to Steven. Since joining them in the conference room, she had yet to address Valerie, who sat across the table from her.

Steven blinked. It appeared Valerie had been right to question whether Traci had a brand identity or even knew what one was. He rubbed the back of his neck. They had a lot of work to do, much more than he'd anticipated. It didn't help that Traci's perfume dominated their confined space. It made the conference room even stuffier. He wished he could open the door, but he didn't trust that the meeting wouldn't explode into an argument.

Steven leaned forward, folding his hands on the table. "Your company's brand identity is the way you want your customers to view your company. For example, do you want people to consider your spa as a fun place or a place to get fit?"

"Why can't it be both?" Traci scowled her question. "A place to have fun while you're getting in shape."

Valerie shifted in her seat. "It's hard for one company to be all things to all people."

Steven nodded. "People who want to have fun won't want fitness trainers pushing them to work out. And people who are serious about their fitness don't want the distraction of social activities."

Valerie nodded. "That's why successful companies cater to a very specific customer base."

Traci gave Valerie a hard stare before returning her attention to Steven. "Well, I don't know what my customer base is."

Steven absorbed that. "How much market research did you do before you planned to open your spa?"

"I did research." Traci's defensive tone was more suited to a four-year-old child than an entrepreneur. "I know Vail is where a lot of the stars go to ski, and they want to get fit for their movie roles."

In college, Traci hadn't wanted to do her homework or study for tests. She'd wanted to get the degree without doing the work. To discover she'd started a business without doing research shouldn't surprise him. But it did. He was surprised and disappointed.

Valerie seemed incredulous as well. "That's the extent of your research?"

Traci turned a vicious glare on Valerie, finally responding to her. "Not everyone has a daddy who'll hand them everything on a silver platter. Some of us have to fight and claw and struggle for every little thing."

"And some of us get married." Valerie's voice was devoid of inflection.

Traci jabbed a finger at Valerie. "Listen—"

Steven held up a hand, palm out. No good could come from this exchange. "Ladies, this isn't productive. Trace, you need to identify your customer base. Do you have a business plan?"

"No."

Steven's eyebrows jumped. "You need a business plan."

"Why?"

"For one thing, it helps you identify your customer base." Valerie's tone was as dry as kindling.

Steven saw the sparks ignite in Traci's eyes.

Traci leaned in to the table, challenging Valerie. "Listen—"

Steven lifted his palm again. "You won't have a successful marketing campaign unless you know your customers, Trace. You should put together a business plan."

Traci pouted. "I thought you were going to do that."

"We can, but we didn't know you'd need our help with that." Steven sat back in his chair, feeling the strain of battling his frustration over this turn of events. "It's going to delay your campaign's launch."

Traci's eyes widened. "By how much?"

Steven turned to Valerie. "A couple of weeks?"

Valerie nodded. "At least."

Traci's eyes narrowed in a hate-filled glare she directed toward Valerie. "You're enjoying this, aren't you?"

Steven tensed as he waited for Valerie's reaction.

Valerie recapped her pen. "No, I don't enjoy giving

clients bad news. Every project this agency takes on becomes personal. Your disappointment is our disappointment. That's why we do our best to set realistic expectations. And, realistically, creating your business plan will set us back at least a couple of weeks."

He wanted to give Valerie a standing ovation. Why had he been worried? Her professionalism was one of the things he admired about her.

Steven returned his attention to Traci. "I'm surprised Walt didn't ask you for a business plan before he helped you open the spa."

Traci's ex-husband might have been infatuated with her, but otherwise, Walter Millbank had proven himself to be a sharp entrepreneur with several successful business ventures.

Traci rolled her eyes. "I didn't have time for all that. I told him he could either invest in the spa or pay me more alimony."

Steven mentally shook his head at his close call. That could have been him, dealing with Traci's extortion at the emotional end of their relationship. He pulled himself out of the past and what might have been. "We'll also need to visit Fit in Time."

Traci's eyes shone with excitement. "That's a great idea. I could show you around Vail and the spa." She lowered her voice and recrossed her legs, the invitation obvious. "And we can christen the hot tub."

Valerie's brows rose. "You're talking to my fiancé, and I'm right here."

Traci ignored her. "Come out this weekend, Stevie. I'll show you a great time."

Steven consulted his BlackBerry. "That's not enough notice." He turned to Valerie. "Would next Thursday and Friday work for you? That's December thirteenth and fourteenth."

Traci curled her bright red lips. "Why are you asking *her*?"

"In addition to being my fiancée, Val's my partner on this project. She'll need to tour the spa as well."

Traci looked dubious. "Can't you just tell her about it?"

Steven arched a brow. "We're a package deal, Trace. We either come together, or we don't come at all."

Traci angled her chin and returned Steven's gaze with hostility. Steven never wavered.

Traci shifted her glare to Valerie. "Then I guess you're coming together."

The lack of warmth in Traci's invitation didn't escape Steven's notice, but he was more interested in Valerie's reaction. Her eyes shone with satisfaction. He knew she'd enjoy her first business trip, despite the client's less than professional attitude.

Steven repeated his original question. "Will next Thursday and Friday work for you, Val?"

A slight smile curved her lips. "That should be fine."

His gaze lingered on her mouth. "Then I'll ask Yamile to make our travel arrangements."

Traci uncrossed her legs. Her scowl in place, she shoved away from the table. "I think we're done here."

Steven rose more slowly. "We'll walk you out."

Traci turned to march from the conference room. Steven exchanged looks with Valerie. She shrugged her brows before preceding him from the room. Traci Greer Millbank must be the agency's worst client in its eighteen-year history.

In the lobby, Traci turned and raised her hands to Steven's shoulders. "I'll wait to hear from you."

She lifted up on her toes, reaching for Steven's lips. Steven stepped back from Traci, setting her hands away from him. Traci scowled at his rejection. Without a glance toward Valerie, his ex-fiancée stormed out.

Valerie turned to Steven. "She won't give up, will she?"

"It doesn't appear that way." Steven turned. He was ready to leave the site of Traci's most recent scene and return to his office. Imagining Yamile's reaction as the administrative assistant watched the show from behind her desk was enough.

Valerie fell into step beside him. "Thanks for insisting that I tour Fit in Time with you."

Steven's brows knit. "We're working on this project together."

"You know I don't usually attend these on-site client meetings."

"You should."

She tossed him a look. "Tell that to Garry."

"I have." Steven shrugged. "He wants to restrict the client visits to him and me, and the final decision is his."

Valerie gave a noncommittal "hmm." They continued to her office in comfortable silence, though she seemed distant from him.

Valerie paused in her office's threshold. "What will you do if Garry tells you to go to Vail without me?"

"He won't."

Valerie gave him a skeptical look. "What will you say?"

Steven crossed his arms and propped a shoulder against the doorjamb. The position brought him closer to her. Close enough to catch a trace of her perfume, to feel her warmth. Valerie didn't step back.

Memories of her in his arms distracted him. But he saw the concern darkening her chocolate eyes and blinked the images away. "Garry won't tell me to go to Traci's spa without you. But, if he does, I'll remind him you and I are working on Traci's campaign together. This trip is more than a client meeting. It's research. You need to be there."

Her brown eyes cleared. He glimpsed the smile within before she turned to enter her office.

Steven reached out, taking hold of her upper arm. Her skin was warm through the thin material of her blouse. "I'm on your side, Val. I give you my word."

Her expression softened. "I'm beginning to believe you." She freed her smile before continuing into her office.

Steven watched her a few moments more before moving away. With her admission, he felt as though he'd just scored the winning basket.

Manuel didn't bother knocking before entering Valerie's office. "How was this morning's meeting with The Ex?"

He was a vintage vision in an orange and black butterfly collar shirt and orange boot-cut pants.

Valerie blinked. "I can hear Donna Summer singing 'MacArthur Park.'"

Manuel sank into a guest chair. He rested his coffee mug on Valerie's desk and adjusted the crease of his pants. "I bought this from an online vintage clothing store." The polyester shirt hugged his thin torso and the shiny pants flared away from his black loafers.

Valerie sat back in her swivel chair. "Another bold fashion choice. It suits you."

Manuel reclaimed his coffee cup. His gaze held hers as he drank his personal java mix—one third coffee, two thirds cream. "Flattery—no matter how well deserved—won't distract me. How did your meeting go? Did Traci show her claws again?"

"Of course." Valerie sipped her apple cinnamon tea. "Steve and I are going to her spa."

Manuel hastily put his mug back on her desk as a coughing fit assailed him. She'd anticipated his reaction. She'd also expected his visit much sooner. She checked the time on her computer monitor. It was well after eleven o'clock. Valerie sipped more tea and waited for her friend's recovery.

Manuel regained his breath. "You're going to Vail? With Steve? For how long?"

Valerie shrugged, masking her excitement over attending a client meeting, no matter how unpleasant the client. "A couple of days. We're going to tour the facility. Traci wants help identifying Fit in Time's brand."

Manuel's jaw dropped. "She's opening a million-dollar-plus facility in less than three months, but she doesn't know her brand?"

"I know it's hard to believe. That should have been the first thing she'd decided."

"Absolutely." Manuel paused. His mouth curved into a salacious grin. "So, one room or two?"

Valerie hesitated with her mug in midair. "What?"

"How are you going to handle your fake engagement? One room or two?"

Heat flared upward from Valerie's breasts. She lowered her mug before the tea splashed onto her desk. The memory of Steven's passionate kiss had been floating through her mind all day. All weekend. She'd told him no public displays of affection, so he'd embraced her in an empty courtyard. Clever man.

Valerie sat tall in her chair and tried to appear in control. "This is a business trip, Manolín. Two rooms."

"But one room would save the agency money."

She ignored the teasing glint in his eyes. "Even if Traci believes Steve and I are engaged, it wouldn't be appropriate for us to share a room."

Manuel laughed. "You are so uptight." He crossed his legs and readjusted the crease in his pants.

Valerie gave his disco-era outfit a pointed look. "I can see why you might have that opinion."

Manuel expelled a long-suffering sigh. "While you're out of town, could you *possibly* convince yourself to have fun?"

"I have fun."

"Yeah. Your twelve- and thirteen-hour days are a barrel of laughs."

"This is a business trip, Manolín. Not a vacation."

He rolled his eyes. "You're not going to be on the clock twenty-four seven. You need to relax. Let your hair down. Get in touch with your inner wild child."

"That may not be a good idea."

"Are you kidding me? It's one of the best ideas I've ever had. Besides, what could it hurt?"

The memory of Steven's heated kiss pressed against her defenses. His taste. His scent. The feel of his arms around her. She didn't think it was a matter of *what* could get hurt; it was a matter of *whom*.

Manuel interrupted her thoughts. "Does Garry know you're going to Vail?"

"Steve's going to tell him."

Her friend winked. "I told you he was a good guy. He'll convince Garry to promote you."

"If anyone could, I believe it would be Steve. Still, I wish I didn't need someone to speak for me."

Manuel shrugged. "Who cares how you get it as long as you get it?"

Valerie rubbed at a sudden tightness in her chest. "It would mean more if Garry weren't pressured into promoting me. I want him to acknowledge that I've earned it."

"*You* know that you've earned it. Isn't that enough?"

She shook her head. "If it's come to the point that someone else has to show him my worth, then maybe it's time I leave."

Steven's sister seemed to think he'd lost his mind. "You're going to *Vail* in *December*? You'd better take warm clothes."

The traffic light turned green. Steven released the brake on his five-year-old BMW and eased onto its accelerator. The Monday night traffic was heavy. "I know what other states are like in the fall, Sis. Not all of the Waves games were at home."

Steven heard Barbara yawn and stretch in the passenger seat beside him. It had been a long day for both of them, ending with Barbara leading science tutoring classes for high school students at the Nia Neighborhood Center.

Her voice was thoughtful as she continued. "Why did Trace open a spa in Colorado, anyway? She was born and raised in Florida."

"I don't think she thought things through, which isn't surprising." Steven kept his eyes on the evening traffic. "Trace was never big on details. She was always too impulsive."

"No, Trace always had a plan."

"What do you mean?"

"The minute you decided to retire from basketball, she whipped out Plan B. The next thing we knew, she was exchanging vows with Walt Millbank."

"I guess there are some details she's big on." Steven's stomach twisted every time he thought of how he'd been played. "I can't believe I was so stupid."

"You were young and ruled by hormones." Barbara's tone was brisk as she dismissed those years of Steven's life. "But now Traci's coming after you again, and you've given her home-court advantage by going to Vail. How are you going to handle that?"

Steven stopped at another red light and turned toward her. "Val's going to be there, too."

Barbara's eyes widened. "The fake fiancée? When you get back, you have to tell me *everything*." Her eyes narrowed. "Will she be armed?"

Steven shook his head with a chuckle. "You make my life sound like a soap opera."

"Steve, darling, your life *is* a soap opera."

"Everything will be fine. Val and I will go to Vail, get the information we need, then come home."

Barbara shifted in her seat to face him. "And what are you giving Val in exchange for her getting in the line of fire?"

"I'm going to talk to Garry about giving her a promotion."

Her brow knitted with sisterly concern. "Are you sure it's wise to set yourself up as her knight in shining armor?"

A corner of Steven's mouth curved upward. "Is that what I'm doing?"

"Laugh if you want, but that's exactly what you're doing. What's going to happen if you aren't able to change Garry's mind?"

Steven shifted his attention to the traffic light. It was still red. He drummed his fingers against the steering wheel. "Val knows there aren't any guarantees."

Barbara's tone was urgent. "I don't think it's a good idea to get between Val and her father. That's a lose-lose situation."

"How?" The light changed to green. Steven gripped the steering wheel and crossed the intersection.

"Whether she gets her promotion or not, you're going to risk one of them being angry with you. I'm surprised you're taking this risk for Val. You're usually so careful to play it safe so people like you."

Steven inhaled a sharp breath. His sister's words were too similar to Valerie's accusations. He shot a quick glance her way before returning his attention to the congested traffic. "You think I'm a people pleaser?"

He heard the shrug in Barbara's voice. "It's understandable. People want to be liked, even obnoxious little brothers."

She was trying to lighten the mood, but Steven couldn't find humor in her teasing. "I've never considered myself that shallow."

"You aren't shallow." Barbara seemed shocked. "You're not a people pleaser because you're shallow or fake. It's because you care."

"It's shallow to care that much about what people think of you." He still couldn't accept that could be him.

"I guess it depends on who the person is and why you want them to like you." Barbara yawned again.

Steven eased his hold on the steering wheel. Once

again his sister had a point. "I sensed the tension be-tween Val and Garry as soon as I joined the agency. I don't know what caused it, but it's time they dealt with it."

"Why do you have to be the one to help them?"

"Why not me? They need to clear the air—about a lot of things, not just their relationship."

"Like what?"

Steven expelled a breath. "A lot. And I want to help them."

"Are you doing this to please Val?"

"No. I'm doing it to please myself."

Chapter 14

"I'm nervous about going to Vail with Steve." *There,* Valerie thought. *I've admitted it.*

She finished loading the dishes from the Sunday brunch she'd shared with Loretta into the dishwasher, prewashing them the way her aunt preferred.

"Why? I thought you wanted to be included in the client meetings." Loretta stirred plant food into the water in the pitcher. "Give me a moment to feed my plants. Then I'll be ready to go antiquing."

There was a spring in Loretta's step as Valerie followed her into the sunroom. She smiled. Antique shopping was her aunt's favorite hobby.

"I'm not nervous because of the meeting. I'm nervous because of Steve." Valerie combed through the collection of CDs Loretta kept near the sunroom. The older woman must have had two copies of every Luther Vandross song ever produced. She picked up *One Night with You: The Best of Love, Volume 2.* Where was volume one?

"What about Steve? Why don't you want to go to Vail with him?"

Valerie looked over her shoulder at Loretta's question. Her aunt stood in front of the four-shelf blond-wood plant stand. Valerie marveled again at the blooming menagerie crowding the simple structure. Loretta crouched to pick up a ficus from the lowest shelf.

Valerie turned back to the CD display. "He kissed me."

"What? Really?" Loretta's voice was a mixture of surprise and curiosity.

Valerie stared blindly at the Vandross CD. "The other day, we were at an . . . off-site meeting, and he kissed me."

Silence grew as Valerie waited for Loretta's response. She flipped the CD over to skim the list of songs—"Always and Forever," "Power of Love." She put the CD back.

Loretta finally spoke. "You don't seem upset."

"I'm not."

"Are you attracted to him?"

Valerie knew Loretta well enough to have anticipated that question. "Yes, and I don't want to be." She faced her aunt.

Loretta put down the ficus. "Why not?"

"Because I'm not the kind of woman Steve Crennell would ever be serious about."

"Then why would he kiss you?"

Valerie shoved her hands into the pockets of her moss green crop pants. "I'm not naive, Aunt Lo. I know he kissed me because he's attracted to me. He wants to spend time with me."

Loretta arched a brow. "I take it you kissed him back?"

"Of course. I'm not made of stone." Valerie's body

flushed with the memory of his heat, his hands and his tongue.

Loretta turned back to the plant stand and lifted her aluminum plant from the bottom shelf. "Then you want to spend time with him, too."

Valerie paced her aunt's sunroom. "He's a very attractive man. A lot of women would enjoy his company."

"And you're no different from them."

"I never said I was. I want to enjoy the company of a handsome, intelligent man and fall in love just like most women."

"Then what's stopping you?" Loretta watered the aluminum plant before returning it to the stand.

Valerie's pacing brought her to the sliding glass doors on the far side of the sunroom. Their sheer curtains were drawn and hooked to the white frame to flood the room with natural light from outside. Beyond the glass doors, a modest wood deck led to a well-manicured lawn. At the back of the yard, two palm trees grew together, joined at the base. Over the years, Valerie had drawn those trees with pencils, charcoal, watercolor and paints.

She let go of the memories and spoke over her shoulder. "I could see myself falling in love with him while he just wants a good time."

Loretta took the CD from Valerie and scanned the titles. She crossed to the portable CD player and slipped in the disc. After poking and twisting a few controls, music started. Luther Vandross's melodic voice sang the opening stanza of "Any Fool Would Know."

Valerie glanced at Loretta. Had the selection been deliberate?

Loretta turned from the CD player and strode back to the plant stand. She picked up the potted African violet and poured enough water to soak the soil. "Why do you think he wouldn't fall in love with you?"

"I'm not his type." Valerie's tone was dry.

"How do you know?"

Valerie turned from her survey of the backyard and the childhood memories it evoked. "Have you seen Steve's ex-fiancée? She looks like a walking wet dream. I, on the other hand, do not."

Loretta chuckled. She resettled the African violet and picked up the prayer plant, the last on the bottom shelf. "Traci Greer Millbank . . . She's pretty showy."

"You've seen her?"

"She's been all over the entertainment news. She's getting one of the largest alimony settlements in history."

Valerie frowned. "I must be the only person in Miami-Dade County who doesn't watch entertainment television."

"Steve was engaged to Traci when he was twenty-two. And he didn't marry her."

"That's because she broke their engagement."

"I didn't hear about him asking her to stay. If he'd really wanted her, he'd have fought for her." Loretta finished watering her jade plant and reached for the hoya. "He played in the NBA. I doubt he's afraid of a little competition."

"I hadn't thought about that." Valerie wandered back across the room.

"It's been three years since he and Traci broke up." Loretta fed the iron cross begonia before watering the seersucker plant. "Are you the same person you were three years ago?"

"I hope not."

The older woman replaced the seersucker and moved on to the foliage lining the top of the stand, beginning with the spider plant. "I'm sure Steve has changed as well."

"But how much?"

Loretta watered the Boston fern. "I didn't know him three years ago. And I've only met him briefly once." She fed the Dallas fern before turning her attention to the passion vine. "If you're afraid of taking a chance on him, then don't. But why do you think you stand less of a chance of him falling in love with you than any other woman?"

Valerie emitted a short, irritated breath. She crossed her arms over her blush bandana shirt. "I can't keep my father's attention. How could I possibly keep the attention of someone like Steve?"

Loretta turned from the plant stand, the water pitcher in hand. "That attitude explains your less-than-active love life."

Valerie moved her shoulders restlessly. "It's always in the back of my mind that, if my father doesn't want to spend time with me, why would anyone else?"

"None of the men you've dated has been Garrison Parker, and neither is Steve."

"This is what they mean when they say, 'Spare no expense.'" Valerie sounded as stunned as Steven felt.

Pictures hadn't done the resort justice and it was still in the preparation stages. How incredible would it be the day of its official opening? From the top of the lobby's entrance, Steven stood beside Valerie and surveyed their surroundings. How could the young woman he'd known in college own a place like this?

Dark red carpeting covered the lobby steps. Across the limestone floor and to the right rose a winding walnut wood staircase polished to near-glass shine. The concierge desk across from them was made of the same shining walnut wood.

"You can tell Walter Millbank that Traci's spending his money well." Valerie stuttered her words.

"Are you still cold?" Steven restrained the impulse to wrap her close and share his body heat.

She shivered as though she'd never be warm again. "I've been to northern cities in the winter before. But we left seventy-degree weather for . . . what? Thirty degrees? I'm freezing."

How was that possible? She was almost mummified in winter outerwear. Her small, slim hands were encased in black leather gloves that disappeared under her coat sleeves. Her cream wool overcoat covered her from chin to ankle. Black leather boots peeked from beneath the hem. And her hair hung loose under a black stretch winter hat.

But as she tilted her head back to look at him, Steven saw the wind had stained her high cheekbones and the tip of her nose red. He slipped his light blue cashmere scarf from his shoulders and bundled it under Valerie's chin. "It's just two days—today and Friday. By the weekend, you'll be back in your own home enjoying seventy-degree weather again."

"Two days. Just two days." She repeated the words like a mantra.

Steven reached for Valerie's rolling suitcase at the

same time she did. "Allow me. My mother would never forgive me."

Her chocolate eyes laughed at him. "If you insist."

She straightened from the case. Steven lifted her luggage, adjusted the strap of his carry-on bag over his shoulder, then walked beside her down the lobby stairs.

He approached the reservations agent watching them from behind the long desk. "I'm Steven Crennell, and this is Valerie Parker. We have reservations."

The young woman's curly red hair bounced as she pounded the computer keyboard. "Oh, yes, Mr. Crennell. You're from Parker Advertising. We've been expecting you." The agent looked up to divide a smile between Steven and Valerie. "And you'll receive a lot of attention since you're the only guests we have."

Valerie returned the young woman's smile. "Has Ms. Greer Millbank arrived?"

The agent nodded. "She's here most weekends." She punched a few more keys. "We have you both here for one night. You're in room two forty-six. And Ms. Parker is across the hall in room two forty-seven."

The efficient young woman ran their credit cards, presented their room keys and supplied a rough map of the resort. "Enjoy your stay," she sang.

Valerie took the keys while Steven carried their luggage. Her perfume, lavender and vanilla, floated over him as they mounted the winding staircase. It teased him, drawing him closer. Tempting him to touch, to taste. Steven tightened his grip on their luggage and focused on the steps.

From the corner of his eyes, he watched Valerie. Had she felt what he'd felt? Was she as aware of him as he was of her? She must be. He hadn't been the only one tangled in the web of their kiss.

They crested the landing between the two sets of stairs that carried guests to the second floor. Valerie folded the resort map and tucked it into her purse. "I thought Traci would meet us in the lobby."

Steven mounted the second set of stairs. "So did I. But I'm glad she didn't."

Valerie smiled as she climbed the remaining stairs beside him. They arrived at the resort's second floor. Steven followed Valerie down the hallway. Their suites were down the hall and around the corner.

Steven glanced at her door. "Can you manage your suitcase on your own?"

Valerie's eyes danced with humor as she held out her hand for her suitcase. "Yes, but thanks for asking."

He relinquished her luggage. "When do you want to meet?"

Valerie checked her watch. "I'll knock on your door after I've freshened up."

Steven studied Valerie. She'd lost that half-frozen look. Her skin was back to its warm golden brown. Her features were animated and her eyes were shining with humor and anticipation. She was beautiful.

"Okay. I'll wait for you in my room." Steven waited until she'd secured her door before opening his own.

He stood in the threshold with his hand on his doorknob, taking in the comfortable sitting area, cozy kitchen, spacious entertainment section and the wide French doors that opened onto a balcony. It was incredible. The resort's suite was as bright and comfortable as a little cottage. If Traci wanted to compete on accommodations, she'd already won hands down, as far as he was concerned.

Steven dropped his carry-on bag beside the door, secured the lock and crossed the suite. His loafers sank into the dark green woven carpet. It was thicker and softer than the carpeting in his home. His tread was soundless as he passed the sitting area and crossed into the cream-tiled kitchen. A bowl of fresh fruit stood on one counter. He lifted the lid of a full cookie jar tucked next to the refrigerator. An interesting, if contradictory, message.

Steven stopped beside the soft cream-colored sofa in the entertainment area. Mounted above the dark-wood fireplace mantel was a forty-eight-inch plasma flat screen television. As a sports fan, he wanted to drop to his knees and weep with joy. As an advertising executive, Steven wondered where Traci wanted her health spa's guests to spend the bulk of their time. On the treadmill or in front of the television? The answer to that question would have a strong impact on Fit in Time's campaign.

He paused in the act of reaching for the remote. Noise carried from the room off the entertainment area. The bedroom? Steven straightened from the coffee table and changed direction toward the doorway.

He reached his destination in a dozen or so long strides—and froze.

In the center of the king-size bed that dominated the room, Traci posed, propped against a pile of pillows. She was topless. The sheets pooled around her hips in a manner that made it clear she was naked underneath as well.

"I thought you'd never get here, Stevie." She stretched her arms above her head as though she'd just woken. The movement lifted her breasts in Steven's direction.

Steven wasn't aroused. He was pissed. "What are you doing here, Trace?"

"Waiting for you."

The bed was swallowed by white sheets and almost buried under decorative pillows.

"I can see that." He scrubbed his face with his hands. He really didn't need this. "Why are you here?"

Traci grinned. "I'd think that was obvious, too." She wiggled her shoulders. Her breasts barely moved.

Tension grew in Steven's shoulders. He needed painkillers and a huge bottle of water. He surveyed the spacious rectangular room with its bright white furniture and matching decor against the dark green carpeting. Traci was like the serpent in the garden of Eden, except Steven wasn't tempted.

"Get out, Trace. I want you to get dressed and get out." He started to leave, intending to give her privacy. Her voice stopped him.

"You don't mean that. I know you remember what it was like, Stevie. You can't walk away from this."

He turned back to the room. "We're *not* getting back together, Trace. Not now, not ever. What will it take to get that through to you?"

She shifted her legs under the covers. The sheets dipped lower. "Come over here and kiss me. A real kiss. Then, if you can walk away, maybe I'll believe you mean it."

"I don't need to kiss you to know that we're through."

"Because of her?"

"Her name's Valerie, and we're together now."

Traci scowled. "For how long?"

"Forever. Now, please leave."

Traci arched her back, lifting her bustline and narrowing her waist. "I can give you so much more than she ever could."

Steven massaged the back of his neck. "This isn't a competition, Trace. This isn't a game. No means no."

Traci punched the mattress beside her right thigh. "What do you see in her? She's freakishly tall and flat as a board."

He gritted his teeth, shoving his hands into the pockets of his full-length cashmere coat. "Get out, Trace."

A knock sounded on the door to Steven's resort suite. He closed his eyes.

"Is that Val?" Traci sounded smug. "Invite her in. I have nothing to hide."

Without response, Steven pivoted on his heels and marched to the door. He took a deep breath, then pulled it open.

As soon as Steven opened the door, Valerie let all her excitement spill out. "What do you think of the suite? Isn't it incredible? I can sleep on this carpet." Her enthusiasm dwindled when he only stared. "What's wrong?"

"Your hair." Steven reached for the locks falling free around her shoulders. He seemed stunned.

Valerie stepped back, raising a hand to smooth the strands. "What's wrong with it?"

"It always surprises me when you wear it loose."

She gave him a suspicious look. Why was he looking at her like that? He seemed hypnotized. "I didn't feel like taking the time to pin it up."

Steven lowered his hand, but his gaze stayed glued to her hair. "Why would you ever pin up something so beautiful?"

Valerie's face grew warm. His words pleased and puzzled her. Why was he saying them? What did he want? She looked him over. "You're still wearing your coat? What's wrong?"

His hands on her shoulders stopped her as she tried to enter his suite. "Val, Trace is here."

She leaned left and right to try to see around him. "Where?"

"In the bedroom." He paused. "Naked."

Valerie froze. Her stomach twisted into knots. But Steven still wore his coat. Her gaze ran over his charcoal cashmere coat, under which was a turquoise crew neck sweater and navy Dockers. "She let herself into your suite, took off all her clothes and slipped between your sheets?"

"Yes." Steven watched her intently. She sensed he was trying to read her mind.

"You should call housekeeping for clean sheets."

After two beats, Steven's expression eased into a smile. "That's not bad advice."

"Hello, Val." Traci's greeting carried from across the suite. She came toward them. The cool rose silk robe poured over her body. Small spaghetti ties loosely held the material together at her hips. Traci was exposed from neck to belly button and from her thighs to her bare feet.

The resort owner stopped beside Steven. Too close. Close enough to make Valerie's hands itch to yank the other woman away.

"How was your trip?" Traci knew her proximity to Steven was driving Valerie insane. Valerie could tell by the gleam in the other woman's eyes.

It was a lot easier playing the outraged fiancée than Valerie would have thought. She gritted her teeth, hoping that would pass for a smile. "I have a better question. Do you enjoy having my fiancé reject you over and over and over again? After a while, I would think pride alone would convince you to keep your clothes on."

Traci's eyes bulged with rage. She slammed her fists onto her well-curved hips, widening the front gap of her robe. "I don't have to listen to your shit. I'm the client."

Valerie spread her arms. "Exactly. You're the client, not the—"

"Val." Steven held up a hand, palm out. "I can take it from here." He turned to Traci. "I'll ask you one last time. Please put on your clothes and leave. If you don't, we will."

Traci turned almost magenta with rage. She struck a pose like a Playboy model, showing off her assets. "You're taking her side against me?"

Steven shifted closer to Valerie. "I'm taking my side, Trace. I've told you before. You and I are over. I'm not going back."

Traci glared at him for a long, tense moment. Finally, she spun and stomped to the bedroom.

With the standoff over, Valerie felt her muscles relax. "Would you really have left if Traci didn't put on her clothes?"

Steven seemed to consider her question. "I don't know. I hope so. I'd already asked her three times to get dressed."

Valerie studied him. He looked like she felt—tired, disgusted, fed up. And he still wore his coat.

She reached out and helped him out of his overcoat. "Steve, how much more of Traci's behavior are you willing to put up with?"

Steve hung his coat in the nearby closet. "This account is important to your father."

"Then my father can meet with Traci. This is too much to ask of you."

"I can handle it."

Valerie threw up her hands. "Stop being a people pleaser. You're compromising yourself, and for what? We've come to a point where you need to decide how much this account is worth."

Chapter 15

"Have you worked for many resorts?" Steven studied the general manager leading the tour of the three fitness rooms. His name was Trent Fischer, and he looked fresh out of college. How much experience could he have running a mid-sized, high-end resort?

"No, but I've had summer jobs in a couple of hotels." The tall, thin blond gave him a huge smile. His brown eyes fixated on Steven as though he expected the former NBA star to produce a basketball from thin air and perform tricks.

Trent unlocked the first fitness room. He entered and turned on the light, illuminating the facility's cramped confines. Steven surveyed the cardio room. It looked like the standard fitness center, one you could find in any business motel. And it wasn't much bigger than his guest suite. Maybe Valerie was right. Maybe Traci would be better off promoting the spa's luxury accommodations over its unimpressive fitness facilities.

Valerie paused beside him. "Trent, were these hotels where you worked independents or chains?"

As he waited for the young man's answer, Steven walked toward the exercise equipment. There were only fifteen machines—five each of treadmills, stair climbers and stationary bikes. Traci must not have expected many guests would use this room.

"I've worked for a couple of small independents and one large chain, but none were quite like this." The younger man shrugged. The muscles under his short-sleeved jersey flexed. He apparently worked out, but at a real gym.

Steven walked between the equipment, which stood in three rows before a mirrored wall. Bikes were in the front, treadmills in the middle and stair climbers brought up the rear. He looked from one to the other of the mounted television sets, which hung from the two front corners of the ceiling. Water fountains braced a couple of walls. A vending machine sat tucked beside the door. It sold water and diet soft drinks.

Steven had seen enough of this room. He rejoined Valerie, who waited with Trent. "What did you do at these other hotels?"

Trent rolled back and forth on his feet. His hands were buried in the pockets of his red sweatpants. "This and that. Bellhop. Busboy."

Between Trent and Traci, there wasn't enough experience to run a lemonade stand, much less a health spa resort. Steven's brows knitted as he calculated the disaster in the making. "You've worked your way up the corporate ladder, from summer bellhop to full-time manager."

Trent laughed his enthusiasm. "Yes, I guess you could say that, Mr. Crennell."

Steven relaxed his brow. "I've asked you to call me Steve."

Trent shook his head emphatically as he led Valerie and Steven from the room. "No, Mr. Crennell. It's an honor to meet you, sir, and I want to make sure you're comfortable."

"I'd be more comfortable if you'd call me Steve. Mr. Crennell is my father."

Steven looked around as they walked across the resort, passing the long, walnut-wood concierge desk. His stomach groused as he paused outside the resort's restaurant. The apple he'd grabbed from his suite's fruit bowl hadn't lasted long. He and Valerie had agreed to have lunch after the tour. Maybe he'd have enjoyed their explorations more on a full stomach.

They turned down a hallway, and Trent led them to the second of the three exercise rooms. The walls were covered in mirrors. "This is the strength training room. As you can see, we have free weights." Trent lifted his arm toward one wall and a mountain of weights in varying sizes. "Weight benches." He gestured across the room to a row of black benches. "And weight machines." He turned to point toward the center of the room and a cluster of heavy-looking equipment.

Stacks of fluffy, white towels stood within easy reach of the equipment. Again, water fountains circled the room, and a vending machine—exact change only—offered additional liquids.

Steven's mind was in a spin. He didn't know where to begin or what to think. Even though Traci admitted she hadn't done any research, surely she couldn't believe these accommodations would attract high-end guests. Steven had stayed at several fitness resorts.

Those facilities had offered more cutting-edge equipment in greater quantities.

He glanced toward Valerie, who sat on a weight bench across the room, watching the view from the floor-to-ceiling windows. What must she think of this? He had to admit, she'd been right.

Steven made an effort to collect his thoughts. "How many trainers do you have?"

"Trace can answer those types of questions better than me." The resort manager looked disappointed that he couldn't help. "All I know is that we're in the process of hiring aerobics instructors, swimming instructors, a ski instructor and some body builders."

Valerie stood from the bench to approach them. "We're just trying to get an idea of the value-added features this resort offers."

"Well, we're going to have a lot of famous people staying here." Trent's voice rose with excitement. "Trace knows a bunch of them, and she's sure she can get them to stay here sometimes."

Valerie stopped beside Steven. "I don't think those famous people would want Traci using them in her advertising materials."

Trent's wide-eyed stare revealed his lack of understanding. "But we wouldn't list them by name."

Steven shook his head. "That doesn't matter. The rich and famous come to exclusive resorts to get away from the paparazzi and gawkers. If you advertise that they come here, you'll be inundated with the people they're trying to avoid."

Now Trent seemed upset. "I don't know whether Trace has any other marketing ideas."

Valerie shrugged. "That's what we're here for. Now show us the last room."

Trent showed them the sauna, indoor swimming pool and spa, all in one room a few paces from the weight room. At the end of the tour, he led them back to the lobby. "Do you have any questions?"

Valerie stopped to shake the general manager's hand. "Not right now, but thanks for your time. The tour was very helpful."

Steven gave the younger man his hand. "We have a lot to discuss before we meet with Trace."

"After lunch." Valerie patted her flat stomach.

Steven nodded. "After lunch."

After bidding Trent good-bye, Valerie continued through the lobby toward the resort's restaurant with Steven. She gave him a cocky smile. "I was right."

The lobby's clock may have claimed it was two in the afternoon, but her body knew it was four. She and Steven had brought fruit from their suites to eat during the tour. She didn't know about Steven, but she was ready for some real food.

"Yes, you were right. I owe you dinner." Steven paced beside her.

Valerie blinked at him. "Why?"

"Our bet, remember? Whoever had the winning advertising angle would be treated to dinner by the loser."

"Traci didn't pick my idea. Although, judging by the decor, she should have." She gestured toward the enormous stone fireplace dominating the lobby's burgundy-carpeted, raised sitting area. "The resort is lovely."

Burnt-umber upholstered, walnut-wood chairs were gathered in groups around coffee tables and end tables. The effect was warm, open and inviting. Valerie planned to try out the large, overstuffed chairs. But not at that moment. Right now, she was starving.

"This isn't a good sign." Steven voiced Valerie's fears as they approached the restaurant.

It looked suspiciously empty. As in, not yet open for business. There weren't any tables, chairs or people. Surely, Traci wouldn't have agreed to let them stay at the resort overnight when there wasn't any food.

Still hopeful, Valerie stood in front of the deserted hostess station and scanned the surrounding area.

"May I help you?"

She started at the male voice to her right. The stranger looked like he'd just put up drywall. He was covered in dust from his close-cropped hair and classic café au lait features to his thick, black work boots clomping against the walnut flooring. His blue jeans were old and faded almost white. Under a heavy emerald and teal flannel shirt, he wore a sweat-stained gray T-shirt. But even under the dirt and sweat, Valerie saw he was young and attractive. Obviously, youth and good looks were the minimum prerequisites for Traci's employees.

His smile was warm and a little curious. "You must be from the ad agency. Welcome to Fit in Time. I'd shake your hand, but mine are dirty." He lifted his large, callused palms so Valerie could see the dust— dried plaster?—herself.

Steven stepped closer to Valerie, placing his hand at the small of her back. "Thanks. We were hoping to get something to eat."

The young man wiped a hand across his forehead. "I'm sorry, sir. But the restaurant isn't ready for guests yet. It should be ready by dinnertime, though. We're bringing in the furniture now."

Valerie checked her watch again. She'd changed it to Colorado time—two hours behind Florida—as she'd waited to leave the plane. It read minutes after two o'clock. "Could we get something to go?" A crust of bread? Anything?

The young man smiled. "No problem. I'll ask someone to bring a meal to your room. Let me just dig out some menus."

Valerie relaxed. "That would be wonderful."

The resort employee disappeared around a wall. After a few minutes, he returned with two menus. "Let me know what you'd like, and I'll ask the cook to make it."

Valerie stepped away from the host stand and surveyed the menu. "I'd rather eat in my room. After Traci's little show this morning, I don't think I'd be able to digest my food in your suite."

Steven grunted. "It doesn't matter to me. I'm hungry enough to eat in the street."

They made their meal selections. The young man phoned in their order, then replaced the receiver. "Your food will arrive in thirty minutes."

Valerie managed a smile. She could eat more fruit while she waited. "Thank you very much."

After Steven added his thanks, she walked with him to the winding walnut staircase that led to their rooms. "Do you think having stairs instead of an elevator is Traci's idea of a fitness bonus?"

Steven chuckled. "The resort's only three floors."

"I've seen more elaborate facilities at travel motels."

"I know. The equipment's not as advanced as our target guests would have the right to expect."

Valerie paused on the landing between the two sets of stairs, one hand on the smooth banister carved from matching wood. "People have treadmills at home."

"And exercise bikes and step machines." Steven continued up the staircase. "But Trace can upgrade the equipment. Trade in what she has for more advanced machines."

They reached the second floor and began down the hallway to their rooms. Valerie hastened her steps, putting distance between herself and Steven's suggestion. "But the resort opens in three months. Even if Traci agreed to upgrade the machines, another shopping spree will cut into our campaign production time."

What motivated his desire for his ex-fiancée's spa to do well? Was it that their agency's success was tied to Traci's? Or was his motivation personal?

Steven kept up with her without any apparent effort. "We wouldn't need to put the campaign on hold. We could work around the machine upgrades."

"Perhaps you could *write* around her changes. But I can't schedule a photo shoot for equipment she doesn't have."

"It wouldn't take that long to bring in new stuff."

Valerie spread her arms. "Even if she agreed to the changes you recommend to make Fit in Time a real health spa, would she have the money? She's already spent so much on this place. Could she afford to invest even more for the right equipment?"

Steven shrugged. "That's for Trace to decide."

"Traci and her ex-husband." Valerie turned toward Steven even as she kept moving. "Do you think Walter Millbank knows how she's wasted his money?"

"I wouldn't say she's wasted Walt's money."

"What would you call it?" She stopped in the hallway between their two rooms.

"Trace has made some questionable decisions. And she obviously didn't do her research. She needs help, someone with more experience to advise her."

Now he was making excuses for her. Valerie rubbed her arms to ease the sudden chill. "Are you that someone?"

He looked startled. "No."

The fist around her heart relaxed. Valerie read her watch again. "Room service should be here in twenty-three minutes."

"Not that you're counting." Steven's smile was tired around the edges. It had been a long day.

Valerie dug her card key from her handbag. "I'm going to check my voice mail and e-mail for messages. Do you want to come in, or would you rather I call you when the food arrives?"

He massaged the back of his neck. "Could you call me? I should check my messages as well."

Valerie turned in the doorway. "Sure." She watched him unlock his door before closing her own. Hunger and travel fatigue caused by their seven-hour flight from Miami combined to weigh her down.

Valerie kicked off her shoes and crossed to the table where she'd set up her laptop and cell phone. She dialed in to check her voice mail as she registered for the hotel's wireless service to check her e-mails.

Twenty minutes later, her eyes began to cross. She logged off the Internet and pulled her sketchbook from her suitcase. She never left home without it. Valerie curled into the fat, burnt-umber sofa, flipped her sketchbook to a clean page and began to draw. A knock on her suite door jarred her from her musings.

She checked the time. At least ten minutes had passed. Valerie realized she was hungrier than ever. *Please let that be room service knocking on my door.*

Valerie rose, stretched, then strode across the room. Through the peephole, she saw Steven standing beside a man in a resort uniform. Between the two men was a cart carrying Valerie and Steven's lunch. She opened the door.

Steven stood aside so the young man could push the cart into the room. "I thought you'd forgotten about me and had eaten my lunch. I opened my door just as the food arrived."

Valerie moved her laptop, giving them more room to eat at the table. "I'd actually forgotten about lunch."

Steven arched a brow. "What were you doing?"

"Drawing."

The resort employee removed the tray covers so Steven could check their orders. His mouth watered at the sight of his hamburger and steak fries. He frowned at Valerie's Greek salad. How could a plate of lettuce quench anyone's hunger?

Steven signed for the delivery and thanked the young man. He carried his tray to the table and sat across from Valerie, who'd already dived into her salad. They ate in satisfied silence for a while. Steven was too hungry to attempt more than a few polite questions about her meal. Valerie appeared to feel the same way.

She sighed as she finished off her salad. "How are things at the office?"

No, not this time. He wouldn't let her use work as a wall between them.

Steven swallowed his last ketchup-drenched steak

fry. "I'm still on my lunch break. I'm not thinking about work right now."

Valerie used her napkin to wipe the corners of her mouth. "Okay. What do you want to talk about?"

He finished his burger. Heaven. "Tell me about volunteering at Miami Children's Hospital."

Valerie folded her napkin and set it back on the table. "What do you want to know?"

He shrugged. "Everything. What do you do there?"

Valerie smiled. "I volunteer in the recreation room. I'm the Crayon Lady." She laughed and her features lit up. Her full lips parted, showing perfect white teeth. Her eyes twinkled and danced.

A warm feeling started in the pit of Steven's stomach. He could listen to her laughter and gaze at her smile for years. "Let me guess. You draw with them."

"Once or twice a week since high school."

"When I was in high school, I went to every basketball camp in Miami-Dade County."

Valerie tilted her head. "It's funny how we took different paths and still ended up in the same place. I saw you when you played for the Waves. You were like art."

Steven watched Valerie leave the table to return her dishes to the cart. He stood to do the same. "I don't think anyone's ever said that about me."

Valerie turned, almost bumping into him. She was caught between his body and the cart. Steven held his ground. Her heat drew him closer. He breathed her scent, lavender and vanilla. Her eyes mesmerized him. He wanted to bury his hand in her ebony hair. Steven reached around Valerie and laid his dishes on the cart.

"What type of art?" His voice was husky. He hadn't

intended it to sound that way. What was she doing to him? And what did he want her to do?

"Modern." She answered without hesitation. "Bold and powerful. Full of energy and contrasts."

"Funny. That's what I feel around you. Restless energy and conflicting reactions."

She searched his gaze. "What conflicting reactions?"

He couldn't resist any longer. Steven reached out and filled his hands with her hair. It was so soft and warm. "Your vulnerability draws me closer, but your temper makes me want to run and hide."

Her smile teased him, tempted him. "Do I frighten you?" She reached out and squeezed his left bicep. "A big, strong professional athlete?"

"Sweetheart, you bring me to my knees."

Steven leaned in and pressed his lips to hers.

Chapter 16

Valerie had wanted this again. Ever since that afternoon in the museum courtyard when Steven had set a fire in her blood, she'd wanted to touch him again. To taste him again. To get carried away with him again.

She pressed closer to his hard muscles under the sapphire sweater that sculpted his chest. Had he worn it to tempt her? Valerie drew her palms up his torso, reveling in every ridge of muscle. She smoothed her hands over his thick, broad shoulders and wrapped her wrists behind his neck.

Valerie moaned as Steven deepened the kiss. She opened her mouth and his tongue eased in. Gently. Slowly. Exploring the curves of her lips, the roof of her mouth before reaching for her own tongue.

Valerie met his touch with some exploration of her own. Cloaked in the innocence of a kiss, she found the courage to test her fantasies. Stroking him. Teasing him. Drawing away, then chasing after him. With her tongue, she simulated what her body wanted to do—if she would dare.

As though he read her thoughts, Steven responded

to her caresses. Smoothing his hands up her back, trailing his fingers down her spine, pressing her hips into him.

Steven pulled his mouth away and pressed his cheek to hers. His chest rose and fell against her breasts with his rapid breathing. Her nipples tightened. His ragged breaths brushed against her ears. Her knees weakened. He lifted his head and scorched her with his heated gaze before sweeping her into his arms and carrying her to the bedroom.

Valerie looked around. Her muscles tensed. As she opened her mouth to stay him, Steven covered her lips with his. This time his touch was soothing, reassuring. She settled into his embrace, choosing to trust the man she'd grudgingly respected for the past eight months.

His long strides brought them to her bed. Steven released her so that she stood in front of him again. He turned, falling backward onto the mattress and pulling her on top of him. They bounced on landing. Valerie's forehead rapped Steven's chin.

"Ouch," he grunted.

Valerie pulled away to check on him. She smiled, seeing he was all right. "Smooth move, Crennell." She straddled his hips.

Steven quirked a brow. "You could offer to make it better with a kiss."

"What about my forehead?"

Steven slid his fingers through her hair and drew her down to kiss her forehead. "All better?"

She lowered to kiss his chin, but he shifted to capture her lips with his. Valerie melted against him, covering Steven like a blanket. His thighs were between hers. Steven cupped Valerie's hips, rocking her against his arousal. Her body grew hungry and wet against the pressure. Her mind clouded until all she knew was need. All she could hear was the beating of her heart, fast and loud. The rhythm became a grind as their bodies strained toward each other.

Steven's right hand withdrew from her hip. He moved it between them and unfastened her pants. He slipped his fingers beneath the band of her underwear. Steven traced the line between her cheeks, then slid a finger inside her.

Valerie gasped. Her body arched into his. She wanted. She needed. She rode the rhythm of his finger, up and down. In and out. A fire burned within her. She felt the yearning so strong that the muscles in her abdomen twisted and pulled. It urged her to join with him and ease the painful ache between her legs. But her mind resisted. It struggled to press reason past their carnal cravings.

Why now? Why here?

Why her?

Why would Steven want her?

Valerie grabbed Steven's forearm, stopping his wicked movements before reason snapped beneath the weight of her lust. "Steve. Stop." Her tone lacked conviction.

"What's wrong?" His voice was heavy with desire.

She pulled his arm free of her and threw herself beside him onto the bed. "I can't go any farther. I'm sorry."

He rolled onto his side to face her. She was grateful for the space he put between them.

"No, I'm sorry. Was I going too fast? I can slow down."

Her thoughts had shattered into tiny shards. She was

having trouble putting the pieces back together again. Why did she need to stop again? Oh, right. "Steve, I'm just not ready to go that far with you. Not yet."

"Why not? We're not strangers. We've known each other for almost a year."

"We've known each other a long time, but we haven't known each other well." With an effort, Valerie returned Steven's intense gaze. It was as though he were combing her mind.

He remained perfectly still. "What do I need to do for you to feel comfortable with me? To trust me?"

Valerie's face flamed. "I trust you, Steve."

Steven studied her for a long, silent moment before he rolled off the bed and onto his feet. He looked down at her as he straightened his clothes. "I don't think you do, Val. I don't think you can separate me from the stereotypes of NBA players. Whatever you think, I don't see you as an easy lay. That's not what I'm about. And there's nothing easy about you."

He strode from the room. Seconds later, the front door closed, quietly and deliberately.

Valerie spent the next two hours working on ad concepts for smaller accounts. She wasn't hiding. She was busy. Although the line between being busy and hiding was razor thin.

She envied Steven's success in bringing accounts into the agency. She was jealous of his friendship with her father. Despite those admittedly petty emotions, she did respect Steven. He worked hard. He came prepared to project meetings, and he didn't have an ego.

She also trusted him—his previous engagement to Traci Greer Millbank notwithstanding. He never shirked responsibility. And he always shared the credit for a project's success.

Steven cared about people. He paid attention to them. He knew she drank tea and not coffee. He noticed when Manuel wasn't wearing his silver chain. Look at his work with the Nia Neighborhood Recreational Center. He paid attention to the kids who spent time there. He played basketball with them, instead of showing off to them.

Valerie tossed aside her sketchbook and uncurled from the sofa. She tugged back on her boots before leaving her suite to walk across the hallway and knock on Steven's door. She was going to explain her hesitancy to him while she still had her courage.

It didn't take long for Steven to answer the door. Without a word, he stepped aside to let her in. That was a good sign.

Valerie squared her shoulders. "I'm sorry. I know you're not a player. I know you'd never treat a woman disrespectfully. You'd never treat anyone disrespectfully. It's just that I keep projecting my issues with my father onto you."

"I'm not your father, Val." His voice was quiet. His eyes were patient.

"I know that."

"I'm not your enemy, either."

"I know that, too."

Steven shoved his hands into the front pleated pockets of his navy Dockers. "So where do we go from here?"

Valerie took a deep breath. "I still think we should take it slow. We work together. This could get complicated."

Steven paused as though considering her words. Finally, he nodded. "That makes sense." He stole a kiss, then circled her to get to his bedroom. "Let's have dinner."

Valerie tracked his movements. "We just had lunch."

"That was hours ago." He waggled his brows. "And I worked up an appetite."

The resort's restaurant had furniture this time. Their host, another attractive young man, led them to a table. The seats were wide, like benches, and soft enough to sleep on.

Valerie opened her menu. "Traci has a lot of men working for her. I wonder how many women work here other than the one at the concierge."

"I don't think she's hired many. Traci's never liked competition."

A companionable silence settled over the table while they read the dinner menu. Their server— another attractive male employee—interrupted them briefly to take their drink orders. Valerie requested a diet soda and Steven asked for root beer.

The server explained the restaurant's specials for the evening, asked if they had any questions, then left to place their drink orders with the bar.

Valerie leaned forward. "It feels weird to have the restaurant's staff waiting on us. We're the only people here."

Steven's lips curved in the sexy smile that made her muscles go lax. "We're probably one of their practice games."

Valerie wasn't very hungry. She wanted something light, but there weren't many light items on the menu. "Her hiring practices and this menu are more examples of Traci not taking this health resort idea seriously."

"What's wrong with the menu?"

Valerie looked at Steven, laughing her surprise. "I don't think most health spas offer the burger and steak fries you had for lunch."

Steven's eyes twinkled with shared humor. "They should. It was delicious."

Valerie returned her attention to the menu. She made her selection just before the server returned with their drinks. She and Steven both ordered the salmon and steamed vegetables. The young man collected their menus and left to put their dinner requests in.

Valerie sipped her diet soda. "It's amazing how much work I got done without the usual office interruptions."

"I'm not going to discuss work on my dinner break."

Valerie suppressed a smile. "For someone so dedicated to his career, you certainly have some rigid rules about when you will and will not talk shop."

"I consider my lunch hour—and even dinnertime when I take work home—mental vacations. We need those, considering the long days we work."

Valerie nodded. "That's a good point."

"Garry doesn't agree. That's why we don't have lunch together anymore."

Valerie frowned. "You don't? The last couple of times I asked Garry to lunch, he said he was meeting someone. I thought he meant you."

"It wasn't me." Steven looked away, spreading his napkin on his lap and drinking more of his root beer.

Then who was her father having lunch with? Valerie shrugged the question aside. What did it matter?

She surveyed the restaurant's dining area. Its burgundy carpeting and walnut wood furniture carried the same warm tones as the sitting area off the main lobby. It was a nice touch. "Traci definitely has an eye for interior design. This room makes me want to get my sketchbook."

Steven picked up his drink. "It makes me want to read."

Valerie returned her attention to him. "What types of books do you like to read?"

"I like a lot of different books—mystery, science fiction, nonfiction, classics."

"Classics?"

He smiled. "Do you have a hard time picturing a baller reading Shakespeare?"

Valerie thought for a moment. "Not if that baller is you."

He lifted his glass to his lips. "I'll take that as a compliment."

"It was meant as one."

Steven's eyebrows jumped. "Two compliments in one day. Keep this up, and I'll have your DNA tested to verify your identity."

Valerie tipped her head back and laughed. "I guess I deserved that. Name one of your favorite authors."

"Alexandre Dumas." Steven didn't even hesitate. "*The Count of Monte Cristo* is one of the best novels ever written."

"Really? I'll have to read it."

Their book discussion carried them right through dinner. When their check arrived, Valerie was stunned by the amount of time that had flown by. She folded the plum cloth dinner napkin and set it to one side on the table. "I'm surprised how many of the same books we've read. Either you're an incredibly voracious reader, or I've read more books than I've realized."

"Probably both." Steven signed the check—presumably

to his room to be expensed later—then set aside the bill. He settled back into his seat and took a swallow of his root beer. "If you do decide to read *The Count of Monte Cristo,* I'd like to know what you think."

"What she thinks about what?" A familiar voice interrupted their conversation.

Valerie looked up as Traci stopped beside Steven's bench. The other woman rested her hand around his shoulder. Valerie took in the cozy picture they made and realized Steven's mini mental vacations had one flaw. The return trips could end with a bumpy landing.

Steven rose from the bench, forcing Traci to release him. He breathed easier. "Hello, Trace. Care to join us?"

Her smile was wide and satisfied, as though he'd offered her more than a seat. "Always the gentleman, aren't you, Stevie? I missed that."

She took his bench, wiggling her bottom onto the seat. Steven circled the table and sat beside Valerie. He rested his arm on the back of her bench. His pretend fiancée scooted over to give him more room. But Steven didn't need space. Not for what he had planned.

He glimpsed Traci's look of surprise before she regrouped.

Traci crossed her arms under her breasts and propped her elbows on the table. The position lifted her cleavage almost to her neck. "What were you two talking about?"

Steven lowered his hand to play with the earring dangling from Valerie's right earlobe. It was slender and cool, like the woman wearing it. Rosy color dusted Valerie's delicate cheekbones and she stiffened beside him. Steven ignored her. She'd catch on sooner rather than later. Valerie was a smart woman.

He forced a lazy tone. "My conversations with Val are private."

The look of indignation that swept across Traci's face almost made him laugh. He turned away and rested his forehead against Valerie's temple. "We enjoyed our tour of the resort, didn't we, sweetheart?" His murmur was loud enough for Traci to hear.

"Yes . . . umm . . . yes. Yes, we did." Valerie shivered against him.

Steven nuzzled her hair. This time he spoke low, for her ears only. "I'm sorry. I know you don't like public displays of affection."

As he'd hoped, Valerie smiled at the comment. Did it bring back memories of the museum's courtyard? He hoped so, and that those memories meant as much to her as they meant to him. The sight of her smile. The sound of her laughter. The feel of her in his arms. Her scent. Her taste. He remembered everything.

"Steven." Traci's tone was as sharp and deadly as a gunshot.

Steven looked up, his movements deliberately slow and distracted. "Yes, Trace?"

His ex-fiancée sneered. "Is it typical for you to grope each other in a client meeting?"

Steven frowned. "Is this a client meeting?"

Traci glared at them. "Yes, it is."

Steven straightened on the bench-styled seating. He tucked Valerie under his arm, keeping her close. Hip to hip, thigh to thigh. He wanted to dispel any ideas Traci may have had about showing up naked in his bed. Ever. Again. And he still needed to call housekeeping for clean sheets. "Okay, Trace. We'll keep this about business. I'd like that, too."

Traci gave him a narrow-eyed stare. "So, what do you think of the place?"

"It's beautiful." Valerie turned her head to survey the restaurant.

Her hair brushed Steven's jaw. He inhaled her herbal shampoo and swallowed.

Valerie continued. "The brilliant colors, the inviting furniture, the rich wood. It's all beautiful."

"If you wanted to promote it as a resort, you're ready right now," Steven explained. "But if you want to advertise it as a health spa—a place for people to work out and get healthy—you'll have to upgrade your fitness facilities."

Traci appeared offended. Again. "What's wrong with that stuff I have now?"

Valerie shook her head. "No one's going to pay twenty-five hundred dollars a night to work out with ordinary equipment."

The health spa owner pouted. "But everyone has equipment like that."

"That's our point. They have better exercise machines at the neighborhood Y, Trace." Steven paused, considering his next words. "Before you started building the spa, did you and Walt discuss the machines and equipment you should buy?"

Traci's head snapped up. "Why should I ask him about my place?"

"Walt works out with state-of-the-art machines every day. He could give you recommendations based on his experience."

Valerie glanced at Steven before questioning Traci. "Didn't Walt invest in your resort?"

"He's a silent investor." Traci fluffed her hair. "He tried to give me advice in the beginning. Write a business plan. Research the market." Traci kissed her teeth. "I don't have time for all that shit. I need to have something of my own. I want to make my own money."

Valerie looked alarmed. "These things take time. You're not going to make money on a business this big overnight."

The shorter woman managed to look down her nose at Valerie. "What do you know?"

Steven saw the same impatience in Traci she'd shown when she'd broken their engagement to marry his teammate rather than wait for Steven to start another career. "Have you ever heard the saying, Trace, 'Act in haste, repent at leisure'?"

Traci rolled her eyes. "You're not my business partners. You're just ad people. Advertise my shit and stop trying to tell me what to do." She glanced at her watch and stood. "I'll take you back to your rooms."

Puzzled, Steven exchanged looks with Valerie. He helped his pretend fiancée from the bench seating. "Thanks, Trace, but we can find our way."

Traci led the way from the restaurant. "It's not a problem."

With minimal conversation, they crossed the lobby and mounted the winding staircase to the second floor. Steven walked beside Valerie as they followed Traci down the hall. He'd wanted to continue the conversation they'd started before dinner, but that would have to wait.

Traci stopped between their two room doors. She gave Valerie a mocking look. "Separate rooms. Interesting."

"This is a business trip." Valerie pulled out her key card and approached her door. Before she could unlock it, the door was pulled open from the other side.

The young sun-bleached blond general manager stood in the doorway wearing one of the hotel's fluffy white towels. And nothing else. He grinned at Valerie. "Where've you been? You asked me to meet you an hour ago."

Chapter 17

"What?" Valerie's slack-jawed expression as she stared at Trent would have been amusing under almost any other circumstance.

Steven paused when he felt Traci's eyes on him. The satisfaction on her face explained everything. He took a deep breath and spoke to Valerie. "It looks like I'm not the only one who'll need to call housekeeping for clean sheets."

Steven saw when realization came to her and Valerie redirected her anger toward Traci.

"You'll try anything, won't you? He doesn't want you."

Traci didn't respond.

Steven placed his hand on Valerie's shoulder. He hoped his touch would keep her calm. Her warmth beneath his palm helped steady him, even as the sight of the near-naked man in her doorway pushed him to the edge of crazy.

He met Trent's gaze. "Put your clothes on and get out."

The younger man turned to Traci. Steven flexed his

grip on Valerie's shoulder. She reached up and covered his hand with hers.

Steven forced himself to relax. "Don't make me repeat myself."

Trent must have seen how close Steven was to the edge. He quickly disappeared back into Valerie's suite. Steven released Valerie's shoulder before he accidentally bruised her.

He turned to Traci, whose satisfaction had fizzled and died. Now she looked bitter and angry. "What were you hoping to accomplish?"

Traci turned to him wide-eyed with faked shock. "Me? Why are you accusing me? Val's the one who invited a complete stranger to her room."

Valerie stepped forward, her hands fisted at her sides. "You put your general manager up to this. You're contemptible. Not only have you abused your position as his boss, but you've sunk into the gutter with your lack of morals."

Traci tossed her hair. "Whatever, bitch. Stevie may not be man enough for you, but he's all the man I need. You hear that, Stevie?" She struck a pose for him, straightening her spine to push out her bust and cocking her hip to one side. "Whenever you're ready to bounce this cheating whore, just let me know, boo, and I'm all yours."

Steven prayed for patience. "I don't believe even for one second that Val would invite a strange man to her room. But I can believe, without any hesitation, that you'd mastermind this farce."

Traci gaped at him. "Why would I do something like that?"

"You know why, Trace."

"You think I want you so bad that I'd try to trick you into leaving her?" Traci waved a hand toward Valerie.

Valerie vibrated with fury beside him. Should he restrain her? He didn't want to break up a catfight tonight. "Don't pretend you wouldn't do something like that, Trace. I saw the look on your face when Trent opened the door. It wasn't surprise. It was satisfaction. You knew he'd be there."

"No, I wasn't surprised that Val would have some man waiting for her in her room, primed and good to go. She's like a bitch in heat. But I wouldn't be satisfied that you'd caught her in the act. That you'd learned how little she thinks of you." Traci stepped forward, reaching out to cup Steven's face. "I'd never want you to be hurt, Stevie. Never. Not by anyone. I care about you."

"Oh. My. God." Valerie took a threatening step toward Traci. "Get away from him."

Trent chose that moment to emerge from Valerie's room. He was pulling on his sweater. Valerie turned on him. "What you did was despicable. Don't you have any self-respect?"

The general manager jabbed a thumb in his boss's direction. His words tumbled out in a nervous rush. "Ms. Greer paid me extra to do it. She said I'd be doing Mr. Crennell a favor. That you're not good enough for him, and breaking you two up would be the best thing anyone's ever done for him. I'm your biggest fan, Mr. Crennell. I'd never knowingly do anything to piss you off."

"Shut up, Trent." Traci roared the command. "You're fired."

Trent's face flushed red. Tears reddened his eyes. "What?"

Steven rubbed his hands over his face. When would this nightmare be over? "Get a good lawyer, kid. You can sue the skirt off her."

Valerie crossed her arms. "A strong wind could blow the skirt off her."

Steven agreed. Traci's latest little black wool dress didn't make it to midthigh. And he doubted she wore anything underneath the tight material.

Trent turned to speed-walk down the hall.

Steven glared at Traci. "We need to talk."

"What?" The shock in Valerie's eyes and tone hurt him.

He drew her away to murmur his plea. "I realize you're upset. I'm upset, too. But Trace and I need to reach an understanding. And, in your current hair-trigger temper condition, you're not helping the situation."

Her tension communicated itself through his fingertips as they braced her slender upper arms. He sensed her mulling over his request in her mind. Steven hadn't wanted them to separate. He'd wanted to present a united front. They were a team. But even though Valerie was a class act, everyone had a breaking point. If Traci continued to call Valerie a bitch and cast aspersions against her character, Steven feared Valerie's dignity would scatter to the winds and she'd rip Traci's hair—extensions and all—out by its roots. He was getting too old to break up hotel brawls.

Valerie crossed her arms and lowered her voice. "I thought I was supposed to protect you from her."

"You don't have to physically be here to do that." Steven felt her relax.

She eyed him warily. "Are you certain there's no chance of your getting back together with her?"

"Positive." He sensed her wavering. Steven held her gaze, communicating reassurance.

Valerie rose on her toes, pressed her fingertips into his shoulder and kissed his lips. "Stay strong. I'll be with you in spirit."

She didn't waste even a glance at Traci as she unlocked her suite and closed the door behind her.

Traci approached Steven, licking her lips. "So, what did you want to . . . talk . . . about?"

Steven unlocked his door. "We're going to talk, Trace. Nothing more." He stood back for her to precede him. Why did he feel as though he were entering a cage with a starving, man-eating jaguar? Could she smell fear?

Steven let the door close behind him. "What will it take for you to understand that you and I are never getting back together?"

She walked toward him, her hips undulating like an ocean wave. Her black dress strained to hold her curves within. Traci leaned her torso toward him and his gaze dipped reflexively to her bountiful cleavage before returning to the expectation in her eyes.

"Do me." Her words were a low, dirty invitation.

Steven put distance between himself and her cloying perfume. "The only thing between us now is business, Trace. That's all I want from you. Your business." He wasn't sure he wanted even that. "If you can't accept that, there's no reason for us to see each other."

Traci followed him. "You're only saying that because you're still upset I broke up with you and married Walt. I'm sorry, Stevie. I made a mistake. How can I make it up to you?" Her tongue circled her crimson lips.

Steven stood between the coffee table and the

flat-screen television suspended above the fireplace. "There's no need to make it up to me. I'm glad you broke off our engagement. If you hadn't, we would've ended up divorced like you and Walt."

Traci reared back as though he'd slapped her. "No, we wouldn't have. We'd still be together. Don't you remember how good it was between us?" She reached out to stroke his chest.

Steven stepped back before she could touch him. He was tired of Traci chasing him around his resort suite as though he were a damsel in a 1930s movie. "It was good until we got out of bed. When you weren't taking my money to go shopping with your friends, you were complaining about how much time I spent practicing."

"We *were* good in bed, weren't we, Stevie?" Traci stalked him. She ran her hands up her body, cupping and squeezing her breasts like a porn star.

"Your show isn't turning me on, Trace." Steven let her see his disgust. "Your tricks worked on me when I was a horny teenager. I'm an adult now. A woman who respects me turns me on. A woman who knows when to use her body and when to use her brains turns me on. You're not that woman, Trace."

Fury blazed in her hazel-tinted eyes. "And Val is? She's this model of womanhood who could screw you till your eyes cross, then bow and scrape to you in the morning?"

"She doesn't bow and scrape."

Traci growled her rage, bouncing up and down on the balls of her feet. "Look at me." She tugged down the neckline of her dress, exposing her augmented breasts. "How could you prefer her to me? How could she be better than me? What does she have that I don't have?"

"Pride." Steven's calm response bounced around the room.

"You bastard." Traci tucked her breasts back into her dress. "Fine. You've made your decision. Fine. I've *heard* you. You don't *want* me. Fine. I don't want you, either."

"Then we understand each other." Why didn't he feel relieved? Instead, he was tense and anxious for her to leave.

"No, we don't. You don't want me. Fine. You can't have me. You can't have any of me. I'm ripping up my contract with Parker Advertising, and I want you out of my resort. Now. Right now!" Traci turned and raced across the room as fast as her black stilettos would allow and slammed out of the suite.

Steven stared at the door. Now he felt relieved.

After checking the peephole, Valerie opened the door for Steven. She watched him walk past her and further into the suite. "It's a good thing the resort isn't open for business yet."

"How much of that did you hear?" Steven crossed into the living area and collapsed onto the overstuffed couch.

Valerie followed him. The first threads of unease brushed over her. "I wasn't trying to hear any of it. But I couldn't miss Traci screaming 'right now' or the slamming of the door." She settled beside him. "What happened?"

Steven closed his eyes and rested his head against

the back of the couch. "Traci wants us to leave the resort. Right now."

Valerie blinked. "Because you won't sleep with her?"

"I told you. She doesn't like competition."

Valerie crossed her arms. "It sounds more like she can't take rejection."

"That, too."

Steven's tone bordered on flippant. His long, lean muscles appeared relaxed as he sprawled beside her on the couch. But beneath the surface, Valerie sensed his tension. She cupped her hand over the back of his as it lay between them on the sofa's cushion. His palm was broader than hers, his fingers much longer. "What aren't you telling me?"

His sigh seemed to travel up from the depths of his soul. Steven turned his head and met her gaze. His eyes were cold, distant. "I lost the account."

"Oh, no." Valerie stopped breathing.

Steven looked away. The spare lines of his profile appeared even harder. He seemed focused on the gray stone fireplace across the room, but Valerie didn't think he saw it. He was very still, as though he'd pulled inside himself. Valerie had witnessed that expression before. It had appeared on television every time a camera operator had found Steven Crennell on the sidelines after a Miami Waves loss. It was the intent look of an elite athlete replaying every turning point in the game to determine how he could have changed its final outcome.

Right now, Valerie was convinced Steven was replaying every word spoken, every action taken since Traci signed their contract, to determine how he could have changed the final outcome of her account.

"You couldn't have prevented this from happening."

She shifted her grip to hold his hand. His palm was rough for someone who made his living behind a desk.

"There must have been something I could have done differently." Steven released her hand. He pushed off the couch to pace the room.

"Perhaps you're right." Valerie angled her head. "You could have slept with her."

Steven grunted. "Short of that."

"Traci's game plan was to give us her account in exchange for you. She didn't get you, so she took back her account. Our mistake was in not recognizing her strategy."

Steven dragged his right hand over his close-cropped hair. "But then the game would have been a nonstarter."

"And a competitor always wants to get in the game." Should she laugh or pull out her hair?

Steven paused, regarding her with surprise. "Yes. I guess that's part of the challenge."

"Another is recognizing a game you can't win." Valerie stood. "Traci wasn't playing with integrity. Accept that there's no way you could have won with her."

Steven resumed his pacing. "My gut tells me you're right. Trace isn't taking anything about this resort seriously, so why would she take the ad campaign seriously? But I hate losing."

"Don't we all." Valerie wrapped her arms around herself. Her frown deepened as her thoughts raced. "Did Traci cancel the account? Or did you?"

Steven's eyes showed his confusion. "She did. Why would *I* cancel the account?"

Valerie shook her head in frustration. "Did you give her an ultimatum?"

He paused, apparently trying to remember the

exact conversation. "I told her if she couldn't work with us, there wasn't any reason for us to see each other."

Her frown cleared. "You cancelled the account."

"What difference does it make?"

"You didn't lose, Steve. Traci forfeited."

Steven stared at her for a silent moment, then exhaled on a chuckle. "I'm still not looking forward to facing your father."

"Garry's not an ogre." She hesitated. "Well, at least not to you."

"He really wanted this account, and he wanted me to do whatever it took to get it."

Valerie arched a brow. "My father doesn't pimp out his account executives."

"That's not what I meant." He sighed and lifted his hand to drag it over his hair. "I've never disappointed him before."

Valerie's heart clenched. "Take it from me. You'll survive."

Chapter 18

Valerie gripped the collar of her cream wool winter coat closer to her neck. A cold breeze seemed determined to sneak into her clothes. "I can't believe this hotel has any rooms left. Its parking lot is full."

Steven pulled her wheeled suitcase and his carry-on bag from the rental car's trunk. The bitter weather didn't seem to affect him as much as it bothered her. "There must be a lot of events in the area this weekend, considering how long it took us to find another room."

It had taken them almost two hours to pack, find another hotel and check out of Traci's resort. They'd contacted half a dozen hotels before this one admitted to having available rooms.

Steven had appeared to be on automatic pilot the entire time. He still was. Valerie was worried, knowing he was brooding over Garrison's reaction to losing Traci's account. At least now he was communicating with words instead of grunts. But his voice was tense and drained. He settled his bag on his shoulder and carried her suitcase.

Since Steven didn't seem inclined to let Valerie handle her luggage, she buried her gloved hands in her pockets and fell into step beside him. "My body thinks it's midnight."

"It's not far off. There's only a two-hour time difference between here and Miami."

Steven's subdued tone increased Valerie's concern. How could she convince him he wasn't a failure?

Valerie walked on. "I'm glad we're going home tomorrow."

"Me, too. It's been one hell of a day." His words were heartfelt.

Valerie sighed with relief when they entered the hotel. The lobby's warmth seeped into her, unthawing her tense muscles.

Walking beside Steven, Valerie approached the front desk. The older gentleman behind the gray marble counter greeted them with a twinkling smile. His shock of white hair and rosy red cheeks made him look like Kris Kringle.

"Welcome to the Vailed Nights Inn. Are ya here for a room?" His enthusiasm coaxed a smile from Valerie.

"Yes, please, if there are any available." She adjusted the purse strap on her shoulder. If she hadn't been in such a rush, she'd have packed the heavy thing in her suitcase and kept only her wallet handy.

The representative winked. "You folks are in luck. We still have one room available."

Valerie stilled. "One? We'll need two."

The representative's pleasure dimmed as he seemed to sense her consternation. His gaze hopped from Valerie to Steven, standing close beside her, as though wondering what prevented the couple from sharing a room. He returned his attention to Valerie, an apology in his eyes. "I'm afraid we only have the one."

Steven stood Valerie's suitcase on its end. "Does it have two beds?"

The older gentleman looked even more confused. His snow white brows knitted in concern. "No. It only has one." His expression cheered as he scanned the computer screen. "But it's a king-size bed. Really, really big."

Valerie's eyes stretched wide. Mental images of her and Steven in a really, really big bed brought a flush to her face. "I'm afraid you don't understand. We're—" She stuttered to a stop as Steven claimed her upper arm.

"Could you excuse us for a moment, please?" Steven escorted Valerie a few paces away. He released her arm and positioned himself so his broad shoulders blocked her from the front desk agent's interested eyes. His big body crowded her. "We should take the room."

Valerie's eyes widened. Her lips parted. "There's only one bed. He must think we're married."

"It doesn't matter what he thinks. I'll sleep on the floor." Steven closed his eyes and rubbed his face. "I don't want to spend the rest of the night searching for a room. I'm tired. And our flight back to Miami leaves at an obscene hour of the morning."

As Steven lowered his hands, Valerie recognized the lines of tension bracketing his mouth, the strain tightening his lips and the fatigue dimming the light in his eyes. His request to book the single remaining hotel room wasn't prompted by his desire to sleep with her. Steven was mentally, physically and emotionally drained.

Her hands itched to cup his jaw and smooth the

frown from his forehead. What could she say to convince him he wasn't a failure? He hadn't believed her when she'd tried before. What could she say this time to reach him?

She held his gaze, refusing to let him look away. "You can't please everyone, Steve. Sometimes you need to do what's right for you."

Steven shook his head. "Let it go, Val."

"You're the one who needs to let it go."

He ran a hand over his hair. "Can we check into the room now? Please?"

Valerie sighed. He was right. "You can take the bed. I'm sure the room will have armchairs I can push together."

"We'll argue about that later, too." With his hand on the small of her back, Steven returned to the concierge. "We'll take the room."

"So much for putting the armchairs together." Valerie sounded dryly amused.

Steven understood what she meant right away. He followed her into the hotel room, carrying her suitcase and his bag.

The room was large, clean and seemed comfortable, but the furnishings were sparse: the king-size bed, one nightstand, an armoire with a television set, a writing table and one desk chair. There were no armchairs.

"I'll take a pillow and a spread, and sleep on the floor." Steven walked farther into the room and set their luggage on the floor.

"The bed is big enough to share." Valerie's voice

came from behind him. "I promise your virtue will be safe with me."

Steven had been lost in his thoughts until he caught Valerie's reference to his virtue. He looked up and saw the teasing—and concern—in her eyes. He found a smile. "What a pity."

"That's settled then." She came closer to him. "The only question remaining is how much longer you're going to beat yourself up over Traci's account."

Why couldn't she leave it alone?

Steven rested his hips against the writing table and crossed his arms. "If our positions were reversed, you'd react the same way."

"Yes, and I hope you'd help me understand that Traci canceling her contract wasn't my fault. That's what I'm trying to get across to you."

Steven stepped around her to pace the room. It was a small space, but he needed movement. "I appreciate what you're trying to do. But this is a process I've always taken after a loss."

"What do you mean?"

Steven walked past her as he circled the room again. "I review every part of the game to identify the action that led me to this point. Maybe there was a shot I should have taken but didn't. Or I should have passed the ball and didn't."

Valerie crossed her arms. "You can't change the past. Even if you took the shot or made the pass, you could still end up with the same outcome."

He shrugged. "True. But I've always analyzed my game. It helps me improve."

Valerie angled her head. "Maybe I can save you some time. I know what you could have done differently in the past."

Steven knitted his brows. "What?"

"You should never have asked Traci to marry you."

"That wasn't one of my better moves." He didn't want to be reminded of that mistake or how his past had come back to torment him.

"How do you go from wanting to spend the rest of your life with someone to not wanting to be alone in the same room with her?"

He tensed. "She played me. I'm not proud of the fact I fell for her game, but I accept responsibility for my actions."

Valerie still seemed confused. "But you won't let her back into your life. Is that because you never really loved her?"

Steven prowled the room again, walking off restless energy. "Why are you asking me these questions?"

"I want to know why someone would stop loving someone else."

Steven stilled. He recognized pain and confusion in Valerie's eyes. "The situation between Trace and me is different from you and your father."

"You and Traci were romantically involved. But both situations are about relationships."

Steven approached Valerie, never letting go of her gaze. "When I say the situations are different, I mean you didn't do anything wrong. Your father loves you."

There was hope beneath the cynicism in her eyes. "How do you know?"

"I can tell."

Disbelief replaced hope. "I must have done something wrong. Otherwise the only reason he wouldn't let me back into his life is that I'm just not worth loving."

Steven stopped. He cupped his hands over her

shoulders and held her tight. Her muscles jumped beneath his palms. A woman's strength. She could give firm support or offer tender concern, even to someone she professed to dislike. Steven didn't doubt that Valerie's father loved her. How could anyone not?

"Believe me, Val. You are worth loving."

He lowered his head slowly, giving her time to put distance between them—if that's what she wanted. P*lease, don't let her back away from me.* He wanted to taste her. He needed to taste her.

Steven held his breath. Valerie's eyelids drifted closed and her lips parted. Steven breathed again.

His lips covered hers. Valerie sighed into his mouth. He swallowed the sound, letting it seep into his bloodstream. His head spun. She wrapped her arms around his shoulders. Her body melted against him, adding to the dizzying sensation. She was soft and slender under his touch, hot and vibrant in his arms.

Valerie's fingers moved up his neck and over his hair. She stroked him, touched him, learned him. In her embrace, he was Steven, not a star. He didn't have to prove his stamina or his strength. He wasn't going to be scored on speed, agility or endurance. This was personal, and it was pleasure.

Steven drew his hand down the curve of her back and held her hips against his. He sipped at her mouth, nipping the corners, running his tongue over her lips. Their texture was moist, full and firm, tempting him to linger.

Steven ran his tongue against the seam of her lips. "Open for me, Val. Let me in."

Valerie parted her lips and Steven slipped his tongue inside. He lingered over her taste, sweet as honey with a hint of spice. She moaned, and he pulsed against her. She pressed against him, and Steven groaned.

His hands slid up Valerie's torso. The firm curves of her body singed the edges of his imagination. His palms cupped the sides of her breasts, testing their weight. He kneaded their fullness through her soft sweater. But his hands grew restless to stroke her bare skin.

Steven stepped back, steadying Valerie as she rocked on her heels. He pulled his sweater over his head and let it fall to the floor.

He caught Valerie's gaze as he brought her hand to him. His temperature rose even as he struggled to remain still. "I want to be with you. But if you want to stop, we have to stop right now."

Valerie stepped back, pulling her hand away from Steven. She took the hem of her sweater and pulled it over her head. Her torso stretched, lifting her breasts. The black lace bra played hide-and-seek with her nipples. The scalloped edges barely covered her breasts.

Steven swallowed before testing his vocal chords. "You're even more beautiful than I'd imagined."

Valerie's brows arched. "You've imagined me in my bra?"

Caught. Steven gave her a wicked smile. "I've seen the way you look at me. I think you've done some fantasizing of your own."

A bright red blush traced her high cheekbones. She angled her chin with an air of defiance. "Maybe I have. And maybe you've looked really good in those fantasies."

"I hope I can live up to your expectations."

Valerie nodded toward his buckle. "Show me what you've got."

Steven chuckled at her playful challenge. "Can you handle this?" His question was only half joking. Was she absolutely certain she was ready to blur the line between their personal and professional relationship? She hadn't been before.

Her eyes darkened. Her lids lowered. "I think I can."

Steven drew the belt from his pants loops. Valerie followed his lead, pulling off her boots and shimmying out of her pants. Her matching silk and lace underpants rode low on her hips. She looked like a Victoria's Secret model. Her limbs were long and toned, her skin golden brown. Steven could watch her for hours. Without conscious thought, he licked his lips. He unfastened his Dockers and kicked off his pants, then made quick work of shedding his underwear and socks.

For several long seconds, Valerie's gaze stroked his naked body. Her reaction made him feel powerful, wanted, attractive. She saw him as a flesh and blood man, not an NBA stereotype.

Valerie came to him, her eyes burning with desire. She extended her hands and drew her fingertips between his pectorals, down his torso. Steven's abdominals quivered with painful pleasure. She wrapped her warm, soft fingers around him, then dropped to her knees. Still holding his gaze, Valerie opened her mouth and took him in.

Steven's eyes widened. He swallowed hard. In his most explicit fantasies of the two of them together, Steven had never imagined this.

Chapter 19

Steven's response to her emboldened Valerie. It gave her courage; it fed her confidence. He'd said she was worth loving. It didn't matter if she believed him. Tonight, she'd live her fantasies—every single last one—with no regrets.

Valerie drew Steven deeper into her mouth. Slowly. She loved the taste of him, the heat of him, the texture of him between her lips. Her pulse sped up as his eyes closed and his head tipped back. She drew her tongue up and around his length. His hips moved with her. His body shivered. Her body ached.

Valerie delighted in the freedom to stroke and caress every inch of Steven's long, hard body. She raised her hands over his taut thighs, sliding around to feel his hamstrings, then up his hard, sculpted glutes. She cupped him, kneaded him. Her fingers dug into his flesh.

Steven tore away from her with a groan. His body shook at the separation. "Not that way. I want to come inside you."

His voice was deep and graveled, rubbing over her

skin. Valerie rose to her feet, licking her lips. Steven's body shook again. Satisfaction made her wet.

He reached out to her with one hand and popped open the front clasp of her bra. He brought both hands to her and peeled away the cups. Her breasts bounced free. He brought her to him, then lifted her against him. His shoulder muscles flexed beneath her fingers. The hair dusting his torso rasped against her skin, an erotic stimulation. Steven opened his mouth and drew in her breast.

Valerie's moan rose from the soles of her feet. He suckled her nipple hard and slow, swirling his tongue around her areola, scraping her flesh with his teeth. Each suckle brought a responding pulse deep inside. Her toes curled and she moved restlessly against him. She tightened her grip on his shoulders. His chest hair was a rough caress, contrasting the smooth, wet feel of his mouth on her. Her panties dampened.

Steven moved to her other breast, catching her nipple with his teeth. He tugged gently. Valerie threw her head back and arched into him. The ache between her thighs drove her crazy. She drilled her fingertips into his shoulders, wrapped her legs around his waist and undulated against his solid abs.

Steven wrapped one arm around her waist and with his free hand, he pulled aside her damp crotch to slip his hand inside her panties. He touched her wetness, caressing her folds before sliding one finger inside her. Two fingers inside her. They moved back and forth while his thumb explored her and his tongue moved up and over her nipple.

In one part of her mind, she was stunned by the noises coming from her. Mewling, begging sounds she'd never made before in her life. A wave of pleasure rolled over her, pinching her nipples.

Valerie gasped and forced her hips to still. "Wait."

Steven pressed his face against her breasts and froze. Valerie unwrapped her legs from his waist. He steadied her as she stood.

"Why?" The confusion in Steven's eyes warmed her. He thought she wanted him to stop, and he was willing to try. Silly man. Her nipples were painfully tight and moisture dripped down her thighs. She wasn't superhuman, and she didn't think Steven was, either.

Valerie shrugged out of her bra and pulled off her panties. She reached for his hands. "I want to finish this in bed."

Steven regained his breath. She was moving them to the bed. When a lady said stop, he had to stop. But, caught up in the moment as he'd been with Valerie, he hadn't wanted to. Her body had been hot, her skin so soft. She'd smelled like sex and flowers. And she'd been so wet. When she'd rubbed herself against him, he'd thought he'd come right there.

Valerie climbed onto the bed, giving him a tantalizing view of round, firm buttocks. She left room on the mattress for him to lie beside her. Instead, he pulled her to him, covered her with his body and kissed her deeply. She moaned into his mouth and his erection flexed against her soft stomach. Valerie parted her thighs to cradle him.

He caught her palms and secured her wrists above her head with one hand, then moved down her body to feast on her breasts. He suckled and licked her right breast, rolling her nipple between his lips while he kneaded and fondled her left breast, pinching her nipple between his thumb and forefinger.

Valerie strained against his hold. Her body writhed beneath him. "Let me touch you." She breathed the plea.

Steven's length strained with desire. He squeezed his eyes closed, struggling for control. "Not yet."

He reached again for her nipple. Valerie moaned and gasped, groaned and sighed. Her music made him harder. Steven slid down her body between her thighs. He lifted her legs, pressing her knees toward the mattress. She was open to him. She was wet for him. Her body moved without conscious thought. Steven lowered his head and kissed her intimately, deeply.

Valerie gasp. "What are you—"

Her words broke off. Steven heard a muffled squeal. He lifted his eyes and saw she'd covered her face with a pillow. He chuckled against her and Valerie's body quaked beneath his tongue. He opened his mouth and kissed her again. Her hips pumped against his lips. Her rhythm quickened and her legs strained as he loved her.

Steven heard her gasps even from beneath the pillow. Her breaths shortened and her volume increased. Steven steadied her hips as they rose higher. Her body arched and tensed beneath his palms. She froze for a moment, then her body shattered against his mouth. Her scream was his applause.

Steven kissed her one last time before sliding up and over her body. She still trembled beneath him. He removed the pillow from her face and revealed her stunned expression.

Valerie blinked. "Oh, my God."

Steven lowered his head and kissed her. He was so

hard, he could barely think. But he needed to. "Give me a minute."

He sat away from her. Several deep breaths cleared his head. Steven stood and padded to their piles of discarded clothes. He pulled his wallet from his pants and found the condom he'd packed in a hopeful moment.

"You're like a Boy Scout. Always prepared." Valerie's husky voice was amused.

Steven carried the condom to the bed. "Are you glad for that?"

Valerie rose to her knees and moved closer to him. She curved one hand around the back of his neck. The fingers of her free hand wrapped around his throbbing member. "Yes, I am." She breathed the words against his lips.

Steven slipped his tongue between her lips. Valerie stroked his length to his tip. Her fingers were slow and gentle. He loved the way she always touched him. She was always aware of him. She seemed as eager to please him as he was desperate to please her. Steven reached between her thighs. She was hot and wet. He squeezed his eyes closed and clenched his teeth. He'd never wanted so badly.

Valerie took the condom from him. She tore the packet, then fit the protection to him. She lay back on the bed, a seductive smile curving her lips as she pulled him with her and spread her thighs. He came to her. Wrapping his arms around her. Covering her lips with his. Pressing his heat into her.

Valerie gasped as Steven entered her. His thrusts were slow at first. Tentative, as though making sure she was ready for him. Oh, she was ready all right. She moved with him. He was big and hard in her. Valerie broke their kiss. She licked her lips as her hunger grew. Steven cupped her hips, shifting them to find her spot. Pleasure shot straight up to clench in her chest. She pressed her head—hard—against her pillow and closed her eyes. Steven's tongue stroked her throat. She felt her wetness flow.

She moved her hips under him, rubbing against him and squeezing him tight. Steven gasped and she squeezed him again. She could feel his heart galloping against her chest. She could hear his panting in her ears. His breath was hot, the sound erotic. He held her to him.

Valerie lifted her hips, rubbing them against him in a circular motion. He pressed into her. She squeezed him tight. He lifted his hips. She drew him back. Steven's breaths came fast and short at their intimate tug-of-war. He loosened his embrace and slipped one hand between them. He touched her there. Valerie's body jerked, then strained tight. She cupped his hips to press him to her. Steven's hips slammed into her again and again and again. They exploded together as they fell back onto the mattress.

Steven raised his hand and slapped off the radio alarm clock. That must be one of the worst noises known to humanity. It also brought an abrupt and unpleasant end to his satisfied sleep.

He rolled over to reach for Valerie. Instead he encountered thin air. Steven opened his eyes and sat up. Where was she? He scanned the empty room. It wasn't that big. There weren't that many places she could be.

The bathroom door opened, and Valerie emerged fully dressed. Not a good sign. She glanced toward

him before crossing to her suitcase. "Good morning."
She mumbled the words.

Steven studied her with a mixture of curiosity and
concern. "Good morning to you, too." He paused.
"Did you sleep well?"

"Yes, thank you. And you?"

Last night, she'd been a generous lover. This morning, she sounded like a well-mannered school girl.

"I slept very well. I was exhausted." The blush deepening the color in Valerie's cheeks was the only sign
she'd heard him. "How long have you been up?"

"Not long."

"You couldn't have gotten much sleep."

"I got enough." Valerie fiddled around in her suitcase. She didn't seem to be looking for anything.

His dread kicked up a notch. "Aren't you going to
look at me?"

Valerie seemed to brace herself before she looked
up. Still, she didn't quite meet his eyes. "You should
get out of bed now. We have to be at the airport by six."

The lack of inflection in her voice. The coolness in
her eyes. Her inability to look at him. All these things
were evidence the distance had returned between
them. Why? What had happened?

Steven rubbed the area above his heart. "What's
wrong, Val? Why are you pulling away from me?"

Valerie closed her suitcase and took her purse from
the dresser. Her movements were restless. "You
should get dressed now."

Steven checked the radio alarm clock. "There's
plenty of time." He returned his attention to her. She
rooted through her purse. "Whatever you're looking
for isn't in your purse."

She shot him a frown. "What are you talking about?"

Steven ripped off the covers and rolled to his feet. "Your courage, your backbone, your spine—whatever you need to tell me why you're giving me the cold shoulder this morning after what we shared last night is not in that purse."

Valerie's gaze skated down his body before returning to his eyes. "How do you want me to act? I didn't think you'd want me to cling to you."

Was she serious? "I'd like you to look at me. Speak to me as though you don't hate me anymore. Touch me."

Valerie dropped her attention to the floor. "I've never been in a situation like this. I'm not completely comfortable."

Steven walked to her and laid his hand on her shoulder. "This is new for me, too. Our pretend engagement took a very real turn last night. Let's take it slow until we're both feeling more comfortable."

Her head snapped up. "What do you mean? More comfortable with what?"

"Our relationship." Her reaction brought Steven's confusion back.

"Our relationship isn't real."

"What about last night?"

"Last night, I thought we were just . . . blowing off steam. You needed sex and I wanted comfort."

Steven backed up as though she'd punched him. "You thought I used you for sex?"

"Didn't you?"

"No. I didn't." He marched to the bed and tore the sheet from its mattress. "But thanks for letting me know you used me as a human dildo."

She gasped. "That's not . . . I . . ."

"Yeah. Draw yourself out of that one." He wrapped the sheet around his waist and held it in place.

She jabbed a finger toward the bed. "What was I supposed to believe? That our fake engagement suddenly became real?"

"Why not?" His fist tightened on the bed sheet. "Why is it easier to believe I'd use you as a handy lay than to believe I'd want to make love with you?"

"Our relationship before the pretense makes it easier to believe that." Valerie spun to pace the room. "We didn't date. We weren't even friends. Suddenly, I'm supposed to believe you have an itch, and I'm the only one who can scratch it?"

"I understand last night may have been too fast. We can slow it down."

Valerie stilled. The anger seemed to drain from her. "Why would you want to?"

"Why wouldn't you?"

"You were a professional athlete." She sounded as though that explained everything.

He waited. "So?"

"You're from a world full of women like Traci Greer Millbank. I'm just plain Val Parker. I can't compete."

Steven scowled. "You don't think I can be faithful?"

"Can you? With women throwing themselves at you all the time? Do you want me to name the professional athletes who've been caught cheating on their wives?"

He hooked his hands on his hips. "I hate to break it to you, sweetheart, but pro athletes haven't cornered the market on infidelity."

"But you have more opportunity." She paced back toward the dresser. "I don't want to be your flavor of the month just to be cast aside when something sweeter shows up."

Never had he tasted disappointment so bitter. "I'd hoped you could see past the NBA image. I know you're not impressed by the money or the fame. But I thought you were able to see the man and not the stereotype."

Valerie frowned her confusion. "I don't want to compete for you."

Steven turned toward the bathroom. He needed to shower before he dressed. "Who said you'd have to?"

"How could you lose the account?" Garrison's reaction communicated disbelief, dismay and confusion. "You and Traci had a personal relationship. This account should have gone smoothly."

Valerie tightened her grip on the arms of the visitor's chair in front of her father's desk. She and Steven had come straight to the office from the airport. It was almost five in the evening, and she was tired. Despite what she'd told Steven that morning, she hadn't gotten enough sleep Thursday night.

In the seat beside her, Steven seemed exhausted, too. He'd been subdued as he'd recapped their business trip for Garrison.

"Steve didn't lose the account." Valerie struggled to keep her tone even. "Traci wasn't taking the contract seriously."

"What's that supposed to mean?" Garrison gave her a hard stare. "I'd told Steve it was a bad idea for you to go along on this visit."

Valerie's chest tightened. It was hard to take a breath. Steven hadn't confided Garrison's response to her joining him on the business trip, but she'd suspected he hadn't been supportive. And now she knew. "Why did you think it was a bad idea?"

Garrison swiveled his chair to face her fully. "Did you and Traci get into an argument?"

Steven answered for her. "Val didn't have anything to do with losing the account." He sounded irritated as well as tired. "Trace was more interested in rekindling our past personal relationship than in planning an ad campaign for her health spa."

Garrison looked surprised. "Why didn't you just tell her you weren't interested?"

Steven smiled without humor. "She doesn't know the meaning of the word no."

Garrison grunted. "You've got to hand it to her. Most people don't get as far as she has without learning how to get around the word no."

Steven inclined his head. "That's Trace."

Garrison quirked a brow. "And she really wouldn't take no for an answer?"

"She really wouldn't." Steven's voice was firm.

Garrison settled deeper into his seat. "Well, you did the right thing, of course. The only thing we as an agency have of value is our integrity."

Steven sat straighter in his chair. "I'm glad you feel that way."

"I told you he would." Valerie was pleased with the outcome of their meeting, even as she was depressed that her father still opposed her professional growth.

Garrison seemed surprised. "Thanks for your vote of confidence."

"You're welcome." Valerie gave Garrison a guarded look. Why wouldn't she have confidence in him? He was the one who didn't believe in her.

Garrison cleared his throat. "I'll let the two of you go. I'm sure you're tired. I'll see you Monday."

Valerie followed Steven from her father's office. She had to hustle to keep up with him as he strode to his office. "Thank you for defending me to Garry."

"I didn't defend you. I told the truth." He never looked at her as he answered. "Professional athletes have been known to do that from time to time."

Valerie almost stumbled from the verbal blow. "Steve, I'm sorry. I never meant to offend you."

"So your offending me was an accident. I feel better knowing that." He crossed into his office.

Valerie followed after him. "You took me by surprise. Please try to understand. I never dreamed you'd want to make our fake relationship real."

Steven stood behind his desk, his hands in his pockets. "And now that you know?"

She hesitated. "I don't think it would be a good idea." It hurt to deny herself even the possibility of what she really wanted, like pulling adhesive tape from her arm.

Steven dropped into his executive chair. "I understand. You're afraid."

"No, I'm not."

"You're afraid of going after what you want. Your relationship with your father has damaged your self-esteem."

A blush burned Valerie's face. Her hands curled into fists. "That doesn't have anything to do with you."

Steven continued as though she hadn't spoken. "That's why you're not leaving the agency, even though you know you'd give your career a boost if you did. Deep down, you're afraid you're not good enough."

"That's not true." *How could he know her so well?*

"Yes, it is. It's also the reason you're afraid to get involved with me. You're afraid you're not good enough to hold the interest of a former professional athlete with scores of groupies lining up to be with him."

"That's a lot of ego you're carrying around. How's your neck holding up?"

"You brought up the groupies, not me." He leaned back into his chair. "But I'll say this one more time, since you appear hard of hearing. I'm not your father, Val. I know your worth."

Valerie's muscles shook, but she struggled to maintain her bravado. "Do you?"

"And I know my own. Don't expect me to beg."

Valerie rushed from Steven's office to escape the accusation in his eyes.

Chapter 20

Steven was wrong.

Valerie flexed her fists as she paced the length of her office. She hadn't stayed with Parker Advertising because she was afraid to go somewhere else. She stayed because it was her family's agency. Why should she leave? She belonged here.

Didn't she?

Her mother and father had worked hard and sacrificed a lot to establish the agency. When her father was ready to retire, she would step in to continue their legacy.

Wouldn't she?

Tired but even more confused, Valerie sank into her chair. She propped her elbows on her desk and cradled her forehead in her hands.

"What have you done with your hair?"

Manuel's words snapped Valerie out of her maudlin contemplation. The graphic artist stood in her doorway. In his warm gold linen jacket, matching pants and mango T-shirt, he looked like an extra from

Miami Vice, the 1980s television series that rocketed Don Johnson to pop culture status.

She couldn't help but smile. "From seventies disco to eighties *Miami Vice.* Is that back to the future on a budget?"

Manuel took his customary seat in front of Valerie's desk. He straightened the seam of his pants. "Don't change the subject."

"That outfit *is* the subject."

"What made you decide to get a twenty-first century hairstyle?"

Valerie touched the loose locks. She remembered Steven's reaction to her hair and her body grew warm. "You can ask me that question in that outfit?"

He gave her a blank stare. "Well?"

She touched her hair again. "I felt like a change."

"Good for you."

"Thanks. I think."

Manuel crossed his legs, straightening the seam of his pants again. "Sorry about Traci's account."

"The rumor mill works fast."

"It always has. How did Garry take the news about her canceling her contract?"

Valerie shrugged a shoulder. "He's disappointed, but he understands Traci isn't interested in a campaign for her health spa."

Manuel gave Valerie a considering look. "And you're okay with that?"

She angled her head. "Why wouldn't I be?"

Manuel shrugged. "I thought you'd resent Garry being so understanding toward Steve. You hate him."

Valerie blinked. "I don't hate Steve."

Manuel looked disbelieving. "You called him your

rival. You said he was a client thief. Did you forget all that?"

"I didn't forget. But 'hate' is a such a strong word."

"I'm curious. Why didn't you use Steve's misfortune to your advantage?"

"How?"

"Traci canceling her contract with us ruined perfect Steve's client track record. Why didn't you use that to hurt his relationship with Garry? You could have been one step closer to your promotion."

Valerie scowled. "Steve's track record is still perfect. Traci was sexually harassing him. He handled himself well, admirably."

Manuel's eyes twinkled as he spread his arms wide. "Well, well, well. Everybody, meet the newest member of the Steve Crennell Fan Club. Welcome, new member."

Valerie arched a brow. "Knock it off. Just because I think he has integrity doesn't mean I'm ready to bring him coffee."

"Ouch."

Valerie's throat tightened as she recalled Garrison's accusation that somehow she was to blame for Parker Advertising losing Traci's account. She rubbed her throat to ease the pain. "Besides, nothing could undermine Steve's relationship with Garry. As far as Garry's concerned, Steve walks on water."

"Well, if Steve's going to be walking all over you, then maybe it's time you found another pond to swim in. John McGee's waiting to welcome you with open arms."

Valerie's shoulders tensed. "If I had another opportunity, I'd take it. I'm not afraid to leave."

Manuel looked around the room. "Did I say you were afraid to leave? I didn't hear me say that."

"This is my family's firm. Why should I leave?"

"Val, read the writing on the wall. When there are more reasons for you to leave than there are reasons to stay, then it's time to go."

"But that's not fair."

"I'm not saying I want you to go. I love you. But you're my friend. I want you to be happy. And, if you're not happy here, I want you to leave." Manuel waved a hand toward the door.

But the muscles in Valerie's stomach twisted to knots. This couldn't be fear. "What if there are a lot of little reasons for me to leave, but one big reason for me to stay? What should I do then?"

"What's the big reason to stay?"

Valerie swallowed. "I'm not ready to leave."

"Then I demanded to be traded to the Knicks."

When Marlon's words penetrated Steven's brain, he jerked to a stop. "You told them what?"

The two men were jogging around the elevated track in the Nia Neighborhood Recreational Center. On the basketball court below, the usual teams of male youths battled for superiority and attention. The kids looked pretty good this Saturday morning.

"I was joking." Marlon's tone crackled with sarcasm.

"That wasn't funny." Steven's nerves were still popping. The image of his friend being traded to their conference rival added to his tension.

"You weren't listening to anything I said, were you?"

"I heard that crack you made about the Knicks." Steven started jogging again, but Marlon's grip on his shoulder brought him to a halt.

Marlon released Steven's shoulder to brace both

hands on his own hips. "All right, man. Don't make me embarrass myself by admitting that I'm worried about you. Snap out of it."

"What are you talking about?" As much as he cared about his friend, Steven had better things to do than decode Marlon's riddles.

"The last time you were this distracted was when you retired from the NBA. What's going on?"

Come to think of it, Marlon was right. Steven had felt this same tension and depression when he'd realized his NBA career had ended and he had to rebuild his life. He started jogging again, trying to put distance between himself and those feelings.

Steven waited for Marlon to fall into step beside him before he answered. "Val isn't the woman I thought she was. She can't separate me from the stereotypes of NBA players. I thought she could."

"What happened? Did she ask you to buy something for her? Did she want you to introduce her to someone?"

"No. But she thinks I'm the kind of man who could sleep with a different woman every night."

Marlon stumbled to a stop. "What? Why does she think that?"

Steven slowed until Marlon joined him again. His rapid heart rate wasn't completely attributable to his work out. "It's not personal. She thinks *all* professional athletes are liars and cheats."

Marlon stared at him for several silent beats. "You're right. She doesn't know you."

The stiffness in his tone let Steven know his friend was offended on his behalf. "For that matter, she doesn't know you, either."

"You know, there's a pattern here. First, you're engaged for *real* to a woman who loves you for your money. Then, you *fake* an engagement to a woman who hates you for a rep you don't even have."

"What's your point, Mar?"

"You're cursed."

"This is my life. Can you *try* to take it seriously?"

"Look, just forget her." Marlon sounded disgusted. "There are plenty of other honeys in the comb."

Steven kept pace with Marlon as they started their fourth lap on the padded indoor track. He wiped the sweat from his eyes. "I don't want to keep fishing. I want to find one woman and settle down."

"Since when?" Marlon sounded incredulous.

"Since I realized all I do is work." Steven picked up the pace, pumping his arms higher as he rounded another corner. His friend stayed with him. "I want more than a paycheck. I want someone to share my life with."

"Then make sure you find someone who's willing to give *and* receive."

Steven slowed. "What do you mean?"

"Look. With Trace, you made all the compromises. You went to the restaurants she chose. You took the vacations she wanted. What about you? What did you get?"

Steven could see his point. "I got my ring back."

"That's the best thing she's ever done for you." Marlon grunted. "Actually, it's the *only* thing she's ever done for you."

Steven shrugged, staring ahead as he paced himself with Marlon's jogging speed. "I'm not going to let one bad experience keep me from making a commitment."

"Look. I don't want you to get impatient and make a mistake."

"You mean *another* mistake. You're never going to let me forget Trace."

"*You* shouldn't let you forget Trace." Marlon grunted again. "You changed yourself to please her. That's not healthy, man. Don't let it happen again."

Steven gave the other man a sharp look. "Is that how you see me, as a people pleaser?"

Marlon shrugged. "Yeah."

Steven almost tripped over his feet again. "Why didn't you ever say something?"

"About what?"

"Never mind."

Marlon shrugged. "Why are you so impatient to tie yourself to someone? You have your family. You're all close."

"Yes, we're very close. We talk often. We get together for dinner at least once a week. Then, at the end of the night, my parents are together. My sister goes home with her husband. And I spend the night with ESPN."

"Is that what this is about? Your family's lined up two by two, so you think you have to be?"

It was more than that. But Steven couldn't explain it. "What's wrong with that?"

"Nothing. But you need to find a woman who's as interested in your happiness as you are in hers. She should want to please you as much as you want to please her. In and out of bed."

There it was again—the accusation of being a chameleon, reflecting other people's needs as his own.

If this was something he'd been doing subconsciously for so long, could he even tell the difference between his wants and what he was doing to please someone else?

* * *

"Esmeralda, that's stupid. Horses aren't *green*. They're *brown*." Indignant ten-year-old Courtney snatched the green crayon from bewildered six-year-old Esmeralda. She slapped a brown crayon onto the recreation room table in its place. Esmeralda stared at the new crayon as though wondering what to do with it.

Courtney was a trying child.

Valerie filled her lungs with a cleansing breath and exhaled. She took the empty seat beside Courtney at the round wood table where the children colored sketches of animals.

She put a gentle hand on Courtney's shoulder to gain her attention. "Actually, Esmeralda is very smart."

Valerie took the emerald green crayon from the older girl and gave it back to Esmeralda. The six-year-old beamed, her big coffee brown eyes glowing. They seemed to brighten the entire recreation room at the Miami Children's Hospital.

Valerie continued. "She knows that, in her drawings, horses can be any color she wants them to be. They can be green." She poked around the crayon box and pulled out another crayon. "Or purple. Or—" She looked at Esmeralda. "What other color do you want your horses to be?"

Esmeralda smiled. "Pink."

Valerie laughed. "Or even pink."

She handed the pink crayon to Esmeralda and watched her color not just the horse but her entire paper dark pink. The little girl still wasn't concerned about drawing inside the lines. "That's beautiful, Esmeralda."

The child giggled, then returned to her master-piece.

Valerie noticed Courtney studying a lemon yellow crayon. Perhaps Esmeralda's influence was breaking barriers for Courtney.

Having ensured peace and stability reigned at the table, Valerie wandered around the room, checking that the young patients had enough crayons and coloring books to entertain them.

"Does the United Nations know about you?" Gloria Shaffner appeared at her side. Her arms were loaded with children's books.

Valerie checked her watch. "It's already noon? These Saturday mornings go by so quickly."

"You're not usually here Saturdays."

Valerie took some of the books from the other woman, then led Gloria to a table in the corner of the recreation room. Valerie claimed the chair with its back to the wall. "Not usually, but I felt like coming in today."

Gloria set her stack of books beside Valerie's pile. Rolling up the sleeves of her mocha frost sweater, she settled into the chair across from Valerie. "I bet the kids were ecstatic. They love you. Especially Courtney. She actually listens to you."

Valerie crossed her legs and surveyed their young charges. From this distance, she could keep an eye on the kids and still speak privately. "She wants to go home." Valerie settled her gaze on the short-tempered ten-year-old. "These play periods aren't distracting her from her upcoming surgery."

"Her second one. Poor thing." Gloria tossed back her heavy auburn locks. "Before you leave, tell me about the campaign."

Valerie's stomach dropped. The campaign they hadn't worked on at all last week? "It's coming along very well. You'll enjoy the presentation."

Gloria's golden brown eyes twinkled. "In other words, you want me to stop asking about it."

Valerie smothered a smile. "We have had this conversation before. Remember? And I said you'd stifle my creativity if you hounded me about it."

Gloria feigned surprise. "I'm not hounding."

Valerie pretended confusion. "Really? It feels like hounding to me." She reached out and squeezed her friend's forearm. "Be patient, Gloria. We'll make our January second deadline and you'll see the presentation then."

At least, she hoped they made their deadline. Valerie didn't want to use the friendship card to ask for an extension.

Gloria sighed. "You know patience isn't my strong suit."

"If I didn't know it before, I know it now."

Gloria laughed. The big, booming sound bounced around the room, drawing the children's attention. When the young patients located the source of the disturbance, they started to laugh, too.

Gloria blushed. "I have that effect on people." She faced Valerie again. "And I will meet Steve Crennell, right? You promised."

Valerie swallowed the sour taste before answering. "I promised."

Gloria squeaked and clapped her hands in excitement. "Oh, wonderful! I'm so excited. I'm really looking forward to meeting him. Can't wait!"

Valerie tried to ignore her friend's antics. "I never

knew you followed sports. When did you become a basketball fan?"

"Oh, I don't watch basketball, but I've seen pictures of Steve Crennell. Yummy!"

Valerie blinked. "Gloria, does Steve's participation in the presentation really make that much of a difference?"

Gloria laughed again. And again, the children joined her. "It doesn't hurt."

Valerie didn't see the humor. "But does it really give us an advantage over the competition?"

Her friend shrugged. "Steve has a strong, positive reputation. By associating himself with your agency, he's sharing his reputation with your firm. It's like a testimonial. You know, Advertising one-oh-one stuff."

"I know what you mean. It's just hard to understand how his reputation can carry more weight than the presentation's quality."

"It's part of the presentation's quality." Gloria leaned forward. "So, what's he like to work with?"

Valerie started to shrug, but changed her mind. Steven deserved her kudos. "He's smart and works hard. I enjoy working with him."

The truth of that statement didn't surprise her anymore. What did surprise her was how afraid she was that he wouldn't want to work with her anymore. She'd accused him of being untrustworthy when he'd proven repeatedly he was a man of integrity.

The bottom of Valerie's stomach dropped again. When was she going to stop allowing her hang-ups to drive them apart?

Chapter 21

"Where is he?" Valerie fretted as she checked her watch for the third time in less than an hour. "I didn't realize I'd need an appointment to talk with my father even on a Saturday afternoon."

Loretta sat at the dining table in the home she shared with her brother. She was reviewing the lesson plan for her senior memoir writing class. "In fairness, hon, he didn't know you were coming."

"True, but is he ever home anymore?" Valerie prowled the perimeter of her father's china cabinet, studying the photographs arranged around the plates, bowls, glasses and cups within. "I'm trying to get closer to him, but he's more of a mystery to me now than he was even a year ago."

"Have you told him that?" Her aunt watched her from above her rimless bifocals.

That seemed to be Loretta's answer to every concern Valerie raised about her relationship with her father.

Valerie spoke over her shoulder. "I would if I could

ever speak with him alone. What's keeping him so busy? Do you know?"

Loretta returned her attention to her lesson plan. "Your father's a very private man. He's been that way since he was a child. It's not one of his most endearing qualities."

Valerie's attention was snagged by a photo in the china cabinet of her and her father dressed for trick-or-treating. She was seven or eight years old. They wore artists' costumes, matching stained goldenrod smocks with lime green berets. Her mother had chosen the outfits and taken the picture.

Her heart tugged at the memory. "He may be a private person, but he told my mother everything."

"Yes, he did. As his younger sister, I've known your father longer. But your mother knew him better."

"But now he's closed himself off from people again. Well, everyone but Steve." Valerie moved on to a photograph from her elementary school graduation. She must have been twelve. The photo was taken two years before her mother's sudden death. It showed Valerie standing proudly between her parents. She was beaming at the camera. They were beaming at her. One happy, loving family. At least for a time.

Valerie moved away from the memories and dropped into a chair across from her aunt. "I just want to make sure he's all right. Has he told you anything?"

Loretta set aside her lesson plan and gave Valerie her full attention. "He seems fine, Val. He's just busy."

"Doing what?"

Loretta picked up her lesson plan again. "You'll need to ask him that."

"I *have* asked. But he's so evasive." She stood to pace

the dining room again. "I'm not being nosy. I have a right to know what's going on in my father's life."

"I agree."

Valerie stilled, glancing back at her aunt. The other woman had sounded so vehement, more vehement than Valerie had expected. "He doesn't tell me anything about his personal life, and he doesn't ask about mine. He seems to prefer treating me as an employee."

Loretta gave a noncommittal hum. "I've told you before, if you want something from your father, you're going to have to take it. Time, attention, information. He won't hand it over to you."

"First, I have to track down the invisible man. And you know that's easier said than done. Then I can try to get him to talk."

"Is it worth the trouble?"

Valerie quirked a brow at Loretta. "What do you think?"

Loretta shook her head. "Only you can make that decision, hon."

Valerie paused beside the china cabinet again, drawn there almost against her will. This time her gaze found a photo of herself at age . . . four? . . . sitting on her father's shoulders. They were laughing and pointing toward the water.

Valerie kept her back to her aunt. "Steve accused me of being afraid."

"Of what?" Loretta sounded surprised.

"Of leaving Parker Advertising. He said that I don't think I'm good enough to find a position with another agency."

Loretta was silent for several moments. "Is he right?"

She turned. "If you can ask me that, you must think he is."

"I know you love your father, but you're obviously not happy working for him. So why do you stay?"

Valerie threw her arms wide. "Why would I leave? My parents built the company. How can I turn my back on that?"

"I'm not saying you should. But why can't you have it all?"

"What do you mean?"

"Why not apply for a senior account executive position with another agency? Then, when Garry's finally ready to retire, if the two of you can come to an agreement, you can take his place at Parker Advertising."

Valerie bent her head, studying the pale gold wall-to-wall carpeting. "I hadn't thought about that."

"Maybe because you were afraid to." Loretta's voice was gentle even though her words felt harsh.

"Maybe." The admission left Valerie feeling more vulnerable than she'd ever wanted to feel.

"What are you going to do about it?"

"I'm going to work on not being so afraid. But I think that's easier said than done."

She echoed the statement she'd earlier voiced about Garrison. Valerie glanced at the china cabinet. "Steve also said he thought I was too afraid to have a relationship with him."

Loretta greeted that comment with silence. It wasn't as though they'd never talked about men before, although those conversations weren't frequent. Until recently, Valerie's social life had been on a ventilator system. "Do you want a relationship with him?" Her aunt's voice was tentative.

Steven was stubborn, bossy and a little cocky. But he

also was smart, funny and—although she hated to admit it—fun to be with. "Yes, I think I do."

Loretta grinned. "Then what are you going to do about it?"

Valerie lifted her purse from the dining table and slung it over her shoulder. "I'm going to work on not being so afraid. And I'm going to see a man about an apology."

Valerie pressed Steven's doorbell and prepared to wait in front of his Georgian style Pinecrest mansion. Wow.

She set the gift-wrapped package on the ground, then dragged her sweaty palms over her faded blue jeans and patted her unbound hair. To distract herself, Valerie looked around while she waited. The rose pink brick walkway that led to his white concrete entrance was almost as long as a city block. She'd practiced her apology twice as she walked to his door. His entranceway didn't do anything to calm her nerves, either. The white concrete arch was an elegant contrast to the black curved wooden doors. She was out of her element. Was it too late to cut and run?

She should have called first. Suppose he wasn't home? She'd call him in the morning. Most people were home on Sunday.

Suppose he had company? She'd leave his gift with him and leave.

Suppose he was alone?

Inside, footsteps crossed hardwood flooring. Valerie closed her eyes and breathed. She picked up the gift package and waited.

The front door opened and Steven stood in the threshold. His silent curiosity ratcheted her tension.

Valerie offered a tentative smile. "I'm sorry to interrupt your Saturday afternoon, but I was hoping we could talk."

Steven stepped back. "How did you know where I lived?"

"Junior partners aren't the only ones with access to personnel records." She paraphrased the response he'd given when she'd asked the same question three weeks ago. Had it really been that long ago?

"I'll make a note about those policy changes." He let her in, then closed and locked the door.

Valerie looked around his entrance hall. Her jaw dropped. "This is incredible."

She crossed the black hardwood flooring, moving further into his home. To her right was a glass staircase with wide hardwood steps. At the midway landing, three narrow windows interrupted the white walls, displaying a glimpse of the side yard before the stairs continued to the second floor.

"Wow." Valerie breathed the compliment as her feet carried her forward.

"Did you come for a tour?"

She spun to face Steven. The amusement on his face was genuine and kind, but she still burned with embarrassment. "I don't know what I was thinking. I'm sorry. It's just so beautiful."

"Thank you." He slipped his hands into the front pockets of his dark olive Dockers.

The movement drew Valerie's eyes to his lean hips, well-muscled legs, and bare feet, back up to his flat stomach and broad shoulders.

Her stomach muscles clenched with the realization

that she knew what this big, strong man looked like under his red violet jersey and nicely fitted pants. Her cheeks burned hotter as her mind drifted back to their last night in Vail.

Steven's question cut the memories short. "What are you doing here?"

Valerie glanced again at his bare feet and slipped out of her beige canvas shoes. "I know it's early—only December eighth—but I wanted to give you your Christmas gift now." She stepped forward to offer him the green and gold wrapped package.

Steven looked at the gift before raising his black velvet eyes to hers. His hands remained in his pockets. "Why are you giving this to me now?"

Was she doing the right thing? Would he understand what she was trying to say? "I want you to know I am listening. It may take me a while to hear you, but I am listening."

Steven hesitated a moment more before taking the package from her. "Thank you."

He led her to a room off the entryway. Was it the family room? Did mansions have family rooms or were they called something else? Valerie didn't notice much beyond the black sixty-plus-inch, high-definition, flat-screen television hanging center stage on the far white wall. He had the Miami Waves game on. French doors guarded either side of the television. Late evening sunlight drifted past the white trim into the room. A long antique white leather sofa sat perfectly centered in front of the television behind a black coffee table. On the far left, a mahogany bar stood behind four matching chairs. That was Steven's destination.

He paused in front of the counter for an update on the game. "Millbank's still off."

Valerie checked the score. She'd been watching the game while she gathered her courage to talk to Steven. "Maybe the coach should bench him."

Steven shook his head. "He just needs to pull himself together."

He examined the package she'd presented to him. Once he seemed to have a sense of her wrapping technique, Steven slipped one finger under the edge of the paper covering the short end of the box. He stroked his hand along the side, coaxing the tape from the wrapping.

Valerie swallowed. She remembered his same slow-hand technique from a hotel room in Vail. She lifted her eyes to his face. Did he?

He used the same technique along the length of the package before pulling apart the paper. The adhesives dropped willingly, revealing the gift inside.

Steven frowned. He turned over the nine-volume set to read *The Works of Alexandre Dumas.* His eyes widened with surprise. "Why did you get this for me?" He asked the question without looking at her.

Steven was very intuitive. Valerie sensed he understood. Still, he wanted the words. She couldn't blame him, although she would rather have drawn him a picture.

"That last night in Vail, you showed me who you are. But I didn't realize it at the time. My insecurities blinded me."

He turned his head toward her. His dark eyes were expressionless. "Who am I?"

Valerie smiled. These words came effortlessly.

"You're a man of integrity, good values and a strong moral code."

"Thank you." Steven inclined his head toward the Dumas collection. "But you didn't have to buy this collection to tell me that. It's a very expensive explanation."

Valerie shrugged a shoulder. "It was worth it. I never should have questioned you. I was stupid and blind. Throughout that whole fiasco with Traci, you handled yourself with dignity." Her smile returned when she detected his blush.

"I appreciate that."

"I don't know what happened with you and Traci after I left you—and I don't need to know—but I'm sure she did her best to tempt you. Still you had too much integrity to cheat, even on a fake fiancée."

Steven leaned against the bar, his arms crossed and his back to his flat-screen television. "You still haven't told me why you were with me that night. I made love to you. What were you doing?"

Valerie's frown cleared. "I wasn't using you like a dildo. I'm sorry I made you think that. I wanted to be with you. I just hadn't thought someone like you would want to be with me."

Steven's demeanor cooled. "You mean an ex-NBA player?"

"No." Valerie paced away from him, impatient with her inability to find the right words. "I mean someone as attractive as you, as successful and confident as you are."

Steven grinned. "You're making me curious about the men you've dated in the past. What were they? Trolls?"

She stopped pacing and gave him a sour look.

"They were nice men, but you notice I'm not with any of them now."

"I have noticed." Steven walked toward her. His feet were silent as he crossed the hardwood floor. "Their loss."

He reached out to touch her hair. Steven's fingers moved through the strands, then over her scalp.

Valerie's thoughts scattered. Her breath quickened. Her heart beat hard and heavy inside her. The hummingbirds nesting in her lower abdomen stirred awake. "Yes, well, I don't know how to respond to that."

Steven smiled. The look in his eyes said the wretch knew what he was doing to her and was enjoying it. "Don't you want to know what I bought you for Christmas?"

She strained to focus. "What is it?"

"It's upstairs."

Valerie's eyes widened. Her jaw dropped. Steven roared with laughter. His hand fell away from her hair as he almost doubled over.

Finally, he caught his breath. "The look on your face."

"What was I supposed to think?"

"I thought you said you knew me." Wicked humor still brightened his dark eyes.

"Oh, now that's not fair. In the middle of foreplay, you tell me my present's upstairs. Any jury would agree the implication was quite clear."

Steven's lips still trembled with laughter. "That was foreplay?"

"What would you call it?"

"I was fixing your hair."

Valerie gasped. "Rude."

"You'll get over it."

With an athlete's strength and agility, Steven swept her off her feet. One minute, she was standing before him; the next, she was cradled in his arms, held against his chest as he strode from the family room and climbed his steps.

She wrapped her arms around his neck and stared out the trio of windows overlooking the side yard. "I've never made love in a mansion."

Steven grunted. "You're making love with me, not my house."

She turned away from the windows to study his profile. "Who said I was making love with either? I thought you were taking me to get my present."

His smile softened Steven's sharp features. He reached the top of the staircase and started down the long, wide hallway. Valerie turned her head to look over the railing to a clear view of the foyer way below.

She frowned at Steven. "Did that even wind you?"

"No." He didn't sound winded, either. Incredible.

She gave his profile a narrow-eyed stare. "Can we do it again?"

"No."

Valerie chuckled, her belief restored that he was indeed human.

The door at the end of the hallway was open. Steven strode toward it. Valerie's pulse picked up and the hummingbirds in her stomach darted around. "I find it interesting that my present just happens to be in your bedroom."

"I didn't know you were coming. I didn't even

realize you knew where I lived." Steven nudged the door wider with his bare foot. "I was going to take your present into work after the holiday party. But since you're here—" He released her legs, allowing her body to slide down his. "Which do you want first? Me? Or your gift?"

Chapter 22

The promise in Valerie's eyes increased Steven's desire. His blood hummed in his ears.

"I want *you*. Steve Crennell. Not the NBA. Not your mansion. Just you." She stepped forward, pulling his jersey from the waistband of his olive Dockers. "Naked. Underneath me."

Steven's shaft pulsed. He helped Valerie raise his jersey over his head; then he pulled her into his arms. "That's a start."

He lowered his mouth to hers, and she opened her lips for him. Steven accepted her invitation. He pushed his tongue into her mouth and sent it on an exploration. He caressed her tongue, her teeth, the sides of her mouth.

Her taste was sweet and intoxicating, like wine. Her scent—lavender and vanilla—filled his senses. Her soft, warm wetness made him restless. It sketched erotic images behind his closed eyelids. Steven drew his palm down her slender, toned body, wanting every inch of her to touch him. His blood pounded louder in his ears.

Steven leaned away, anxious to remove Valerie's clothing. She'd looked beautiful in the black blouse and skinny blue jeans that accentuated her long legs—legs he'd wanted wrapped around his waist from the minute she'd crossed his doorway. But now he wanted her bare, soft skin against him.

He tossed her blouse . . . somewhere, then watched as she shimmied out of her jeans. It amazed him what this seemingly conservative woman wore under her clothes. Valerie straightened, revealing barely there yellow underwear. Beneath his increasingly tight pants, Steven's manhood nodded its approval.

"You are so beautiful." He traced a fingertip around her dark nipple, visible through her bra's gauzy material. Her nipple tightened beneath his touch. Steven's mouth went dry.

Valerie reached out to him, caressing his pectorals and drawing her fingers through the hair on his torso. She unfastened his pants and let them drop to the floor. "So are you."

Steven's stomach muscles quivered. With Valerie, he was strong and vulnerable at the same time. He knew the woman in his arms, but she continued to surprise him. She challenged him and drove him insane. She touched him and made him ache. Anger and contentment; joy and sorrow. She drew from him a confusion of reactions that nevertheless led to the same conclusion—he wanted to be with her, head, heart, body and soul. For this day and night. And for forever.

Steven unhooked the front clasp of her gauzy bra and freed her breasts from the cups. He cradled their soft weight in the palms of his hands. Valerie flattened her hands over his pecs, touching him as he touched her. Kneading him as he kneaded her.

She leaned into his hands, rose up on her toes and parted her lips for him. Steven kissed her. Valerie took hold of his tongue and drew it deep into her mouth, suckling it, caressing it in a simulation of a more intimate act.

Steven kicked away from his pants and walked her backward toward the mattress. With his hands around her taut, warm waist, he lifted her onto the bed. Her breasts bounced with the movement. Steven swallowed. His gaze lifted to hers and the heat in her eyes scorched him.

There was no doubt in his mind that, this time, Valerie saw him and only him. Not his past glory or future plans. Not his NBA fame or fortune. She wasn't even aware of the insecurities her father may have seeded in her mind. She was Valerie. He was Steven, and the only thing between them was their underwear.

Steven leaned his torso over her. He pressed his cheek against hers. Then he ran his tongue around the shell of her ear. Once. Twice. She shivered beneath him. When he dipped his tongue into her ear, she stiffened and moaned.

"By the way, that's foreplay." Her voice was a whisper.

Steven chuckled beside her ear and she shivered again. "No, I'm just fixing your hair."

Her laughter caused her breasts to rub against his chest. Steven kissed her ear, then bit her earlobe. Valerie skimmed her fingernails over his shoulder blades. The wicked sensation bowed his body into her. She arched up to meet him.

She feathered wet kisses along his jaw and licked his chin. "Tasty."

He found her mouth and kissed her deep. He slid one hand beneath her hips to press her against his growing arousal. "Very." He breathed the word against her lips.

Valerie moaned, pressing her palms against his shoulders until Steven moved back.

His gaze searched her face. "Did I hurt you?"

Her smiled relieved his fears. "I want to be on top."

In response to her words, Steven's hips pressed into hers before he found the strength to roll away.

Valerie shed her panties before climbing on top of Steven. She pressed her knees against his lean hips and ran her fingertips over his six-pack abs. She wanted to take a bite out of him somewhere. Everywhere. But she'd get to that later. She shook back her hair, arching her spine, and felt Steven move beneath her.

She smiled at him. "Liked that, huh?"

He ran a hand up her left thigh. "What's not to like?"

Valerie laughed. The heat in his eyes, the intensity in his expression, made her feel special. Valued. Worth loving. This time, she wasn't focused solely on the sensations she wanted to give and receive. This time, she was open to him. She wanted to be with him, physically and emotionally. Spiritually.

She wanted to feel him, but she especially wanted to see him. His muscles, braced between her knees. His torso kissed by the soft light of the setting sun as it filtered across his bed. The pulse skipping at the base of his throat. His expression, so intent. He watched her as though he wanted to pull her very essence inside of him. She saw all of that.

Valerie leaned forward and inhaled his scent. Hot sandalwood. She licked the spot where his pulse raced. Steven's hands cupped her bare buttocks, massaging her flesh, then moved up her back to her waist. Valerie trailed kisses down the center of Steven's chest, pausing to kiss and tease his nipples. When they grew into points, she rubbed the pebbled flesh with her palms. The intimate sensation made her restless.

She continued downward, past his flat abs to his navel. Her tongue played in and around the indentation while her fingers stroked his body. The well-worked muscles of his abdomen undulated beneath her hand. His fingers dug into the mattress.

Valerie moved even lower to the waistband of Steven's briefs. She licked around the edges, then slipped a finger underneath. She glanced up and saw Steven rolling his head on his pillow. His breathing quickened.

She came up on her knees and pulled his underwear from his hips. His erection sprang free—full, hard and pulsing. Valerie leaned in to stroke its length with her tongue before pulling the briefs from Steven's legs. Steven kicked his underwear free of his ankles. He scooted down the mattress, hooked his hands under Valerie's arms. Then dragged her back up his body and onto his face.

Valerie gasped as Steven's mouth closed over her in a deeply intimate kiss. An almost painful pleasure shot up her core. Valerie arched her back and drove her fingers into her scalp to keep her head from exploding. Her hips rocked against him, unconsciously finding a rhythm to match his mouth. Steven's broad, strong palms held her hips in place as he suckled, nibbled and licked her. She didn't need his anchor. She wasn't going anywhere as long as he was touching her.

The magic of his lips and tongue made her eyes cross. Valerie arched back even further, pushing her hips forward. Her body tensed. Her muscles tightened. Wave after wave of pleasure crashed over and through her. Through the storm, Steven held her tight. Pressing deeper. Keeping them connected. Valerie's body convulsed. Her muscles went lax and she screamed as her body collapsed backward onto him.

Tiny aftershocks still registered deep inside her. Steven gathered her to him and rolled onto her. He kissed her hard and she tasted herself on his tongue. She sighed, loving his weight on top of her. His scent. Their taste.

Steven rolled off her. He lay beside her, breathing hard. "Condom." He slid across the mattress.

Valerie heard him rummaging in his nightstand for the protection. Her body screamed for him to hurry. Finally, he returned to her with the item in hand. Valerie took it from him. She rose and once again straddled his hips. With shaking hands, she opened the wrapper, then rolled the condom onto him. Steven pressed himself into her hands, arching his back and pressing his head into his pillow. He rolled them to switch positions and kissed her.

Steven entered her, smooth and deep. Stretching her gently. His touch set off more tremors and Valerie shivered around him. She gasped and he deepened their kiss. Steven pulled out to his tip, then pushed back even farther. Valerie moved with him, her body straining toward another climax.

Steven broke their kiss. He lowered his head to catch her nipple. Valerie fed her breast to him, urging him to suckle her harder. He transferred his attention to the other breast, loving it the same way. All the while his hips continued their strong, steady strokes, pushing Valerie to the edge of reason from multiple pleasure points. Her moisture flowed and her tension built. She was ready to explode.

Steven lifted his head and pressed his cheek against hers. He tightened their embrace, pulling her closer. Moving them harder. His breathing hitched in Valerie's ear. She pressed her head against the pillow and lifted her hips to grind against him. Steven grabbed her hips and pushed into her once. Twice. Valerie tipped back her head and screamed. Steven stiffened, flowing into her, and then collapsed.

Steven was crushing her. He'd shifted so only his torso rested on her, but he was still heavy. She didn't mind, though. His weight felt good. She could feel his heartbeat against her breast. She didn't mind that, either. It felt good, too.

Valerie gave him a hard hug. "Believe it or not, I hadn't intended for that to happen. I just came to apologize."

"Apology accepted." He breathed the words against her ear. It tickled.

"What a comedian."

Steven stretched across her to turn on a bedside light. "Hang around. I'm just warming up."

Valerie blinked at the light. She surveyed the mattress, its tangled sheets and scattered pillows. "This bed is enormous. It could probably get its own zip code."

He hooked an arm around her waist and rolled over, pulling her on top of him. "Will you stay the night?"

She heard the uncertainty in his tone. Funny, if

she'd heard that note in his voice yesterday, Valerie might have thought he'd wanted her to leave. But now she recognized this famous ex-NBA player who could have any woman he wanted was afraid she'd reject him.

Valerie made herself more comfortable on top of him. "I'd like to, but I don't have a change of clothes. Or my toothbrush."

"All right. I'll take you home in a while."

"There's no rush." She braced her forearms on his chest to prop herself up. "My car's parked in front of Casa Crennell. Why don't you come home with me?"

"But you don't live in a mansion." His eyes teased her.

She gave him a dry look. "If we park your ego in the garage, you just might fit."

"If you're going to be insulting, I won't give you your gift."

Valerie gasped, staring at him wide-eyed. "I forgot all about that."

Steven crossed his arms beneath his head. His smile was wide and smug. "Really? Why?"

Valerie tapped his chest. "What an ego." She rolled off him, fluffed a pillow behind her back and pulled the sheet over her breasts. "Go get my present."

Steven heaved himself off the bed. "Whatever my lady commands."

"Ooh, I like that."

She watched the flow of muscles in Steven's back, buttocks and legs as he crossed his room naked. She admired his strength and the discipline it took to maintain it. No, he didn't play basketball professionally any longer. But, if it weren't for his knee, he could compete tomorrow.

He opened the door to a walk-in closet that, from her angle, appeared to be the size of her master bedroom. He disappeared for several moments, then reappeared with a large, rectangular box.

Valerie's mouth dropped opened. "What's in that?"

Steven paused before reaching her. His voice was amused. "The expression on your face tells me you think it's too much. Before you refuse my gift, remember the Alexandre Dumas collection in my family room. I know how much that cost."

Valerie scowled at him. "Don't be tacky." She waved him forward. "Give me my gift."

Steven handed her the large box and sat on the edge of the bed. He was so comfortable with his nudity. Valerie was torn between studying him and paying attention to the cheerful raspberry and white gift-wrapped box.

Valerie focused on the box. She weighed it with her hands. "It's heavy."

"Maybe to you."

"Ooh. Tough guy." She ripped the wrapping from the box. Or at least she tried to. "You used a lot of tape."

"I saw the way you tore open your gift last year. I thought I'd give you more of a challenge this time."

Her look promised retribution. Valerie folded the remains of the wrapping paper and set it aside, then lifted the lid. Her mouth dropped open in a silent "Oh."

Stephen shifted closer to her. "Well? What do you think?"

Valerie touched the smooth, gleaming cherrywood box inside. She lifted it onto the bed and raised the lid.

Several shelves extended outward, displaying water-colors and acrylic paints, charcoal and colored pencils.

She blinked back tears and raised her eyes to his. "This is one of the best gifts I've ever received. Thank you."

She slid the box aside and scooted closer to Steven, raising on her knees. Valerie wrapped her arms around his neck. Steven returned her embrace. "I'm glad you like it." He sounded surprised.

"I love it." She squeezed him tighter.

"You act as though no one's ever bought you art supplies before."

Valerie leaned back, letting her arms slide from his shoulders. "Not since my mother passed away. For the past ten years, my father's given me gift cards. Very nice, very expensive gift cards."

"Garry doesn't strike me as much of a shopper." Steven released her.

Valerie stroked the lid of the cherrywood box. "I'm not any better. Last year, I bought him gourmet coffee."

He looked askance. "For your father?"

Valerie gave him an embarrassed smile. "We don't know each other as well as we should. But I decided years ago, it's the thought that counts."

"That's true." He didn't sound as though he agreed, though.

"I can understand why that idea wouldn't sit well with you. You're so observant of other people. It's a very attractive quality. That's probably how you're able to make other people happy so easily."

Steven frowned. "I don't understand what you mean."

Valerie tilted her head. "You knew I loved the

museum because you took the time to notice two postcards on my desk. You realized when Manolín wasn't wearing his silver chain. You knew that I preferred tea to coffee, something my father doesn't know. You're very observant of other people."

Steven shrugged. "It's not that hard."

"Maybe not to you, but it is to some people."

Steven covered her hand with his. "What's your point?"

Valerie glanced at the cherrywood box containing her new art supplies before returning her gaze to Steven. "I don't want to disappoint you again."

"You won't."

"How do you know that?"

"The only way you could disappoint me is by giving in to your insecurities and doubting me or yourself again. If you start feeling that way, tell me and we'll talk it through. Fair enough?"

"Fair enough."

"Good." Steven stood. "It's getting late. I'll get my stuff together so we can spend the night at your place."

"Okay." Valerie grinned. She rose to her knees and let the sheet drop to the mattress. "But first, how about one for the road?"

Chapter 23

"The weekend's over." Valerie looked at her bedside clock. The LED display read almost half past nine PM. "We have to go to work tomorrow."

Valerie sighed. She and Steven had spent a beautiful weekend together. Now that it was Sunday night, discomforting images of Cinderella after the ball wavered in and out of her mind.

Steven cuddled her closer to his side. The hair on his chest tickled her nose. "Then go to sleep."

He sounded half asleep himself. After a night of languid loving, she was pretty sleepy, too. Her head rested on his chest. His heart beat slow and steady under her ear. Hypnotizing. Her arm rested across his warm abdomen. The hair on his torso tickled her skin. Her right leg was bent across his hard thighs.

Valerie took a deep breath and pushed the words past reluctant lips. "You should go home, Steve."

He stirred under her. "Why?"

Valerie propped herself on his chest and looked down at him. "We need to keep our personal and professional lives separate. It would be hard for me to do that if I woke up Monday morning wrapped around your naked body."

All traces of sleep disappeared from his chiseled features. He eyed her with suspicion. "Are you feeling insecure again?"

She held his skeptical gaze so he could see the truth. "This isn't about insecurities."

"I'm not creeping around. We're not doing anything wrong. There's nothing to be ashamed of."

"I know that. I'm not saying we should hide our relationship. But I'm not flaunting it, either."

"How is spending the night together flaunting our relationship?"

Valerie rolled off him to lie on her back. She pulled the sheet over her bare breasts. "Try to understand, Steve. I don't want you to go, but this is new to me. I've never had a relationship with someone I worked with."

"Neither have I." Steven's tone was dry.

Valerie's lips curved. "No, I bet you haven't." Sobering, she rolled onto her side and studied Steven. "Don't you spend Sunday night mentally preparing for Monday morning? With you lying beside me, it will still feel like the weekend."

"I'm not going to be your weekend lover."

"I just need a little time to adjust to having an office romance. I'm not looking forward to people gossiping about us."

"You're the owner's daughter. Even if they gossip about you, they'll do it behind your back."

"That's a comfort."

He was silent a moment. "I don't understand how my leaving tonight is going to help you prepare for

the morning. But, if you want me to go home, I will."
Steven stole a kiss, then stood to dress.

Valerie smiled her gratitude. "Thanks, Steve."

"It's a good thing I followed you in my car yesterday. Otherwise, you'd have to take me home." Steven
pulled on his clothes in silence.

Valerie shrugged into the robe she'd plucked from
the closet and waited to follow him from her bedroom. They descended the stairs, then crossed the
hall into her living room.

She held her robe tight around her. "Drive safely."

Steven unlocked her front door, then turned to
look at her. His eyes bore into her, seeking to read her
mind. Valerie opened for him. She didn't have anything to hide.

He gave her one last hard kiss before crossing her
threshold. "Lock up behind me." And he pulled the
door closed.

Her heart tore a little, but Valerie told herself she
was doing the right thing. She needed to get used to
becoming lovers with her rival. She had to get comfortable with being in an office romance. She wanted
time to fall in love with Steven Crennell.

Valerie wandered back to her bedroom. It wasn't
even ten o'clock, but that was the room in which she
needed to be. Its buttercup walls, pale gold curtains
and carpeting, and raspberry bed sheets welcomed her.

Valerie crawled under the covers and pulled
Steven's pillow into her arms. It smelled like him.
Warmth and sandalwood. After a few restless moments, she climbed back out of bed, padded down the
hall to the living room and searched for her new copy
of Alexandre Dumas's *The Count of Monte Cristo*.
Steven said it was one of the best books ever written.

She wanted to learn more about the man she was falling in love with.

The ringing phone jerked her from the story. Valerie blinked and looked at her bedside clock. It was almost eleven o'clock. She blinked again. She'd been so wrapped up in the story that she'd lost track of time. Steven was right—it was a great book.

The phone continued to ring. Almost afraid to hope, Valerie lifted the receiver. "Hello?"

"Miss me?"

She melted back against the headboard of her bed. "Yes."

Steven's heart jumped, part surprise, part pleasure. "Say the word, and I'll come right back to you."

"Don't tempt me." Her voice, soft and low, made him feel as though he were back in her bedroom, back in her arms.

"But you are tempted? I'm surprised you'd admit it."

"I like to keep you off guard." She chuckled and he felt its echo vibrate low in his belly.

"I think that's your specialty, keeping me off guard. You've got me back on my heels."

"You give me too much credit."

"What are we doing tomorrow night?"

"I'll cook us dinner."

Steven exhaled the breath he hadn't realized he'd been holding. Yes, his question had been a test. He'd wanted proof Valerie was telling the truth when she said they weren't going to be weekend-only lovers. And she hadn't hesitated to provide him with reassurance.

He breathed easier. "On one condition."

"I'm offering to make you a home-cooked meal,

and you're putting conditions on it? What's wrong with this picture?"

"This can't be a working dinner." Steven spoke firmly. He didn't want there to be any misunderstandings.

"I didn't intend it to be. I know you don't like talking about work while you're eating."

The muscles in Steven's neck and back relaxed. "I just have one question, then."

"What's that?"

"What are you wearing?"

Valerie's laughter rolled across the telephone line. Her joy wrapped around him, flowing into him like champagne. Steven wanted to feel this way all the time. What would he do if her insecurities reared up again? Would he be able to reassure her that she was worth loving?

"The slogan we've agreed to for the Good 'N Healthy campaign is 'Healthy. Confident. Strong. From the inside out.'" Valerie's hands covered the two creative concepts she'd laid on Steven's office desk.

Steven's gaze drifted to Valerie's hair. She'd worn it loose again. It fell in straight, dark strands past her shoulders. How would she react if he rose from his chair, walked around his desk and drew his fingers through the thick locks? He'd better not. His actions would weaken her confidence in their ability to keep their professional and personal lives separate.

His attention dropped to the back of her hands—long, slender fingers and warm, golden brown skin. He remembered the way she felt, the way she touched him. The way she made his heart race.

Steven shifted in his seat and returned his gaze to Valerie's face. "Let's hope we have more luck with Good 'N Healthy than we had with Trace. I don't want to lose another account."

"We didn't *lose* Traci's account. She decided not to work with us." Valerie flipped over the art concepts and pointed to the first sketch. "I used the three fanned diamonds in the company's logo as a design element. They frame each scene."

Valerie pointed to the first diamond in the series and the female character inside. "In this scene, it's morning and the customer is getting ready to take an herbal supplement. In the second scene, she's making a presentation to executives at work. In the final scene, she's staying out late with friends."

Steven took the sketch from Valerie. "Each scene represents health, confidence or strength." He made the remark as though speaking to himself.

Steven studied the sketches. It was amazing how much motion, emotion and depth Valerie conveyed in a rough, black-and-white pencil sketch. In the first diamond, the female customer twisted open the bottle, excited to be on a healthy regimen. In the second scene, the customer, looking confident, delivered her presentation to business executives. The last diamond showed that, even after a long day, the customer had the energy or strength to go out with friends.

"Your illustrations speak for themselves without the words." Steven set aside the first concept and studied the second sketch.

"Thank you." Valerie pointed her pencil toward the page in Steven's hands. "That's the same concept, using a male customer."

In the first diamond, the male customer held the Good 'N Healthy bottle. The second diamond showed him as a television news reporter covering a breaking news event. In the final diamond, he was grocery shopping.

Steven frowned. "Does he have to be grocery shopping?"

"Is that not macho enough for you?"

He gave her a dry look. "That's not fair. You know I don't have a problem breaking gender stereotypes."

Valerie knitted her brows in confusion. "Then what do you want him to do?"

Steven looked again at the sketch. "Something other than grocery shopping. Maybe draw him picking up the dry cleaning."

"That last diamond represents strength. You don't need strength to pick up dry cleaning."

"You don't need it to go shopping, either."

Valerie arched a brow. "Obviously, you don't do much grocery shopping."

Steven waved a hand above the sheet with the female customer's sketches. "She's going out with friends after work. Why can't he do the same?"

"I want them to be distinct to show the supplement has universal appeal. That's why they have different careers."

"Let's have him do something else with his friends." Steven picked up his pen, rolling it between his fingers. "I know you don't want him to exercise because we're trying to stay away from sports."

Valerie's eyes widened. "But he could go to a sporting event."

Steven sat up. "After work with his friends."

"Perfect." Valerie scribbled something on the

sketch. Then she sat back with a sigh. "I feel good about this campaign."

He leaned back. "I think we've come up with a strong advertising concept."

Valerie looked quizzical. "I wonder if this is what my parents felt like when they were just starting out."

"Is that why you're working for your father? Were you hoping to take your mother's place?"

Valerie shook her head. "No one could take my mother's place. But I'd hoped to find my own space and to help grow the firm they built."

"You said 'hoped,' past tense. Have you changed your mind?"

"Over the past few months, my doubts about ever being able to find a place here have grown."

"Is it because of me?" Steven stopped twirling his pen. He couldn't move a muscle as he waited for her answer.

"I used to think so. But Garry's reaction to Traci canceling her contract made me realize that, even if you weren't here, he wouldn't have a place for me."

His heart hurt for father and daughter. "I want you to stay—for personal and professional reasons. But, if you aren't happy here, you should leave."

A half smile lightened Valerie's expression. "You sound like my Aunt Lo."

Garrison had introduced Loretta Parker Post to Steven. If the senior partner hadn't told him Loretta was his younger sister, Steven wouldn't have realized Garrison and Loretta were related. They were such different personalities.

He tightened his grip on his pen. "A second perspective just like mine? Maybe we're right." Steven paused as Yamile Famosa sauntered into his office without knocking.

The receptionist-cum-administrative assistant and her little blue dress rounded his desk and offered him a stack of envelopes. "Here you are, Steve. I brought you your mail." Her sultry tone implied she was offering him something else.

He took the correspondence from her. "Thank you, Yamile. But in the future, I can get my own mail just like everyone else."

She gave him a wet dream smile and laid her hand on his chest. "It's no problem. I'm happy to give it to you."

Even if he'd been deaf, he couldn't have missed that double entendre. Steven removed Yamile's hand from him. "No, thank you, Yamile."

He watched the shifting light in her coal black eyes and saw when his dual meanings became clear to her.

Yamile wrenched her wrist free of Steven's hold and stormed from his office.

Valerie pursed her lips. "That went over well."

Steven exhaled. "It had to be done."

"I agree. But was that for my benefit?"

Steven's eyebrows jumped. "Why would you think that?"

Valerie shrugged a shoulder. Her hand lifted toward the nape of her neck. "For eight months, she's been coming on to you, and you never said a word. It's only now that we're seeing each other that you've told her to stop."

"This didn't have anything to do with you. I just got tired of her chasing me around the office."

"Why didn't you say something sooner?"

He frowned at Valerie. Why was she making such a big deal over this? "I didn't think it was worth it."

"Or maybe you didn't want to upset her. But now you've accepted that her behavior is inappropriate and that your comfort is more important. Good for you."

He sighed. "I'm not a people pleaser."

"Maybe not anymore. Now you're putting more importance on your happiness."

"You could be right." Steven recalled Marlon's words. *You need to find a woman who's as interested in your happiness as you are in hers.* Maybe he'd found her.

Valerie stood, taking the concept sketches with her. "I'll make the changes, then finalize the art."

Steven waited until she was at his office door. "Val?"

She turned, her dark hair swinging behind her. "Yes?"

"When I come over for dinner tonight, I'll let you chase me around your condo."

Valerie's hand shot to the nape of her neck again. Steven smiled. She kept forgetting her hair wasn't wrapped in a bun.

She dropped her arm and gave him a cocky smile. "I may just catch you."

"I'm counting on it."

What a long day, but he was looking forward to the evening. Steven saved the campaign proposal he'd been drafting, logged off his computer and raised his arms high above his head.

"That stretch would be a lot more impressive if you got naked first."

Steven spun his chair toward the familiar voice in

his office doorway. Traci leaned against the door-jamb. A black and yellow leopard-print tank top and matching hot pants clothed her curves. Six-inch strappy black stilettos gave her petite frame height.

He cleared his throat. "What are you doing here?"

"Hi, Stevie." Traci entered his office and took one of the two guest chairs facing Steven's desk. "Is that any way to greet a former flame?"

They'd had this conversation. Steven held on to his patience. "Trace, I—"

She burst into laughter. "You look so serious." Traci paused to take a breath. "I'm not going to bite you, Stevie. Unless you want me to?"

"I don't."

Traci shrugged, a wicked grin curving her lips. "Your loss. I give good bite. But that's not what I'm here to talk about."

Steven knew her hesitation was deliberate—an attempt to add drama to the moment. For now, he'd play along. "What are you here to talk about?"

Her expression became almost resentful. "I'm here to apologize. I shouldn't have tried to use our contract to convince you to get back with me. Even though I think you should get back with me."

Surprise fossilized him. "Did someone put you up to this?" Although he couldn't imagine who.

Traci looked affronted. "Why would someone have to put me up to apologizing?"

Steven gave her a disbelieving look. "When was the last time you apologized for anything?"

She crossed her arms and legs. Her full, red lips pouted. "Whatever. So, anyway, I apologize."

"Apology accepted." He was too stunned to say anything else.

"Good. That's settled." She swung her right leg, which was suspended over her left leg. "So, when will I see the ads for my health spa?"

Steven shook his head, trying to clear his thoughts. "We don't have a contract anymore. Remember? You canceled it."

"Then uncancel it. My spa opens in three months."

Steven sensed her desperation. Traci was anxious to work with them again. If nothing else, time—or the lack of it—was on his side. Steven was getting a second chance to contract her account for the firm. Garrison would want him to jump at the opportunity, but he wasn't a people pleaser. At least not anymore.

"If we're going to work together, we're going to have to set some ground rules."

Her frown returned. "Don't worry. I won't try to get into your pants again. Unless you want me to?"

"I don't." His tone left no room for possibilities. "But I was referring to your business plan. You need one."

"I know. Walt is helping me with it."

Surprise parted Steven's lips. "You've been in contact with Walt."

"We've had dinner a couple of times. I told him you broke our contract and said I needed to decide whether I wanted to be a really great hotel or a spa."

"I didn't break our contract. You did."

"Whatever. So, Walt got his business manager to help me write a plan, and we decided on a plan. I'm trading in the equipment I have and getting all new stuff."

"All right. Now we have a direction." Steven tried to read Traci's eyes. "Are you and Walt getting back together?"

"I don't know." Traci uncrossed and recrossed her legs. "I appreciate his help with my business, though."

"He still loves you."

Traci burst into laughter. The sound was confident, almost cocky. "I know. Ever since the divorce, his game has been crap."

There wasn't anything amusing about that. "What are you going to do about it?"

"Why are you all up in my business, Stevie?"

"Walt is a former teammate. I'm concerned for him. And, with his game off, I'm concerned for the team."

Traci rolled her eyes. "Walt and I are talking. We had some good times. He's a great guy. Probably better than I deserve." This time, her laughter was self-conscious. "Maybe we'll get back together. Maybe we won't. What about you and Val?"

"What about us?"

"Have you set a date yet? For the wedding, I mean."

"No, not yet."

Traci raised a brow. A smile began to bloom. "Trouble in paradise?"

"No, Trace. Things are better than ever between us."

"Really?" Traci stood. "You'd better be careful with that one. Because one thing I know for sure? She's too good for you."

Chapter 24

At the sound of voices from her father's office, Valerie hesitated in his doorway. Steven had arrived first for their Tuesday morning meeting with Garrison. She could see her father over Steven's shoulder as the two men stood facing each other. Garrison's desk stood between them.

Her father stared at something in his hand. "Two tickets to Cirque du Soleil. Thank you, Steve."

"You're welcome."

"How much do I owe you?"

Steven lifted a hand. "Consider it an early Christmas present."

Valerie crossed the threshold. "Who's the second ticket for?"

Silence dropped into the room. Valerie noted the two men's different expressions. Steven seemed regretful. Garrison looked guilty. She took in her father's heightened color. Why would he be uncomfortable? It was a simple question.

Garrison settled into his executive chair. His gaze

was glued to his desk. "I haven't decided yet. Let's get the meeting started."

Valerie felt the sting of her father's dismissal. She breathed deep and let the feeling pass over her. If he didn't want to discuss the tickets with her, that was his prerogative. But then why would he discuss it with Steven?

Steven's expression shifted to disappointment. He glanced at Valerie before claiming one of the visitor chairs. "As I explained in the e-mail I sent last night, Trace wants to emphasize her health resort's fitness features. She's going to get more innovative exercise equipment."

Valerie took the chair next to Steven's. "Is Walt going to help her?" She was proud of how steady she sounded. But she couldn't guarantee the emotions tearing her up inside wouldn't explode at any moment.

Steven's eyes communicated his care and concern. "Yes. And she's sending us a copy of the business plan Walt's manager helped her write."

Valerie looked away before the tears came. "Is she going to delay her resort's opening?"

Garrison joined the conversation. "We don't need an extension. We can work with this time frame."

Valerie almost laughed. Who was this "we" to whom Garrison referred? It had been months since he'd done any work on the firm's accounts.

She forced herself to meet his gaze. "Yes, we can work with this schedule. But if it's possible to get more time, I'd like to use it. I'd rather launch the campaign well than launch it fast."

Steven interjected. "It wouldn't hurt to at least ask for an extension. As Val's pointed out before, we can't create the promotional brochure without a list of equipment, which Trace hasn't purchased yet."

Garrison heaved an irritated sigh. "Fine. But I don't want it to seem as though we can't get the job done. We have a reputation for completing projects on time and on budget."

Valerie turned to Steven. "Have you sent her a replacement contract?"

Steven shook his head. "I want to review it again before sending it to her."

"Good. You can ask about the campaign launch date in the context of the contract. That way, it doesn't look as though we're asking for more time. You could say you're updating the replacement contract before sending it to her."

Steven smiled. "Good thinking."

"It makes sense." Garrison nodded. Was that approval in his eyes? "Anything else for Fit in Time?"

Steven scanned his notes. "No, that's it."

"Good." Garrison sat up straighter in his chair. "What about Good 'N Healthy? What progress have you made?"

Valerie gave Steven and Garrison copies of the more polished campaign sketches. "We're using the same concept—'Healthy. Confident. Strong.'—for different customer base examples. The first is a woman. The second is a man."

Steven picked up the explanation. "They both start their day with Good 'N Healthy. But they need confidence and strength for different purposes. This underscores the universal benefits of the natural supplement."

Garrison looked up from the sketches. His grin was for Steven. "Brilliant."

Steven inclined his head toward Valerie. "The concept was Val's idea."

Valerie felt her cheeks warm at Steven's words. "We came up with the slogan together."

Garrison gave Valerie a considering look. "This is what you meant by diversifying our campaigns. I see your point now." He returned his attention to his junior partner. "What's the next step with this campaign?"

"Val and I are presenting the campaign to the Good 'N Healthy marketing executives January second."

Garrison caught Valerie's gaze. "Do you have any concerns about making that deadline?"

Valerie stiffened at the sarcasm in his tone. She angled her chin. "It's going to be tight, working on the Fit in Time and Good 'N Healthy campaigns simultaneously, in addition to the other projects we have. We need another account team."

Garrison looked away. "Well, when you win the lottery, let me know." He turned to Steven. "Anything else?"

"Nothing from me." Steven turned to Valerie. "Do you have anything?"

"No, thanks." She closed her notepad, folded her sketches and stood to leave.

Valerie walked out of Garrison's office with Steven. She waited until they were down the hallway from her father's office before she spoke. "Do you know who the second Cirque du Soleil ticket's for?" She didn't think he was going to answer her.

"I might." The words sounded as though someone had pulled them from him.

"Who is it?"

Steven wouldn't meet her eyes. "What makes you think he's not taking you?"

Valerie led him into his office. They couldn't continue this discussion in the hallway. She closed the door so they wouldn't be overheard.

Valerie faced him. The notepad and folded sketches were clenched in her right fist. "Come on, Steve. If you're going to lie, at least do it well."

He looked wary. "I didn't lie. I asked a question."

"Okay. I'll take your question seriously. I don't think I'm the one my father's taking to Cirque du Soleil because, three weeks ago, he couldn't even meet me for dinner at his own house."

Steven moved past her to stand behind his desk. He added his notebook and his copies of the Fit in Time sketches to the piles of paper on its surface. "Val, ask your father."

"You heard him. He basically said it wasn't my business."

"Then why don't you leave it alone?"

Valerie studied Steven, trying to read past the distance he was forcing between them. "Why all the secrecy?"

"Ask your father." There was a quiet inevitability in his tone.

"It's not my Aunt Lo. She would've told me. So he's taking a friend. What's the big deal?"

Steven's answer was a stoic silence.

Valerie's eyes widened. "He's taking a *girl*friend?" He still wouldn't respond. "How long have they been dating?"

Her entire body felt cold and brittle from shock. How had her father gotten so disconnected from her?

He was leading an entire facet of his life—of his heart—separate from her. How could he do that?

"Val, you've got to talk to Garry. It's not fair to put me in the middle."

"You've known about this all along? He'd tell *you* but not his *daughter*?"

"I don't think he was comfortable asking his daughter dating questions."

She paced to the window, then spun back to him. "*You've* known about her since before they were dating? Why didn't he tell *me*?"

"I don't know, Val. I've asked him that myself."

Valerie stopped pacing halfway to the door. "And what did he say?"

Steven shrugged. "That he would tell you. But it was obvious to me he never did."

"Then why didn't *you* tell me?"

"You needed to hear it from him, Val."

She continued pacing toward the door. "Technically, I still haven't heard it from him." Valerie stopped. She was less than a foot from the door. Her back was to Steven. "What does that say about the way he feels about me? What does it say about our relationship?"

Footsteps came closer to her. Steven cupped her shoulder and turned her into his embrace. Her crossed arms were between them, holding her notepad against her.

"It means Garry doesn't know the treasure he's missing." He spoke into her hair. "But don't give up on him, sweetheart. It's not too late for him to learn."

"It's been twelve years, Steve. How much longer am I supposed to wait?"

Steven leaned back. His face was blurry above her. Valerie blinked back her tears to clear her vision.

He kissed her forehead, then her damp cheeks. "Talk to Garry. Maybe he has a good reason for not telling you sooner."

Valerie snorted, wiping the tears from her cheeks. "Like what?"

"You won't know unless you ask him."

"And what am I supposed to ask him? 'How long have you been seeing this woman?'"

Steven feigned a wince. "Hopefully, you'll think of something a bit more tactful to start the conversation."

"You're the wordsmith. I just draw pretty pictures for a living. Words don't come as easily for me."

"You've never had a problem expressing your feelings to me. You were always quite clear."

Valerie rolled her eyes. "Very funny."

Steven kissed her lips. "I have faith in you."

Valerie absorbed his confidence, his strength, then stood on her own. "I'm glad someone does."

Valerie stood in Garrison's doorway for the second time in less than an hour. She'd left her notepad and sketches in her office, so her arms hung free at her sides. She cleared her throat to gain his attention.

Garrison glanced away from his computer monitor. "What is it?"

Valerie took a seat. She didn't think her knees would support her another second. "What is she like?"

He frowned. "Who?"

"The woman you've been dating."

Garrison sighed. With a couple of strokes of his keyboard, he saved the document he'd been reading. He pushed away from his computer desk, then slid his chair around to face her. "Steve told you?"

"No. I guessed." Valerie knotted her fingers together in her lap to stop her hands from shaking. "I should have guessed sooner. All the lunches and dinners. The weekends I came by, but you weren't home. What's her name?"

Garrison stared at her, searching each feature. What was he looking for? Approval? Disapproval? Indifference? Which did he want? Valerie played it safe and kept her features expressionless.

"Bethany Jackson." Garrison's reply was spare. It was the response of someone under interrogation who feared giving away too much information.

"How long have you known her?" She needed the answer but was afraid to receive it.

Garrison hesitated again. "About four months. Maybe five."

Valerie swallowed. That long. "Has anyone met her?" It felt so strange asking her father whether she was the last person in his life to meet his girlfriend. It shouldn't even be a question.

Garrison's gaze wavered before falling away.

A deep breath loosened the constriction in Valerie's chest. "Steve's joined the two of you for lunch, hasn't he?"

"Yes."

"And Aunt Lo?"

"She's met Beth, too."

Everyone around her had met this mysterious Bethany Jackson. Sorrow morphed into resentment and heated to anger too quickly to control. "Why haven't I met her? Why can't I be a resident of Garry's world?"

Garrison sprang from his chair. He braced his knuckles on his desk to glower down at her. "Don't judge me, Valerie Grace. Don't you dare judge me until you've walked in my shoes."

Valerie surged up to meet his anger. "I feel like *I'm* the one on trial here, *Dad*. And you've already judged me. But what was my crime? What have I done wrong?"

"Don't be ridiculous." Garrison crossed his office to shut his door.

Valerie turned to keep him in her sight. "I'm being ridiculous? It doesn't strike you as strange that everyone knew you were dating but me?"

"I didn't think you'd want me to date."

He was lying to her, and that hurt. "Mom's been gone for more than twelve years. I didn't expect you to be alone for the rest of your life." She forced her shoulders to relax. "When can I meet her?"

"I'm not ready to introduce you yet."

"Why not?"

Garrison crossed his arms over his chest. He avoided Valerie's gaze. "I don't know."

She wasn't buying it. "Yes, you do. But you won't give me even that much."

"You'll meet her soon enough."

Valerie unclenched her teeth as she stood. "I'm done with waiting. There isn't a place here for me. I have to accept that now. I'm going to find a place somewhere else." She turned and walked with unsteady steps across Garrison's office. Tears of anger and sorrow burned her throat. She held her head high as she walked past him.

"What does that mean?" Her father's voice followed her.

Valerie called her answer over her shoulder. "I quit."

Chapter 25

"You knew Dad was seeing someone, didn't you?" Valerie asked Loretta as her aunt let her into her father's home. She turned to watch the older woman—her confidant of the past twelve years—lock the front door.

Loretta searched Valerie's eyes for several heartbeats before answering. "Yes." Her aunt seemed relieved that the waiting was over.

Valerie was glad Loretta wasn't being coy, although that behavior wasn't in her aunt's nature. She blinked faster to keep the tears from falling. Loretta wrapped her arms around her, holding her steady until the storm passed.

Valerie used her hands to dry her face. "Let me guess. You didn't tell me because you thought I should hear the news from him, no matter how long it took."

Loretta led her into the kitchen and sat with her at the table. Her aunt watched her closely. "Did your father finally tell you?"

"No. I guessed." Valerie stood and crossed to the

stove. She shook the kettle. It was empty. "Would you like a cup?"

"Yes. Thanks. How are you feeling?"

She filled the gleaming black appliance for two cups of tea, then put the water to boil. "I'm glad that he's dating. They've been together for five months. He must be serious about her."

"And?"

Valerie wandered the kitchen. The cheery yellow paint didn't lighten her mood. "And it stinks that I had to guess he was dating. You knew. Steve knew. But the entire five months he and Bethany have been dating, he could never find a good time to tell me? I don't buy that."

"What did Garry say?" Loretta sounded subdued, as though disappointed by the way Garry had handled the situation.

Valerie picked up her pace, circling the kitchen. "He fed me some line about being afraid I wouldn't approve of his dating, as though my approval matters to him."

"I told Garry you wouldn't be upset. I also told him your mother would be happy for him, too."

Valerie tried to imagine her mother's reaction to Garry's dating. Her pacing slowed with happy memories; then she stopped and said, "I think you're right."

"Of course I'm right. She was my friend long before she was his wife."

Valerie rejoined Loretta at the kitchen table. "That's one of the reasons I don't believe he was afraid I wouldn't approve of his dating. But he refused to tell me the truth."

Loretta covered Valerie's right hand with her left

one as it rested on the table. "I told him to tell you about Beth. He assured me he would, but he wouldn't say when."

Valerie let the quiet settle over the kitchen, losing herself in her thoughts as she replayed her discovery in Steven's office and the scene in Garrison's.

The kettle screamed. Valerie rose to make two cups of tea. "I'm not surprised that he'd put off sharing anything about himself with me. He's kept me at a distance for so long. I don't think he knows how to talk with me anymore."

Loretta accepted the hot mug from Valerie. "How did you leave it with him?"

Valerie sipped the hot tea with care. "I quit."

Her aunt's eyes grew wide. "You quit? The agency? What did Garry say?" Her words tumbled over each other.

"I didn't wait for him to say anything."

Loretta stared at her in stunned silence. "He probably doesn't believe it. *I* can't believe it."

"You've been encouraging me to leave for weeks."

"But I didn't think you'd do it. You can be as stubborn as your father."

Valerie sipped more tea. It was a little cooler. "It hurts more to stay than to go. At least, it hurts more today. But I'm ready to move on, work for somebody else."

"Take your time. This is a big decision. Before you make it, be certain of what you're looking for."

"Oh, I know what I'm looking for. A place where I can flourish and feel respected instead of confined."

"Where's that?"

Valerie swallowed a larger sip of the tea. "I have a few ideas."

Steven stopped in front of Valerie's empty office for the third time that hour. Her computer was off, but her office light was on. Her chair was tucked under her desk, but proofs were spread across its surface. He checked his watch. It was after noon. She usually had lunch around this time.

He approached Manuel, whose desk faced Valerie's office. "Have you seen Val?"

Manuel shrugged into his white sports coat. With his matching white pants and red wide-collared shirt, the man looked like photos Steven had seen of John Travolta in *Saturday Night Fever.*

The graphic designer pushed his ergonomically correct gray chair under his desk. "She walked out about an hour ago. I haven't seen her since."

Steven rubbed the back of his neck. He could feel the tension headache building. "Did she say anything to you?"

"No, but she looked royally pissed. What happened?" Manuel's tone was accusatory. He looked ready to take on whomever had upset Valerie, and he didn't seem to care whether that person was almost a foot taller than him. The message was clear. If Valerie and Steven had a fight, Steven would be on his own. Manuel wouldn't split his loyalty.

"I don't know what happened." It was the truth. Steven didn't know. But whatever had transpired between Garrison and Valerie must have been worse than he'd anticipated.

Manuel gave him a doubting look. "If she doesn't

come back this afternoon, I'm going to call her tonight." There was a threat in his words.

Steven sighed, glancing at his watch again. Only a few minutes had passed. "I'm going to see if I can find her now. I'll check her house. I won't be able to concentrate until I know what's going on."

The other man's frown eased. "Good. Tell her to call me right away. I'm worried about her—and the ad concepts gathering dust on her desk." Manuel's joke would have gone over better if it weren't for the concern weighing his words.

Steven nodded. "I'll let her know."

Forty minutes later, Steven waited for Valerie to open her front door. His heart stuttered when he saw her. Her dark hair was tousled as though she'd dragged her fingers through it too many times to remember. Her chocolate eyes were red and swollen.

Valerie pulled her fingers through her hair as she let him in.

Steven drew her into his arms, caressing her back with gentle hands. "What happened?"

"I quit." Her words were muffled against his chest.

Steven jerked still. He leaned back to meet her eyes. "Are you serious?"

Valerie slipped from his embrace and led him further into her living room. "When I asked him why everyone had met his girlfriend but me, he lied."

"What did he say?

"He said he didn't know."

"But you think he does?"

She stopped in front of her orange sofa and spun to face him. "Of course he does."

"Why do you think he hasn't introduced you to Beth?"

Valerie's expression crumbled. Tears poured down her cheeks. Her sobs were silent. "Because he doesn't want me in his life."

Two large strides across her brown carpet brought him right back to her side. He wrapped her in his embrace, pulling her closer, holding her tighter as her body shook with misery. "That's his loss, Val."

"Those are just words, Steve. What do they even mean?" Her voice was thick with sorrow.

"It means he doesn't know the value of who he's turning away."

Valerie twined her arms around his neck. "Thank you." Her voice hiccuped.

Steven was silent for a long moment, lending her his strength and support. He kissed the top of her head. "What are you going to do?"

"I've accepted JTM Agency's job offer."

For the second time in less than half an hour, Valerie had shocked him. Steven's arms dropped away. "You're going to work for McGee?" The words left a filthy taste in his mouth.

Valerie stepped back. "He's been after me to work for him for a long time. You know that. And he says I'd be a valuable member of his team. That's what I want. For someone to give me the chance to be a valued team member and make a contribution to their company."

Steven rubbed the back of his neck. "I've never trusted that guy."

"Because Garry's never trusted him?"

Steven gave her a sour look. "I've been known to have independent thoughts once in a while."

Valerie reached out to rub Steven's arm. "I'm sorry. Why don't you trust him?"

He took a moment to weigh his words. "I know McGee appreciates your talent. You've received a lot of awards for your designs and campaigns. But is his interest in you personal or professional?"

"John comes across as flirtatious."

"Because he is."

"If he gets inappropriate, I'll just set him straight."

Steven didn't doubt she could handle herself with McGee. But he didn't want her to have to. "If you go to work for your father's biggest competitor, you may never be able to repair your relationship with him."

Valerie turned back to the window. "My relationship with Garry can't be fixed."

"He'll be furious once he learns you're working for McGee."

"He should have thought about that before he pushed me away."

"I know you're right, but I wish you could have found somewhere else to work. There are a lot of other agencies, and you have a great portfolio."

"I'm not worried about Garry." Valerie shrugged one shoulder.

He was worried enough for both of them. "When do you start?"

She hesitated. "I told John I'd start tomorrow. Wednesday."

Steven's eyes widened. "Tomorrow? You're not taking time off between jobs?"

Valerie paced away from the window. "To do what? Reconsider my decision? I've either thought about leaving Parker Advertising too much or not enough."

"I understand."

She turned to face him. "I'm going to do a presentation to Good 'N Healthy on JTM's behalf."

Steven's brows stretched upward. "The one we developed?"

"Of course not." She sounded offended. "It wouldn't be ethical to present our campaign as my own. I'll come up with something new." Valerie returned to the window.

Steven followed her. "What does your leaving Parker Advertising mean for us?"

She searched his gaze. "As far as I'm concerned, the only thing that changes is that we won't work together anymore."

Steven smiled. "Well, if we won't be seeing each other during the day, we'll have to make the most of our evenings."

Valerie quirked a brow. "Do you mean all this time, you *haven't* been making the most of our evenings?"

"That's not what I'm saying at all." He pulled Valerie into his arms. "Would you like me to prove it?"

Wednesday, Steven walked into Garrison's office for their morning meeting. He chose his usual guest chair. "It's just you and me today." He watched Garrison for the other man's reaction to that statement.

Garrison frowned. "Where's Valerie?"

"She quit yesterday. Remember?"

Garrison waved a dismissive hand. "That was a temper tantrum. She wasn't serious."

Steven held on to his patience. "Yes. She was."

Shock blanked the other man's expression. "So now she's unemployed. How is she going to pay her bills?"

"She'll be fine." Steven watched Garrison even as

the older man studied him. How did Valerie's father feel? Angry? Sad? Indifferent?

"She's found another job, hasn't she? With whom?"

Steven gave a humorless laugh. He adjusted his posture, resting his left ankle on his right knee. His pose was relaxed, but his body was tense. "What irony. Val left because you were keeping secrets from her. Now she's keeping secrets from you. How does it feel?"

Garrison narrowed his eyes. "What's gotten into you?"

The other man would do better to ask Steven what he'd lost. The answer would have been, "my patience."

"Garry, it's time you told your daughter why you're keeping her at a distance. I'd like to know, too."

Garrison fell back into his chair. The movement was restless and impatient. "How am I supposed to do that when she's not here? Where is she?"

"The agency isn't the only place you can talk to her. Try being her father sometimes instead of always being her boss."

Garrison gave Steven a speculative look. "You sound very protective of her. Are you in love with my daughter?"

"Your daughter is a remarkable woman."

"I'll take that as a yes. Does she know?"

"Does she know *you* love her?"

Garrison's curiosity turned to anger. "I'm her father. Of course she knows."

"There's no 'of course' about it. Val left the agency because she believes you don't want her in your life."

Pain flashed in Garrison's eyes. "That's ridiculous."

"Not entirely. Spending time with Val isn't high on your list of priorities, is it?"

Garrison's eyes narrowed. "That's between me and my daughter. Who is she working for?"

"Talk to your daughter. I'm not your informant." Steven's tone remained firm.

Garrison's frown darkened. "Damn it. Is she working for McGee?"

"Ask Val."

"It doesn't matter. She's not here anymore. Fine. You're still giving the Good 'N Healthy presentation."

Steven's eyes widened. "I don't have time to come up with another campaign. Besides, Val is giving a different presentation to Good 'N Healthy."

"Let her. We'll give our presentation."

Steven shook his head. "Garry, I just told you, I don't have time to develop new creative."

"Use the one we have."

Steven looked at him in amazement. "I can't do that."

"Why not?"

Steven hesitated. "That's Val's campaign. She came up with the concept and the creative."

"She developed the concept and creative for Parker Advertising. That proposal is mine, and I want you to present it to our prospective client January second."

The look in Garrison's eyes told Steven the debate was over. He was the boss, and he wanted to present Valerie's advertising campaign proposal as their own. Steven's feelings about the decision didn't matter.

Steven stood to leave Garrison's office. How would Valerie react to what he was going to have to do?

Chapter 26

Valerie read the caller identification on the phone in her JTM Agency office. According to the display, the call had been transferred from the receptionist's desk. Who would be calling on her first day at the agency? Was it Steven? The idea sent a thrill of pleasure through her.

She lifted the receiver. "Valerie Parker." She winced at how sickeningly happy she sounded.

"Until I heard your voice, I couldn't believe you'd gone to work for my competitor. What are you doing there?"

Valerie froze. Ice ran down her spine. Her father's voice was short of commanding. Had Steven told Garrison where she was? Why?

Valerie squared her shoulders and blew out a breath. "It's nice to hear from you, too, Garry. How are you?"

"What possessed you to work for McGee?"

"He offered me a job."

"You had a job. Here." He sounded as though he were speaking through clenched teeth.

"And now I'm working for an agency that appreciates me. Thanks for calling, Garry." She started to disconnect, but Garrison called to her.

"Why are you doing this?" He was asking, not demanding.

Valerie hesitated. "I want to be part of a team instead of on the outside looking in. I want to find someplace where I belong."

"You belong here, at Parker Advertising. Your name is Parker, isn't it?" His irritation was showing again.

She wasn't feeling long on patience, either. "You think I belong with Parker Advertising? Is that why you're *calling* to ask me to come back rather than coming to see me?"

"Coming to see you means I care more? That's ridiculous."

"There's more to being part of a family-owned company than sharing the owner's last name."

"That's not why I'm calling." His voice was cool.

"Why are you calling?"

"To tell you I won't be emotionally blackmailed into ending my relationship with Beth."

The breath went right out of Valerie. He couldn't have hurt her more if he'd reached through the phone and slapped her across the face. Her voice emerged as a thin whisper. She cleared her throat and tried again. "That's not what I'm doing."

"Yes, you are. You're using Parker Advertising as leverage to get me to choose between the family and Beth."

The receiver shook in Valerie's hand. She braced her right hand on her left elbow to help support her hold on the phone. "Is that why you didn't tell me about Bethany? You thought I'd want you to choose between us?"

"That's what you're doing now. You're trying to get me to decide between you."

"I would never do that. I want you to be happy. Maybe in time you'll see that." Valerie disconnected the call. It wasn't necessary to hear whether Garrison believed what she said. She no longer cared.

"You've been really quiet." Valerie gave Steven a glass of lemonade, then curled up beside him on her sofa. "I thought I'd be the moody one tonight because of Garry's phone call. But you have me really worried. What's wrong?"

Steven sipped the lemonade, then gave her a sober look. "Garry wants me to give the Good 'N Healthy presentation."

Valerie put her hand on Steven's thigh. "I'm sorry, Steve. Between Traci's account and everything else on your plate, I know you're swamped. Maybe Manuel could help you come up with another presentation." She was excited for her friend. Manuel would appreciate the opportunity and rise to the occasion. She started to tell Steven that, but he interrupted her.

"You don't understand. He wants me to give the presentation you developed."

Valerie stilled. She sat back, letting her hand slide from Steven's thigh. "But you're not going to give it."

The six-foot-four-inch, two-hundred-plus-pound, former professional athlete gave her a helpless look. "Val, I don't have a choice."

"Why not?"

He looked confused, as though he couldn't understand her question. "Because Garry wants me to give the presentation."

Valerie studied the strain lines around Steven's eyes and mouth, the regret in his eyes. "But you don't want to."

"Of course not." He popped up from the sofa and began to roam her living room. "It's your presentation. I told Garry that."

"Then why are you going to give the presentation?" Valerie pressed her back into the sofa and watched Steven pace in front of her. "If you don't think it's the right thing to do, why are you doing it?"

"I told you. Because Garry told me to." Steven dragged a hand over his close-cropped natural. "When your coach tells you to do something, it's for the good of the team. If you don't do it, the team suffers."

"Garry isn't your coach. He isn't even your boss. He's your partner." Valerie wanted to pull her hair out. "You've invested in the company. I think you have more leverage than the average employee."

He stopped pacing. He braced his hands on his hips with a sigh. "The name on the door is Parker Advertising."

Valerie straightened from the sofa. "When are you going to get that changed?" She didn't wait for him to answer. "You're going to give Good 'N Healthy our presentation—the presentation I directed—because you're trying to please my father."

Steven tossed back his head. "Oh, not this again."

"That's exactly how I feel." Her blood was heating. She hid her rising temper behind sarcasm.

"You created that campaign for Parker Advertising. It's not yours."

She stepped back as though from a blow. Valerie was looking at a stranger. "If you really believe that, why don't you want to do the presentation?" He just stared at her. "You've gone back to your people-pleasing ways, once again at my expense."

Steven narrowed his eyes. "What do you mean by that?"

Valerie turned away and walked toward her window. She stared at the carpet of green grass and the soaring palm trees in front of her condo. "Garry gave my prospect, Good 'N Healthy, to you and you took it to please him." She turned away from the window. "Now Garry wants you to give my presentation to my prospect. And you're doing it to please him."

"That's not fair, Val."

"No, it's not." She faced him. "I'm not asking you to please me by not doing the presentation. I'm asking you to do what you think is right. Do what pleases *you.*"

Steven paced away from her, rubbing the back of his neck. "It would please me to keep my job."

"What about me, Steve? What are you willing to do to please me?" Valerie walked toward him.

Steven gave her a blank look. "This has nothing to do with you."

The pain in her chest took her breath away. Had she even known this man? "You don't think you have to please me because you think I'll always be here." Anger gave her the strength to cross to the door. "I've had enough of people expecting me to respect their feelings when they can't be bothered to consider mine."

Steven turned to track her progress. "I've considered your feelings."

"I mean outside of bed." She yanked open her door. "It took me years to realize my father was never going to treat me with regard. I'm not wasting that amount of time with you."

Pain and anger flashed across Steven's face. "I do respect you, Val. You know that."

"Prove it. Follow your instincts and tell Garry you won't do the presentation."

Steven heaved a frustrated sigh. He turned away, then spun back. "This is business, Val."

She heard her father in those words. Her temper grew. "Fine. Then come up with another campaign."

"I don't have time."

She held the door wider. "Neither do I."

Steven's gaze moved between hers and the door. Seconds felt like minutes. She didn't want him to leave, but she was tired of fighting for herself. Fighting to prove her value. Fighting to prove her worth.

Slowly, Steven crossed to the door. He stopped at the threshold. "What do you want me to do?"

"The right thing."

He rubbed his neck again. "This is business, Val. It doesn't have anything to do with how I feel about you."

"Maybe not to you." Closing the door was like ripping a hole in her heart.

"What's on your mind, player? You've got no game today." Marlon scowled at Steven in a mixture of concern and frustration.

"Sorry, man." Steven wiped sweat from his eyes. He had to focus on the game, not on the sound of Valerie's door closing behind him. The sound hadn't been loud, but it had been final. And it had echoed in his ears since Wednesday night when they'd gotten together for a meal and ended up in an argument instead.

Marlon braced the ball on his hip. "Don't apologize. Just tell me what's wrong. You called me for a Saturday pickup game, and I'm out here playing myself."

Steven shifted his feet, trying to adjust the weight bearing down on him. "I deserved that."

"I know."

"I must be out of practice."

"This has nothing to do with rust, player. I've seen the way you drill the young guns who shadow you around the center. You act like they're all first-round draft picks."

Steven tried for the smile his friend was after. "I'm not that hard on them."

Marlon's gaze was piercing. "You've got the same look on your face that Millbank was walking around with. The-lights-are-on-but-no-one's-on-the-court."

Steven stiffened. "I hadn't realized I was so easy to read."

"How long have I known you?" Marlon didn't wait for a response. "You and Val have a fight?"

Steven paced a tight circle under the basketball hoop. His sneakers squeaked on the polished hardwood floor. The few kids who'd taken to the stands to watch him get schooled had left when he and Marlon started talking.

Steven stopped. "I think we're over." Saying the words made it hurt more.

Marlon was silent for a moment. "I'm sorry, man. Was she a red light after all?"

"No. She was solid gold."

"Then what happened?"

Steven began pacing again. "Garry wants me to make the presentation to the natural foods company."

"The company she brought to your agency? And she got pissed off with you because Garry told you to come up with the proposal?"

Steven stopped pacing to look at his friend and former teammate. "Yes. That one." Why was there a tone in Marlon's voice? "Val and I decided to use her campaign. It was better than mine. The problem is Val's gone now."

Marlon interrupted. "She left her own father's company? That can't be good." He crossed to sit in the stands, settling the basketball next to him.

Steven followed, sitting beside him. He propped his elbows on the bench behind him. "You're right. It's not good. Garry wants me to present the campaign Val developed."

"Ouch." Marlon leaned forward, turning to meet Steven's gaze. He folded his hands between his knees. "Did you tell him no?"

Steven's eyes widened. That had been Valerie's reaction. What was wrong with everyone? "I can't tell my boss no."

The other man shrugged. "Why not? You don't want to present Val's proposal as your own. Either tell Garry no or come up with a new proposal."

Steven was speechless for a moment. "What would happen if you told Coach no?"

Marlon shrugged. "He'd probably fine me. But I'd write the check happily, if I thought I was right."

"Val didn't create the campaign proposal for herself. She created it for Parker Advertising, so technically, it *is* our proposal."

Marlon cocked his head to one side. "That doesn't

even sound like you, man. Are you channeling Garry? Is that why Val kicked you to the curb?"

Steven stood, pulling his fingers through his hair. "This is business."

"I don't see it that way, man. This is a battle for your immortal soul."

Steven turned to frown at his friend. "This is serious."

"As a heart attack." Marlon sat back, crossing his ankles in front of him. "Who do you want to be, dog? You want to be your own man and do what your gut tells you? Or are you going to be Garry's lapdog?"

"What?" Steven's head was spinning.

"You say it's all about business. How's that going to work out for you on those long, lonely nights? Of course, there are several versions of ESPN now. There's ESPNU—"

"I'm not basing my business decisions on my sex life."

Marlon pushed himself off the stands. He crossed to Steven, putting his hand on the junior partner's shoulder. "There's no doubt about it. Whatever you decide, there'll be far-reaching consequences. And not just for you and Val, but for Val and Garry."

Steven saw a new side to his old friend. Marlon was a slob and had no concept of time. But he'd just given Steven new insight into his dilemma with Valerie and Garrison.

Chapter 27

"You didn't think I'd let you celebrate Christmas alone, did you?" Loretta crossed the threshold into Valerie's condominium and kissed her niece's cheek. "Merry Christmas, hon." She continued toward the kitchen, carrying two reusable grocery totes.

Valerie locked her front door, then followed the older woman into the kitchen. "Merry Christmas, Aunt Lo. What's in the bags?"

Loretta set her belongings on the round maple table. "Cornish game hens and vegetables. I didn't know whether you'd have anything for dinner."

Valerie stood beside her aunt. "Soup and sandwiches."

Loretta gave Valerie a wide-eyed stare. "For Christmas dinner?" She made tutting sounds as she unpacked the bags. "The game hens are already cooked. We just need to reheat them. Give me a hand with the vegetables."

Valerie preheated her oven, then took a chopping knife from her counter display to cut the vegetables. "What's Garry doing?"

"*Your father* is having dinner with Beth."

Valerie hadn't missed the mild chastisement in Loretta's tone. She washed the asparagus. "Weren't you invited?"

"They invited me. But no one likes being a third wheel."

Valerie put down the asparagus and the chopping knife. "In other words, you didn't want me to be alone." She crossed the room to give her aunt a hard hug. "Thank you, Aunty."

Loretta took a container of apple juice from the silver refrigerator and poured two small glasses. "Well, you are my favorite niece."

Valerie chuckled, returning to the stone white kitchen counter. "I'm your only niece." She chopped the ends from the asparagus and added the seasoning.

Loretta offered a glass to Valerie. "How's the new job?"

Valerie swallowed a sip of apple juice. "I quit yesterday."

Loretta coughed, stepping back from Valerie and doubling over. Valerie put a hand on her aunt's shoulder to help steady her. She frowned. The older woman couldn't be in danger if she had enough breath to cough. Still, Valerie supported her until her breathing returned to normal.

Loretta dried her eyes. "You what? Why? What happened?"

The oven chimed, letting Valerie know it had heated enough to cook the vegetables. "Steve was right. John is a lecherous toad who won't take no for an answer." She settled the tray in the oven. "I said it. I wrote it. I even sent him an e-mail, which included the definition of sexual harassment. It didn't matter. He was more interested in *collaborating* than in working."

"The pig. What are you going to do now?"

Valerie rested her hips against the counter. "Look for another job."

"You're not going back to the agency?"

Valerie shook her head. "I have to move forward. What happened with John was upsetting, but it didn't shake my self-confidence the way it would have even a month ago. I didn't question my design abilities. I realized John was at fault. That's one good thing I got from Steve. He helped reinforce my confidence in my work."

"Have you heard from him?" Loretta sipped the juice. It seemed to go down much easier this time.

"No, and I don't expect to." Valerie finished her glass of apple juice, then crossed to the fridge and poured another for herself and her aunt. "We both think we're right and the other person's wrong. He thinks *his* presenting *my* campaign proposal is about business. I think it's bullshit."

Loretta's eyes clouded with concern. "Look at it this way, Val. If the person who invented the secret recipe for Coca-Cola left, would you expect the company to stop making the soft drink?"

Valerie frowned at her glass of juice. "No."

"And what about the people who came up with Mc-Donald's special sauce recipe? If they left, would that be the end of the Big Mac?"

Valerie turned away and shoved the Cornish game hens into the oven. Warming the main dish was a cover while she considered counterarguments to Loretta's valid point. "It's galling. I got the agency the opportunity to present to Good 'N Healthy. I came up with the campaign proposal."

"And you chose to leave Parker Advertising."

Valerie's eyes grew wide. Whose side was her aunt on? "I couldn't stay."

Loretta cupped her hand against Valerie's cheek. "I know, hon. It just worked out that the final straw for you came before you had the chance to pitch the proposal. There's always a trade-off. No decision is easy, is it?"

Valerie turned and drummed her fingers against the kitchen counter. "You think Steve and Garry are right, don't you?"

"I didn't say that. But I did want to show you that different perspectives were involved. There are always at least three sides to every story—your side, the other person's side and the truth. You have to keep your mind open to other perspectives."

Valerie frowned at her aunt. "Why do I have the feeling you're not just talking about ad campaigns?"

Loretta's smile was mysterious. "Because you're a smart woman."

Valerie sighed. "You think I should go back to Parker Advertising, don't you?"

"Returning to the agency doesn't have to mean you're going back to the situation you were in before. Talk to your father. Make him understand why you left and tell him what you want. You said yourself you're not the same person you were a month ago."

Valerie folded her arms. "I guess it's worth a try."

"What do you have to lose?"

"You mean, what else?"

By her count, Valerie had already lost her job, her

father and her lover. That's a high price to pay to find yourself.

Want ads. Valerie always had assumed she'd work for her family's company and wouldn't have to worry about searching the want ads. See what happened when you assumed? She sipped her tea and scrolled through the advertising industry association's online job bank.

Her front doorbell sounded, interrupting her depression over the few listings she'd found on the local job site. As she rose from her desk in her upstairs office, Valerie wondered whether she'd have to move to find employment. On the other hand, maybe Friday listings were always thin. And it was the day after Christmas. Perhaps advertising companies had better things to do during the holiday season than post position openings.

Valerie padded to the window overlooking her front door. She coughed as her tea went down the wrong way. Was that Garrison standing on her steps with his arm around a woman? She stumbled back before they looked up and found her gaping in the window.

Oh, my God! Her father was going to introduce her to his girlfriend—while she was braless and wearing the rattiest T-shirt and shorts in her closet.

Valerie sped out of her office and down the hall to her bedroom, peeling off her stained lead gray T-shirt as she ran. She dug a raspberry lace bra from her lingerie drawer and snapped its front clasp as she jogged to her closet. She pulled a sage green tank top from one hanger and dragged it over her head.

The bell rang again as she dropped her tattered pool blue shorts and yanked her espresso capris off another hanger. Valerie stopped to glance in the oval, pewter-framed vanity mirror above her maple dresser. Her hair—twisted and pinned to the top of her head—was a fright. She didn't have time to fix it. With her fingers, Valerie scraped back the tousled locks and tucked a few strands behind her ears. Then she spun away.

She flew down the stairs and crossed the entryway. The doorbell rang a third time. Valerie took a steadying breath, smoothed her clothes, patted her hair, then opened the door.

Garrison frowned. "Didn't you hear the doorbell?"

Valerie heard the irritation in Garrison's tone. It was hard not to respond to it. "Yes, I did. That's why I'm answering the door." She stepped back to let in her unexpected guests. Her gaze dipped to the midnight blue department store bag in her father's grasp before jumping to his face. "Did you take the day off?"

"I took the week off. Steve's minding the store." Garrison cleared his throat. "Valerie, I'd like you to meet Bethany Jackson. Beth, my daughter, Valerie."

The hand she offered the statuesque, middle-aged woman in front of her wasn't quite steady. And her gift of gab, which had always made networking easy and fun, had deserted her. What should she say to her father's girlfriend?

Bethany's grip was firm and warm. Her smile was friendly. "I've wanted to meet you for a long time."

Valerie was conscious of the slender woman's conservative appearance. Her gaze took in the simple flip of Bethany's short chestnut brown hair, the scoop-neck ivory blouse, and cerulean blue wide-leg trousers. She stopped on the faux leather snakeskin sandals. The stilettos were hot pink.

Valerie relaxed and squeezed the other woman's hand. "It's a pleasure to finally meet you. Please come in."

Her legs were numb as she led Garrison and Bethany to her living room and waited while the older couple settled onto the sofa. "I'll get us some apple juice."

Valerie escaped into the kitchen. She stared sightlessly at the refrigerator door while she collected her thoughts. Her father and his girlfriend were in her living room. Should she slice some fresh vegetables to serve with the apple juice or would the apple juice be enough?

Why was she fretting over vegetables and apple juice when her father and his girlfriend were in her living room?

Why was she freaking out over her father and his girlfriend waiting in her living room?

Valerie reached for the refrigerator handle, the first step toward clearing the clutter from her mind.

"What do you think?" Her father's voice scattered her thoughts to the wind.

Valerie's heart leaped into her throat. She spun to face him. "Garry." His name shot out with her breath. "Beth's in a strange place. She's probably nervous. Don't you think you should have stayed with her?"

"She'll be fine." He shoved his hands into the front pockets of his cocoa brown twill pants. "What do you think?"

Valerie squared her shoulders, ready to address those cluttering thoughts one at a time. "I think it's strange that you chose to introduce us now. Why did you wait until *after* Christmas?"

Garrison shrugged his shoulders under his antique white polo shirt. "I thought you were still angry with me."

"I think it's more likely that *you* were still angry with *me*. You said you wouldn't let me emotionally blackmail you into choosing between me and Beth. What changed your mind?"

She read the defiance in the still-fit-over-fifty lines of his form.

Garrison angled his chin. "Beth wanted to meet you."

His words stung. Valerie took a mental step back. "It didn't matter what I wanted, but Beth's wanting to meet me made the difference?"

Garrison's expression tightened. "That's not what I said."

"Well, that's how it sounded."

"You're twisting my words."

Valerie paused as her thoughts cleared further. "Beth said she's wanted to meet me for a while. What was the problem, Garry? Why did you make us wait?"

Garrison started to speak and then checked himself. His eyes scanned her features; then he looked away. "Do you need help with the juice?"

Disappointment burned in her chest. "No." She watched him leave her kitchen.

Minutes later, Valerie carried into the living room a tray of apple juice, cut vegetables and salad dressing as a dip. Valerie sat in the armchair closest to the kitchen and watched Bethany and Garrison help themselves. "How was your Christmas?" She opened their conversation with the elephant in the room. Garrison didn't even look at her.

Bethany swallowed a bite of a carrot. "It was lovely.

We brought your present." She nudged Garrison with a slap to his thigh. "Get it for her, Garry."

Garrison stood to retrieve the midnight blue department store bag. "Merry Christmas. Belated."

Valerie frowned. She hadn't realized the package was for her. It was awfully big for a gift card. "Thank you." She unwrapped the scarlet and gold box. Her jaw dropped and her eyes stretched in surprise. "What a lovely nightgown. Thank you."

Bethany beamed. "Garry wasn't sure you'd like it. But I knew you would. Every woman wants baby doll pajamas."

Garrison paused with the glass of juice in his hand. "I don't think this is a conversation I should hear between my girlfriend and my daughter."

Bethany laughed and slapped his thigh.

Valerie studied the hot pink baby doll pajamas. No, it definitely wasn't Garrison's style. Bethany's influence over her gift brought both relief and amusement. She looked forward to watching her father's girlfriend shake up his life.

Valerie folded the pajamas back into the box. "Thank you very much. I love them. I'm afraid I don't have anything for you, though. I wasn't expecting to meet you."

Bethany shook her head. "Please don't let it worry you. I told Garry we shouldn't drop in on you unexpectedly, but he said you wouldn't mind."

Valerie's eyes widened. "No, I'm happy to finally meet you." She studied her father, who was staring at his half-empty glass of juice. What was he feeling?

Bethany smiled. "Then that's your gift to me. I was nervous about making a good impression on Garry's daughter."

Valerie glanced at Bethany's hot pink stilettos. "I can tell you make him happy, and that's all that matters."

Bethany's smile trembled and she ducked her head. "Don't make me cry. Let's see what you got for your father."

Valerie caught Garrison's gaze. She'd finished his gift. She'd even wrapped it. Why was she now hesitating to give it to him?

Garrison turned away to dip a celery slice into the dressing. Was his hand shaking?

Valerie took a deep breath and pushed herself from the armchair. "I'll be right back."

She crossed the living room and mounted the stairs. At her bedroom, she lifted the large canvas wrapped in plain scarlet paper from her closet and lugged it carefully down the stairs.

Bethany turned at the sound of Valerie's approach. "Goodness. What is that?"

Valerie gave her a mischievous grin. "It's a . . ."

Bethany threw out both well-manicured hands. Her brown eyes widened and her jaw dropped. "Don't tell us!"

Valerie and Garrison burst into laughter at the other woman's reaction. Valerie looked at her father in surprise. When was the last time they'd shared a laugh?

Garrison stood and came around the sofa. "I'll open it here. There's no need to carry it farther."

Valerie released the package. It hadn't seemed that heavy when she'd mounted it. "Thanks. Merry belated Christmas."

Garrison met her eyes. "Thank you."

Bethany joined them. She bounced once on her toes. "Come on. Come on. Open it."

Garrison smiled at his girlfriend, then knelt to carefully and slowly peel away the red wrapping paper.

The painting was a replica of the photo her aunt had given her the last time they'd visited her mother's grave. In the painting, Valerie was a toddler, wiggling in Garrison's arms and laughing up at her mother. Marilyn stood behind her husband's shoulder, beaming a loving smile at her baby daughter. One of Marilyn's hands curved around Garrison's shoulder. The other hand rested softly on Valerie's chubby arm. Garrison sat with Valerie held safely in his care. In the painting, Valerie had captured Garrison's expression perfectly—his love, joy and pride for her.

"Oh, my God." Bethany put a hand over her mouth, muffling her voice. Her free hand grasped Garrison's shoulder. "That's such a beautiful painting."

Garrison stared at the artwork in silence.

"Do you recognize it?" Bethany asked.

"Yes. I remember the photo. I remember the day. Excuse me." Garrison lunged to his feet and rushed into the kitchen.

The portrait fell against Valerie's thighs. She stared at Bethany in surprise.

The other woman nodded toward the door. "I think he needs you now."

Valerie propped the painting against her sofa and hurried after her father. As she neared the kitchen door, she heard sobbing. Deep, agonized sobs she'd never heard before in her life. Garrison stood with his back to the room. He was leaning against the white stone counter, his head in his hands. Crying.

She walked up behind him and wrapped her arms

around his waist. She rested her cheek against his back. "I didn't mean to make you cry. I'm so sorry. So very sorry." Her voice was a whisper. Valerie didn't want to intrude on his privacy, but she couldn't take the sound of his tears.

After a few moments, Garrison quieted. "You look so much like her. Every time I look at you, I see her. And it hurts so much."

Valerie went lax with surprise. She dropped her arms and stepped back. "Why didn't you ever tell me?"

Garrison turned to her. His face was ravaged by tears. "What good would that have done? There's nothing you can do about the way you look." He ran a hand restlessly over his face. She could still hear the tears in his voice. "When she was alive and the two of you would play together or draw together, those were beautiful moments. You were a little replica of your mother. I have pictures of those moments here." Garrison pressed a fist to his heart. "And here." He touched his temple. "After she died, sometimes it hurt so much to look at you. It hurt so much. When you cried, I saw her crying. When you laughed, I saw her laughing. When you drew, it was like she was in the room again. I needed to push the pain away, but I never meant to push you away, too."

Valerie wiped away her own tears. "Why did you take so long to tell me?"

Garrison closed the gap between them and wrapped her in his arms. "I couldn't see what I'd done or what I was doing. I was blind. The years passed. You seemed to be doing well, so I stopped worrying whether I was doing the right thing."

Valerie felt his tension and heard his hesitation. "What is it, Dad?"

"Then I met Beth. I'm falling in love with her. But I realize I can't have a future with her if I'm still holding on to my past."

Valerie leaned away. "You don't have to forget Mom to love Beth."

Garrison released her to pace the kitchen. "That's not what I mean. I didn't introduce you at first because I was ashamed that I'd fallen in love with another woman. Every time I thought of telling you, I could see your mother's face."

Valerie stepped forward and placed her hand on her father's back. "Above all, Mom would want you to be happy."

"If I'd been the one to pass first, I wouldn't like the idea of your mother falling in love with another man."

"Obviously, Mom wasn't as unreasonable as you are."

Garrison heaved a deep sigh and turned to face her. "Lucky for me."

Valerie smiled. "Beth seems like a very nice person."

His eyes sought approval. "Do you really think so?"

Valerie nodded. "Anyone who'd wear those shoes with that outfit is comfortable with herself and the people around her. I'm sure we'll get along just fine."

Garrison chuckled. "It's a new outfit, but she refused to get new shoes."

"Good for her."

Garrison cupped her chin. "I'm the world's biggest fool for taking so long to tell you how much I love you and how very proud I am of you."

Valerie swallowed back more tears. "I love you, too, Dad. And I'm proud of you."

"I understand why you left the agency. Professionally, it was the right move. And, personally, I know I pushed you too far away. Make sure McGee—that little piece of shit—treats you better than I did."

"Didn't Aunt Lo tell you?"

"What?"

"I quit. I don't work for John anymore."

Garrison's eyes widened, then narrowed with suspicion. "What did that little creep do?"

It troubled her that Steven and Garrison had read John so much better than she had. Must be a guy thing. "Dad, I'm fine. It's a long story. The short version is I don't work for JTM Agency anymore."

Garrison rubbed his hand across his forehead. "Then come back and work for me."

Valerie hesitated. "Are you asking me back because of the Good 'N Healthy presentation?"

Garrison blinked. "No. Steve's already cancelled the meeting with the client. He said he doesn't have time to come up with a new proposal, and he won't pitch yours."

Valerie's jaw dropped. "What?" She breathed the question.

"I know. It was a bad business decision, but he felt strongly about it, so I let it go. He's a partner. I've been thinking of making him a full partner."

Valerie only understood half of what her father had said. She was still trying to wrap her mind around the fact that Steven had said no. "Why didn't he want to make the presentation?"

"He said he didn't feel right presenting someone else's work as his own." Garrison shrugged. "I told him he was taking things too personally, but he didn't want to do the presentation, so we cancelled."

Incredible.

Garrison continued. "Val, I'm not asking you to come back because of the presentation. I'm asking you to come back because Parker Advertising is your home. It doesn't feel the same without you."

Valerie remembered her aunt's words. "I'd like to return to Parker Advertising, Dad. But things will have to change."

Garrison nodded. "If you give me a second chance, I promise things will be better."

Valerie threw her arms around his shoulders and held on tight. "Welcome back, Dad. You've been away too long."

Valerie froze inches before the door of Steven's office. She'd had a great visit with Garrison and Bethany. She'd even made them lunch. But now— a little more than an hour later—her muscles wouldn't follow her mind's command to take that final step forward. Watching Steven work behind his desk, her nerves came charging back.

The radio beside him shattered the silence with a play-by-play of the Miami Waves game. The home team was on a run to extend their lead.

Steven's head was turned away from her as he reviewed invoices. His thick shoulders stretched his lightweight wine red sweater. Valerie's fingertips tingled with the need to explore those muscles. She ached to press against his broad back.

Abruptly, Steven looked up, meeting her gaze as though he'd known he'd find her there. He blinked. "I thought I was alone."

Valerie swallowed to dislodge her heart from her

throat. She tipped her head toward the radio. "Millbank's back on his game."

Silence stretched. Valerie's heart beat even faster waiting for Steven's response. Would he respond?

He lay down his pen with deliberate movements. "His reconciliation with Trace must be going well." Steven turned off the radio and sat back in his chair. His piercing stare belied his relaxed pose. "Why are you here, Val?"

No more stalling. She wiped her sweaty palms on her silver corduroys and willed her legs to carry her forward. Valerie eased into one of Steven's guest chairs. Her confidence took a slight boost now that her unsteady knees no longer had to support her. "We need to finish up the Good 'N Healthy campaign proposal." Her words were breathy and uncertain. Did Steven notice?

He shook his head and looked away. "I cancelled that meeting."

Valerie tried to recapture his attention. "I know. Dad told me. But I called Gloria this afternoon and rescheduled the meeting. We have another week."

Steven frowned. He pushed his long form away from his desk and paced to his windows. Late afternoon sunlight soaked his office. He hooked his hands on his jeans-clad hips. "Why?"

She swallowed again. It was a fair question. How would he react to her answer? "I want to start over with Parker Advertising. Dad and I have—finally—cleared up our misunderstandings." She paused, took a deep breath. "And I want to start over with you."

Steven turned to her. "I didn't cancel the presentation because of you."

Her body iced over. Valerie forced her stiff lips to form words. "I didn't want you to cancel for me."

Steven crossed his arms and settled his hips against the window's ledge. "I know. You wanted me to cancel for me. You thought I was doing the presentation to please Garry, even though I didn't agree with him." He shrugged. "You were right. *That's* why I cancelled."

"You did it to please yourself."

He nodded once. "Yeah. It felt good."

Valerie was still confused. "Then what's wrong? Why are you pushing me away?"

Steven shook his head. "I want you back, Val. But what happens the next time we disagree? Will you accuse me of not valuing you? Will you close the door on me again?"

Valerie frowned. "I can count on one hand the number of times we've agreed this past year."

A reluctant smile tugged at a corner of Steven's firm lips. "I thought we'd only worked together eight months."

She ignored him. "You're a man of integrity, Steve. Whenever we disagreed, your arguments were based on what you believed in, not what someone else wanted you to do. All I want is for you to remain true to yourself."

"No more people pleasing?"

Valerie cocked her head, sending him a look that tempted and teased. "Unless the person you're pleasing is me."

His dark gaze warmed her blood. His deep voice mesmerized her. "Always."

Valerie shivered. She closed her eyes for just a moment. When she opened them, Steven stood in front of her. His smile communicated an intimacy and a promise that made her toes curl.

Steven offered her his hand. His touch was warm, firm and steady, a perfect reflection of the man. "I am hopelessly and deeply in love with you."

Valerie melted as she stepped into his arms. In his embrace, she felt loved and best of all valued. She wrapped her arms around his neck. "I love you so much, not only because of who you are, but because of who you helped me to be."

"You helped me, too. I hadn't even realized I was a spineless people pleaser until you told me."

She pulled back to scowl into Steven's grinning face. Valerie smacked the hard muscles of his left shoulder. "I never called you spineless."

He kissed her forehead. "Literary license."

Steven lowered his mouth to hers. Valerie parted her lips and took him inside of her. All of him. His warm, sandalwood scent. His sinfully sexy taste. His muscles, firm and taut beneath her touch. Here in his arms, held tight against his body, was where she belonged. Where she always wanted to be, loving him and feeling worthy of love in return.

Don't miss Patricia Sargeant's
Sweet Deception

Available now wherever books are sold

Turn the page for an excerpt from
Sweet Deception . . .

Chapter 1

"Can you fulfill a woman's sexual fantasy?" Joan Brown challenged Ronald Montgomery. She felt confident confronting the arrogant thriller writer in her role as Cleopatra Sinclair, newly published erotic romance author, as they participated in this writers' conference author panel.

Ronald stared at her blankly. "I beg your pardon?"

He even sounded like an uptight, elitist author. Her disappointment escalated. Joan channeled her Cleopatra persona to turn up the heat. She gave the best-selling author a sultry stare. Her gaze stroked him from the top of his close-cropped natural hair to his dark and chiseled features, piercing coal black eyes, and broad, hold-me-tight-against-you shoulders.

"You look as though you could make a woman's sexual dreams come true. In fact, while we've been sitting here on this panel, I've been fantasizing about you."

"Excuse me?" Was there a touch of interest in his shocked response? That was probably her imagination. Her very vivid imagination.

"You look great in jungle print, by the way. But you ruined the image when you insulted the romance genre."

She was amused and annoyed as Ronald shot a look at the now silent audience, a standing-room-only crowd of aspiring and published male and female authors.

He seemed uncomfortable. "This isn't the right time or place to discuss your fantasies, Ms. Sinclair."

Joan regretted that he couldn't use her real name, but she managed to stay in character. "Your mother should have warned you not to play with fire if you don't want to get burned, Mr. Montgomery." She licked her lips to turn up the heat.

Ronald wasn't the only author on the panel to tweak her temper, though. She'd come to this conference thirsty for acceptance. She'd been looking forward to this once-a-year opportunity to share experiences with other authors. Instead, Ronald and their fellow panelists—a tough-talking female mystery writer, a patronizing male science fiction author, and an irreverent male horror novelist—had condemned the romance genre with halfhearted disclaimers of "nothing personal." Those authors now shrank into their seats behind the long wooden table. *Wise.*

But Ronald was the one at whom Joan had taken aim. She'd been gathering her nerve to ask him to share a drink—maybe even dinner—after the panel. Well, hell hath no fury like a romance author insulted.

Joan propped her chin on her fist and sent him a steamy look. "I know you're *just* a thriller author." She paraphrased his earlier words and threw them back at him. "But tell me, do you have the imagination to fulfill a woman's sexual fantasy?"

Every muscle in Ronald Montgomery's body went on red alert at that question. Cleopatra Sinclair's velvet voice taunted him. Ronald had asked himself that same thing every day for the past three months, ever since his breakup. He was still looking for an answer. "Yes, I do have the imagination to fulfill a woman's sexual fantasy." *Don't I?*

Shocked laughter popped like champagne corks around the room, magnifying his self-doubt. Female authors—approximately 90 percent of the audience—watched with glee. Their male counterparts regarded him with pity, shaking their heads as though to say, "Buddy, you've brought this on yourself."

Yes, he had.

Ronald looked at Cleopatra, her wide milk chocolate eyes, pouty pink lips, and siren red dress. He'd verbally struck at her in retaliation for another woman's betrayal. But she'd turned his attack against him, forcing him to face the insecurity that had eaten at him for months.

The problem was, in addition to being embarrassed and annoyed, he was also captivated and aroused. He was thirty-two, but Cleopatra had him blushing like a twelve-year-old boy. The hot looks and flirtatious talk probably were retribution for his earlier criticisms. Still, they made him feel desired as he hadn't felt in many long months. He could feel the ice around his heart melting, and it scared him.

Ronald resisted the urge to drain the glass of cold water inches from his fingertips. But Cleopatra wasn't so inhibited. Her eyes were bright with defiance as they held his. She lifted her glass and took a long, slow drink. Her throat muscles contracted once, twice. Then she replaced her glass and ran her tongue over her moist lips. *Sweet heaven.*

Cleopatra took aim again. "Then why do you believe romance novels give women unrealistic expectations of relationships? Does the message of female empowerment threaten you?"

The tide was shifting in her favor. He saw his defeat in Cleopatra's eyes. Ronald spoke loudly and clearly to be heard above the audience's grumbling. "I don't have any problem with female empowerment. In fact, I support it."

"Are you disgusted by stories of healthy, loving relationships?"

He'd thought he'd been part of one. "Of course not. I—"

"Are you turned off by happy endings?"

"No, I—"

"Perhaps it's the fact that romances make up well over fifty percent of all mass-market paperback sales. Is it professional jealousy?"

Ronald laughed, surprised by his genuine amusement. "I'm very satisfied with my sales. I've been on several of the best-seller lists, and my books are being adapted into a TV series."

"Then your distaste for romance novels is baseless."

"I don't see their literary value. They're like *Playboy* for women."

The anger glowing in her eyes should have set half the room on fire. "Characters in a romance novel may not save the world like a thriller hero, but they're saving something just as valuable. Each other."

"Romances have a fantasy view of—"

"Haven't you ever been lonely? Or afraid? Or filled

with self-doubt? Haven't you ever needed someone to help you through a crisis of self?"

How did she know? Could she see it in his eyes? Had he said something that gave him away? Now he was afraid to even open his mouth.

Cleopatra didn't need his answer. "Why are these stories of any less value than stories of supersecret government agencies disarming nuclear warheads?"

The panel moderator saved Ronald from having to respond.

"This is a truly fascinating debate." The frazzled woman checked her wristwatch as she hustled to the front of the room. "But I'm afraid we need to wrap up the discussion. We want to save time for at least a few audience questions."

Cleopatra arched a brow at him. Her gaze still smoldered with anger. Ronald inclined his head. The erotic romance author had earned this victory. Would she allow him to even the score?

Cleopatra's entrance into the crowded hotel cocktail lounge that evening captured Ronald's attention. She mesmerized him as she sauntered to the bar, apparently unaware of her audience. Her long, toned legs were bare from mid-thigh. And her five-alarm red dress wrapped her like a hot breath.

Ronald excused himself from a table of mystery and thriller writers to join her. In her strappy red stilettos, she was maybe three inches shorter than his six foot two. "To the victor go the spoils?"

Cleopatra turned. Her wavy raven locks swung behind her golden shoulders. Ronald wanted to run his fingers through them. With recognition came a sultry smile. "Pardon me?"

Did she know her effect on him? Was he having any on her? "Buy you a drink?"

She blinked her long-lidded eyes, bright and warm with awareness. "Thank you. I'll have a diet cola."

Ronald hesitated. That was unexpected. He'd judged Cleopatra to be a cosmopolitan or even apple martini drinker, something feminine and alcoholic.

Dismissing his surprise, Ronald ordered her soda and asked for a beer. Her neatly clipped nails, polished bloodred, grazed his skin as she took the glass from him.

That wasn't an accident.

Cleopatra walked away. Ronald took a swig of beer before following her.

She led him through the crowded bar and past occupied tables. Cleopatra leaned against a far wall and sipped her drink. Her gaze swept the packed room, with casual curiosity. Then she turned her full focus to him.

It was hypnotic to be the recipient of someone's complete and undivided attention. Mesmerizing and, for him, rare. Ronald couldn't look away. "I'm sorry about the panel discussion."

She shrugged a slim shoulder, covered only by her dress's red spaghetti strap. "I should be used to it. People who aren't familiar with the romance genre assume it's pornography. Some of our stories are sexy, but they're *not* pornography."

"I'll take your word for it." Ronald considered her shoulder as he drank his beer. Would it feel as soft and smooth as it looked? He tightened his grip on his mug to keep from touching her.

Cleopatra shifted her attention from his eyes, allowing her scrutiny to linger on his chest before continuing down his body. He blushed. Never before had a woman checked him out so thoroughly.

When her lips moved, he realized she was talking. "Excuse me?"

"You've never read a romance?"

"No."

"You should try one. You're far too tense." She sipped more diet cola without releasing his gaze. Her warm brown eyes were casting a spell on him.

"Which would you recommend?"

"Any of mine would do you a world of good." There was blatant seduction in her voice.

Ronald propped his shoulder on the wall beside her, bringing himself closer to her soft, powdery scent. "How long have you been writing?"

"A long time, but I've only been published a few years. I haven't reached your *New York Times* best-seller status."

"Have you considered writing in another genre?"

A winged brow lifted. "Why would I do that?"

Uh-oh. He'd offended her again. "You were talking about making the lists."

"Romance authors regularly appear on the lists. Do I need to quote industry statistics? I come prepared to these conferences in case I meet people just like you."

"What do you mean?"

"Uninformed. Unaware. Unenlightened."

"I apologize. Again. I didn't mean to offend you."

"Making the lists isn't the primary reason I write. It would be nice. But I write because I have something to say."

"What's that?"

She shifted to face him, moving nearer. Her eyes were dark and mysterious in the bar's dim lighting. Her body heat warmed him. Her perfume clouded his mind. Was he starting to feel light-headed?

"What do I have to say?" She leaned closer still. Her voice was a wanton invitation. "That sex between consenting adults may be naughty, but never bad."

Ronald hunched his shoulders, coughing to keep from swallowing his tongue.

Joan was enjoying her Cleopatra persona, perhaps too much. Under the suffocating watch of her minister father, she'd never flirted so outrageously. Even though she was twenty-six years old, a business owner, and living on her own, her father's approval was still important to her.

But her home in Columbus, Ohio, was almost twenty-three hundred miles from this Los Angeles writers' conference. It was the perfect opportunity to let her hair down. And the ever-so-delicious Ronald Montgomery seemed to be the perfect man with whom to lose her inhibitions.

Ronald had stopped coughing. His reaction would have intimidated Joan. Wait. Who was she fooling? Joan wouldn't even be in this bar. She'd be hiding somewhere with her sketchbook or laptop.

But for this night—the last night of the conference—she wasn't Joan. She was Cleo, and Cleo wanted to play. "What's your position on that statement?"

Ronald cleared his throat. "It depends on the consenting adults. Is either in a relationship with someone else?"

Very clever. He was good at this game. "No."

"That's good to know."

She laughed. "Go ahead and ask me."

"What?"

Joan ran an index finger lightly over the hand Ronald used to grip his empty beer mug. The lure of his warm skin made her want to touch even more of him. His wrist. His forearm. His do-me-baby chest. "Ask me if I've ever tried the positions I've described in my books. That's what everyone wants to know."

"I haven't read them."

"I won't hold that against you later."

Ronald's eyes flared. "That's very generous of you." His voice had deepened.

Her ability to get a reaction from this man amazed her. Joan had felt an instant attraction when the moderator had introduced them. She'd shaken Ronald's hand, and she hadn't wanted to let it go.

Even as he'd angered her during the panel, she'd been aware of him. He'd been sexy in a navy blue double-breasted suit. The intelligence in his coal black eyes, the clean lines of his chiseled features, the width of his shoulders, and the length of his hands had appealed to her. A man like him—successful, worldly, and hot as hell—would never notice Joan. But he'd bought Cleopatra a drink.

Joan felt empowered—and excited. "Generosity is important in all facets of life."

"I've always believed the same. If you give often and generously, the pleasures you receive in return can be greater than you've ever imagined."

He'd taken her breath away. Could she keep up? She didn't know, but she wanted to try. "More than you've ever dreamed of?"

"Much more."

"A kindred soul." Joan stroked his hand again and

felt a ripple of awareness throughout her body. "I wonder how much more we have in common."

Her words were husky. Was his heart beating as fast as hers? Joan looked up and saw his Adam's apple bob. *Good*. She wasn't the only one feeling the heat from this game.

Ronald's voice was rough. "Do you think variety is the spice of life?"

"I choose my seasonings very carefully. If they don't improve the dish, I don't include them."

"Another shared preference. I like to taste the full flavor of a dish on my tongue. It enhances the experience."

If his words weren't obvious, the passion in his eyes made his message clear. Joan had never believed it possible that words alone could bring her to arousal. But her body heated, and she felt herself melt. "To the victor go the spoils?"

His slow smile made her thighs tremble. "Not spoils, but treasure." He offered her his hand, and she followed him from the bar.

The elevator took an eternity to carry them to Ronald's hotel suite in the high-rise. It was the last night of the international writers' conference, and everyone had somewhere to go.

When they arrived at his suite, Ronald unlocked the door and allowed Joan to precede him. "Do you want a drink?" He walked past her, toward a small refrigerator.

Joan leaned against a nearby wall. "I'm not thirsty, but thank you."

Something in his voice told her he wasn't taking this night lightly, either. It was in his body language, a subtle uncertainty; in his actions, a hint of distraction.

Perhaps those were her feelings, and she was projecting them onto him? Ronald lifted a bottle of water from the fridge and downed a healthy swallow. No, she was right. He was nervous, too.

She pulled off her stilettos. Her eyes half closed with the blissful relief of taking off the high-heeled shoes. She left them in a corner and wandered farther into the suite. Her stockinged feet sank into the plush tan carpet.

Ronald's accommodations included a small kitchenette with a microwave oven, a living area with a television, and a work space with an ergonomically correct chair. Appearing on best-seller lists had its perks.

Joan joined Ronald in the kitchenette. She was eye level with his broad back. At the touch of her hand on his upper arm, he turned to face her. Joan traced his face with one finger, his high forehead, sharp cheekbones, square jaw softened by full, sensual lips. She would love to draw him.

Sliding her hands inside his suit jacket, Joan felt the warmth of his body against her bare arms. *Delicious.* She slipped the garment free. "I don't think our hunger can be satisfied in this room."

Ronald wrapped his arms around her, leaning closer to rub his lips against her neck. "And you call yourself an erotic romance writer?"

Joan caught her breath and dropped his jacket to the floor. "What were your plans for this room?"

His laughter was warm and wicked against her ear. Heat swirled in her belly. "We'll talk about that later, after we know each other better."

"Good, because right now all I want to hear you say is, 'I have protection.'"

He molded her body against him. His erection pressed against her belly. "I have protection."

The sweetest words she'd ever heard.

Joan stood on her toes, and Ronald bent to meet her. When their lips touched, it was soft and sweet. *Heaven.* She nibbled across his mouth, enjoying his taste and texture.

Easing her hands over his shoulders, Joan pressed her fingertips into the thick, deep muscles beneath Ronald's dress shirt. All that strength and power reacting to her. She was damp with arousal.

Joan wanted to strip Ronald's shirt off and study him. But she also wanted to sink herself further into the feelings drowning her. His erection nudged her abdomen, and she chose to dive into the sensations.

She wrapped her arms around Ronald's neck, lifting herself against him. As she sighed, parting her lips, Ronald penetrated her mouth with his tongue. Her nipples puckered, seeking his touch. Joan rubbed against him, her breasts against his chest, her heat against his, hoping to soothe the ache. It wasn't enough.

She wanted the erotic attention of Ronald's tongue but needed to feel his bare skin under her palms. She leaned away and hurried to unbutton his shirt. Ronald stepped back, shrugging out of it, and discarded his undershirt. He stood before her, naked to his waist.

He was a spare feast of sable brown skin and sculpted muscles—deep shoulders, sinewy arms, molded pecs, and hard abs. His chest was covered with fine hair that narrowed as it traveled to his navel, disappearing beneath the waistband of his navy pants.

Joan blinked. "I think I've seen you in a museum."

Ronald chuckled, adding boyish charm to her adult

fantasy. He returned to her. Joan inhaled his scent, warm and musky. He reached behind her and, with one smooth movement, unzipped her dress. The rasping sound was final. There was no stopping now.

Good.

The bodice of Joan's dress fell forward, leaving her upper body naked but for her black strapless bra. The fire in Ronald's eyes singed her.

He unfastened her bra, drawing the undergarment from her in a slow caress. "You're so beautiful. A treasure." He whispered the words.

"So are you." She reached out, smoothing her fingers through the crisp hair on his chest, pressing her hands against his hard pectorals. "Strong and handsome. Like a sculpture."

Ronald palmed her breasts as she unbuckled his pants. Then he slipped her dress over her hips. When they were both naked, he carried her to the bedroom.

Ronald laid Cleopatra on the bed and put his wallet on his nightstand. For a moment or two, he just gazed at her. She was a fantasy, full breasts, small waist, round hips, and long legs. But beyond her physical attributes, the way she looked at him with unabashed desire warmed him. It made him feel wanted and welcomed.

He lay beside her, watching her closely, afraid that at any moment he would lose her attention. What if she became distracted and withdrawn? He couldn't survive that. Not this night. Not this woman. He nuzzled her neck, breathing in her soft scent—soap, a fragrance, and Cleopatra. What could he do to keep this connection?

Listen to her.

The answer seemed so simple, yet said so much. He

moved against her. Her soft sigh, he touched her again. Her gasp, he shifted higher. Her moan, he came closer. And when she arched into him, he knew he'd found her spot.

Ronald pressed his face into the curve of her neck. "Stay with me. Don't drift away."

"I'm here with you. I won't let go."

He followed her body's curves with his mouth. Over her breasts, along her waist, and into her navel. Her skin was silk, smooth and soft. He wanted to touch her forever. He smelled her heat, and it made him harder.

When he drove his tongue into her navel, she raised her knees, pressing her thighs against his arms. He felt her tugging at the sheets.

"Where do you want me?" His lips moved against her torso. Her stomach muscles quivered.

"Between my thighs."

"When?"

"Now."

Ronald raised himself above her, but Cleopatra pressed him back. Her voice was urgent. "Not that way."

Her gaze on his was sharp, intense. She was seeing him and nothing else. She was aware of him and no one else. That knowledge scorched him, made him want her even more.

He rolled back onto the mattress, and Cleopatra straddled his hips. "Where's your condom?"

Ronald reached for the nightstand and pulled one of the condoms from his wallet. He started to open it.

Cleopatra took his hands. "Let me."

She slid down his legs and cupped him. Her hair teased his hips. But instead of covering him with the condom, Cleopatra wrapped her lips around him. The unexpected caress, hot and moist along his shaft, drew a groan from Ronald's chest. His hips rose from the mattress, and his body stiffened. He was lost in what Cleopatra was doing to him with her tongue, lips, and fingers. It had been so long since someone had touched him like this. Had anyone ever made him feel this way?

Cleopatra moved away, and the loss of her heat made him groan again. She rolled the condom onto his rock-hard erection, then shifted over him. Her hair swung forward, brushing against his face. With one of her slender arms on either side of his head, Ronald felt caged in. It wasn't a bad feeling, he thought. In this position, her breasts were inches from his lips.

Ronald lifted his head and suckled her nipple. Cleopatra arched into him, rubbing herself against his belly. He cupped her hips with both hands and held her against him. His penis throbbed.

He switched breasts, giving the other equal devotion. Cleopatra's panting became a moan. Ronald released one hip and shifted his hand between them to touch her.

Cleopatra gasped. "Not yet. I want you inside me."

She slid down his body and positioned him at her entrance. Her touch was gentle and her movements slow, despite the pulse he saw beating double time at the base of her throat.

Seated above him, her dark hair tangled around her shoulders, her body trim, her curves full, and his penis poised to enter her, Cleopatra was an erotic image he wanted burned into his memory.

Then she moved him. His tip had slipped just inside her when she stopped. Ronald clenched his teeth and clutched the sheets. Cleopatra closed her eyes, arched her back, pushed her hips forward, and lowered the rest of the way to his hilt. Ronald lifted his hips to meet her. They stopped. The feeling was too intense. He had to catch his breath.

Cleopatra began to move, slowly finding a rhythm. Ronald helped her, his hands on her hips, guiding her. Her breasts bounced in time with their movements. He shifted his hands up her torso to hold them, loving the way her nipples grazed his skin.

She pressed her hands against his, kneading her breasts with his palms. She dragged his hands down her torso and led him to her lap. He knew what she wanted, his touch, inside and out. He traced his fingers to the juncture of her thighs. Her inner muscles clenched, tightening their hold on his shaft. He touched her with his thumbs, and Cleopatra gasped.

She bent her torso backward, her breasts pointing toward the ceiling. Ronald drove deeper inside her and harder against her. She pumped him faster, her muscles squeezing him. Ronald closed his eyes, concentrating on pleasing her and pleasuring himself in the process.

She urged him, praised him, begged him. And when Cleopatra screamed her climax, her body shuddering against him, she pulled him with her. His body drained into her, and she stayed with him, stroking him, caressing him, warming him. Melting away the cold.

Look For These Other
Dafina Novels

If I Could
0-7582-0131-1

by Donna Hill
$6.99US/**$9.99**CAN

Thunderland
0-7582-0247-4

by Brandon Massey
$6.99US/**$9.99**CAN

June In Winter
0-7582-0375-6

by Pat Phillips
$6.99US/**$9.99**CAN

Yo Yo Love
0-7582-0239-3

by Daaimah S. Poole
$6.99US/**$9.99**CAN

When Twilight Comes
0-7582-0033-1

by Gwynne Forster
$6.99US/**$9.99**CAN

It's A Thin Line
0-7582-0354-3

by Kimberla Lawson Roby
$6.99US/**$9.99**CAN

Perfect Timing
0-7582-0029-3

by Brenda Jackson
$6.99US/**$9.99**CAN

Never Again Once More
0-7582-0021-8

by Mary B. Morrison
$6.99US/**$8.99**CAN

Available Wherever Books Are Sold!

Check out our website at www.kensingtonbooks.com.